As the blast of light flashed through the dimness, Jorge saw an old woman standing in the circle. She was dressed in a ragged Zapotec costume and held a gnarled staff.

"There has been death," she shrieked. "There has been a death and there will be more. If Tombo Siete is violated further, all will die. The Old Ones are offended. All will die!"

●

Praise for Gene Snyder's earlier novel, MIND WAR

"Fast-moving and terrifying!"
—CHARLES L. GRANT,
EDITOR OF SHADOWS

"A fast-paced tale where fiction becomes stranger than truth."
—JIM BERRY,
AUTHOR OF BEYOND THE SPACE OF TIME

GENE SNYDER

TOMB SEVEN

CHARTER BOOKS, NEW YORK

TOMB SEVEN

A Charter Book/published by arrangement with
the author

PRINTING HISTORY
Charter edition/October 1985

All rights reserved.
Copyright © 1985 by Gene Snyder
This book may not be reproduced in whole
or in part, by mimeograph or any other means,
without permission. For information address:
The Berkley Publishing Group, 200 Madison Avenue,
New York, New York 10016.

ISBN: 0-441-81643-6

Charter Books are published by The Berkley Publishing Group,
200 Madison Avenue, New York, New York 10016.
PRINTED IN THE UNITED STATES OF AMERICA

Acknowledgments to Dr. Irving Strouse, for medical data; Dr. Sam Zimmerman, for excellent dental research; Ms. Ellen Levine for monumental negotiation skills; Nancy, Laura and Michael for support above and beyond the call of duty; Dr. Albert Eyde for contributions to the original concept; Mr. Mel Parker, editor extraordinaire, for patience and faith.

G.S.

**To the memory of
Doctor Jorge Perez-Hererra**

PROLOGUE

Oaxaca, Mexico.

Julio Mendoza was bored, hot, and tired. It was the beginning of his third tourist circuit of the day through the Monte Alban ruins, and the gringos were acting as usual. Stringing out from the more than mile-high altitude of the mountaintop, they stopped, gawked, and took photos, barely listening to his narrative.

"Please, ladies and gentlemen, try to stay together. Don't wander from the group." He cleared his throat and started the speech he could now do in his sleep. "As you can see from this vantage point, Monte Alban is a mountain whose top has been flattened and built upon...." He gestured across the nearly half a mile of plateau containing mammoth pyramids and other ancient structures. The center, grassy court could have contained more than ten football fields. "While what you see before you is massive, it is estimated by the government, which chose to cease excavation some years ago, that less than ten to twenty percent of the ruin has been unearthed." There were a few whistles, oohs, and aahs from the tour group.

"But..." The interruption came from a middle-aged, plump American woman in a gaudy, flowered dress and a straw hat.

Julio grimaced. "Yes, Senora?"

"Excuse me, but as we got off the bus, I saw a group of people digging over there." She gestured to a small saddle of land some quarter of a mile from the main peak.

"Ah, yes, Senora. You are most observant. That is an American group doing some work at the Tomb Seven area ...but we will get to that later. Ladies and gentlemen, please follow me. The first structure that we see is called the Ball Court. It is—"

"Senor? Senor?" Cocho was near sixty and far too old to be a digger. He wheezed and coughed as he descended through the dark, steep tunnel that served as the current Tomb Seven dig.

"Senor? *Dónde está usted?*" Where are you? There was no answer. He continued to work his way downward until he got to the bottom of the shaft. He cursed to himself. The last thing he needed at his age was to make an extra trip up and down the dig to remind some gringo that lunch was ready.

He played his flashlight across the bottom of the tunnel until the light caught something.

Cocho froze as he saw what his light had exposed.
Madre de Dios!

The light shook in his left hand as he automatically crossed himself with his right. After a second he turned, and forgetting his age, started to scramble back up the tunnel in terror.

"Ugo? Ugo?" The eerie echoes of his own voice bounced back to him from the clay walls as he scampered upward, screaming for the head digger. "Ugo? Emergencia!"

As he got to the mouth of the dig, he stumbled and fell. Ugo dashed to him but Cocho was so winded that he could not speak. All he could do was stare wide-eyed at the tunnel mouth and point with terror to the bottom of the shaft.

"Why do they call it the Ball Court?" It was the same American woman again, and Julio felt himself counting the number of days it would be before he would be back at the university for the Fall semester.

"It was called that"—he pointed to the sloping pit containing two stepped sets of seats that led to a narrow arena floor some thirty feet below—"because it was thought to be a place of sport. Two teams of players would play a game with a leather ball...not unlike soccer. The games were important as the losing team, it is thought, was sacrificed to the gods." He paused, hoping that he had sated the woman's curiosity. "The age of the ruin is uncertain. It is known that the Zapotecs lived here, and the Mixtecs. The earliest dates for construction have been placed at three thousand B.C., although the entire dig might well be far more ancient than that. To your right..."

"*Despacio...cuidado.*" Slow...careful. Ugo made sure that he and the three other diggers, who were working their way down through the steep, slippery tunnel did not set off an earthslide. It took them more than fifteen minutes to get to the bottom. Their lights played across the bottom of the well until they came across what old Cocho had found.

"*Dios mio,*" one man whispered. He crossed himself and started to back up the tunnel. The second digger simply turned and dashed past him, scrambling upward. Ugo turned and fixed his light on the third and last digger, forcing him not to flee.

Julio had completed the circuit of the ruins and was starting to lead the ragtag group back down the hill to the bus.

"You never told us about why they call that"—she gestured into the distance—"excavation over there Tomb Seven." It was, of course, the same American woman. It wouldn't have been so bad if her voice was less petulant.

Julio breathed deeply to retain his calm. "I am sorry, Senora. I forgot to mention that. It is called that because seven tombs stacked vertically were found there. That American group is tunnel-digging beneath the lowest of them in search of further ruins." He remembered the part of his speech that he had skipped over in his haste to finish with the group. "The Tomb Seven area is rich in local folklore *and myth. Among other things, it is believed by the local Indians that the entire area of the tomb is cursed."*

Ugo moved forward making sure that the last digger stayed with him. He dropped to one knee and played his light across the corpse of the gringo on the mud floor of the dig. He checked for a pulse though he was sure that there would be none. The body was still warm to the touch, and that was eerie. The dead American was stretched out on his back, his arms outspread as in a crucifixion. His hands were balled into tight fists, and strangely, there seemed to be no marks on the body. He had not been hit by a falling rock nor did there seem to be any evidence of accident.

It was the face that was terrifying. The mouth was open as if in midscream and the eyes were wide with horror.

The third digger edged forward. He leaned close to Ugo and whispered, as if to speak aloud would be to awaken the corpse.

"El maldición de Los Viejos." The curse of the Old Ones.

The digger got to his feet and backed away, gripping his crucifix and mumbling prayers. Ugo stared at the body for a long moment. Could it be? He tried to push away the thought and the cold ball of fear that had started to knot his stomach.

On the crowded bus the American woman looked at her guidebook, seeking the next stop of the day. She looked out the window, peering through a cloud of dust back in the direction of the ruin.

She grunted to herself. "Foolish natives and their silly superstitions."

1

Dr. Jason Farewey cursed quietly to himself as he waited for the policeman to approach his car. He could see the still flashing lights of the New Jersey State Police car which was parked behind him as he glanced in the rearview mirror. "Bloody damn," he mumbled to himself as he fished for the registration of the rented car in the glove compartment. Seconds later the state trooper came abreast of his driver's door.

"License and registration, please."

Jason handed the trooper the folder from the glove compartment as well as his international driver's license and his passport. The trooper stared at the last two curiously.

"You're a—"

"Yes, officer, I'm a visitor here. I arrived at Kennedy Airport this morning and I was late getting to a conference. I expect I was going a bit too fast. Sorry."

The trooper recognized the man's tone as one of command. He was not sheepish or apologetic, simply forthright, with just the slightest hint of frustration. He flipped the international license to the back cover.

"What language is this?" he asked.

"Welsh, officer."

"Hmm," the trooper mused for a second. He looked down at the man in the car. The driver was tall and muscular, with a shock of reddish hair, a deep tan, and piercing blue eyes. The stare carried the same quality of command as the man's voice. The face betrayed fatigue and the same hint of frustration as had the man's voice.

"Well, you're right about going too fast. You were clocked at sixty-four in a fifty-five." He paused for a second, thinking of the time it was going to take him to backtrack the license through the Trenton computer system. He looked back to the license and noticed something.

"Are you a doctor?"

"I'm an archeologist. I was headed up to the Moreland Research Institute for the conference I mentioned. As I said, I was running quite late."

"That the big place in Hunterdon?"

"That's correct, officer."

The trooper shrugged, handing back the papers. "Well, all right. Let's just call this a warning. Hunterdon's only ten miles up the road. Just keep to the speed limit, understand? In New Jersey we're serious about it."

Farewey managed a smile. "Yes, officer. And thank you very much."

Minutes later Jason was moving west again. Keeping one eye on the speedometer and one on the exit signs, he swore quietly to himself in Welsh. Why the hell was he coming to the conference in the first place? He had little respect for radical approaches to archeology. He remembered that Dr. Jerry Tanner, the director of Moreland Research, had once quipped to him at a conference that he was the Cotton Mather of the field. Jason had responded that Tanner was the field's Houdini. It was soon after that Tanner had invited him to the conference. Perhaps it was the challenge of confronting Tanner that made him accept. But at the moment, he could only wonder if the trip was worth the delay at airports, surly customs people, and New York traffic, not to mention being stopped by a policeman. Wistfully, he wished he were in the field, working at a dig somewhere.

He had spent most of the last ten years in various digs in several parts of the world. He had finished his Ph.D. at twenty-two and had spent the better part of the last decade building a reputation as one of the most brilliant men in his field. The key to his reputation was meticulousness and diversity. Unlike many of his colleagues, Jason had generalized rather than specialized. He was as at home in the Yucatan jungle as he was in a North Wales bog.

Lost in thought, he almost missed the exit, seeing the Hunterdon sign at the last second. He swerved up the ramp, hoping that the same policeman didn't see him do it.

The Moreland Research Institute was impressive, though anachronistic, Jason thought, as he drove through the front gate and stopped at the security booth. It was centered around a huge old British manse once, Tanner had said humorously in his letter, owned by a Welshman. But to either side of the mansion stretched a number of ultramodern glass and steel research buildings. For the brief decade of its existence MRI—as it was called by the Americans—had grown enormously, though the thrust of their projects was, sadly for Jason, foolish. Parapsychology, paraphysics, para-this and para-that were things wasted on Jason. Still, he thought, I am here, aren't I?

He registered at the main desk and was shown to comfortable quarters on the second floor of the old building. A quick glance at the conference program told him that there had been little missed in the morning program—introductions, general directions, little more. He was pleased to see that he had arrived in the midst of the midday break and that Tanner was not due to speak until the early afternoon. He unpacked the single, small carry-on shoulder duffel with which he had traveled across much of the world. He put the single wash-and-wear suit and solitary dress shirt on a hanger on the inside of the bathroom door. Efficient to the core, Jason used the shower for more than just cleansing. It would push away some of the jet lag and take the wrinkles from the suit all at the same time.

Less than an hour later, program in hand, Jason entered the half-filled lecture hall only a moment before Tanner started to speak. Jason immediately recognized some of the faces in the audience and was surprised to see several of them. A number were archeologists even more traditional than he. Even old Paul Dhalquist was there, the most traditional of statesmen in American archeology.

Tanner's delivery was superb, as far as Jason was concerned. But he found it hard to separate it from its topic. Psychics working together with archeologists was something Jason found more than difficult to accept. Part way through the talk, Jason saw Dhalquist get slowly to his feet.

"Dr. Tanner."

Tanner stopped and his eyes moved to the older man. He didn't seem the least bit disturbed at being interrupted.

"Yes, Dr. Dhalquist?"

The old man folded his arms. Jason saw the action as a fuse being lit.

"Well, Dr. Tanner, all of this, ah...information and speculation is quite...interesting. However..." The old man took a long pause. He seemed to be standing in front of a group of graduate students in a Harvard lecture hall.

"Is there any shred of real *empiric* evidence for these... what shall I call them...postulations?"

There was dead silence in the hall, and Jerry Tanner took his own long pause before answering. Jason thought Tanner must feel like he was talking to the pope.

"Yes, Doctor. There is. Granted, there isn't a huge body of data yet. But that's why MRI asked all of you to come here. We need your help to establish procedures and parameters for the effective integration of psychics into archeological research...." He paused. "On an experimental basis, I mean. Consider the time wasted in a dig that requires large-scale searches and forays. Think of the precious foundation money lost in exploring blind alleys and leads that are little more than rumors...."

Dhalquist unfolded his arms. "How different is all of that from using all of this *witchcraft* you have been expounding about, Doctor? No. Proven technique is proven technique.

Personally and professionally, I have not seen one thing that would change my viewpoint a single iota."

Jason watched as Tanner again paused. He knew that there might be a confrontation with Dhalquist simply because of the man's reputation. He was a bit surprised that it had happened so soon. He also knew of Tanner's rapier wit and he watched as, at the podium, Tanner flushed ever so slightly. Finally, he responded to the challenge.

"Isn't that the same statement that the papacy made to Galileo, Doctor?"

There was a brief burst of nervous laughter in the hall. It quieted suddenly as Dhalquist started to speak.

"I see no reason to remain at a conference where scientific technique and logic are squashed in favor of barroom levity. I am leaving and I suggest that those of my . . ." He gestured around the hall. ". . . *rational* colleagues do the same."

Dhalquist turned and left. At least half of the others did too. When the exodus was finished, Jason remained in his seat. He was not about to get back in his rented car and drive to the airport or stay at a local motel until he could get a reservation. Besides, there was something about Dhalquist's indirect accusation that to remain was to be irrational that was challenging to the stubborn Welshman. He could see that, at the podium, Tanner, though not flustered, was clearly tense. Jason got to his feet.

"Dr. Tanner?"

"Yes, Dr. Farewey?"

"We can't forget that psychic study has had its Cardiff giants, can we?" His reference was to a nineteenth century hoax; a large human form sculpted in granite which was buried, then "discovered" and billed by pitchmen as a petrified prehistoric giant.

Tanner didn't hesitate a second. "Ah, Dr. Farewey, Cardiff is in your country and it was a team of Welsh archeologists and anthropologists that first testified to the authenticity of the giant. I believe it took several months before they discovered it was a fabrication."

Again there was a wave of laughter in the hall, and Jason found himself joining in.

"Touché, Doctor," he found himself saying while still laughing.

The balance of the address dealt with applications of psychic archeology that MRI had developed and the results of some field tests. Jason found the results sketchy. It seemed that psychics were spotty in their accuracy. Jerry Tanner was quick to point out, though, the MRI contention that such skills could be trained to be more accurate through practice. Again Jason was skeptical, though the relentlessness of Tanner's data and delivery was starting to get to him. As the address ended, there was a scattering of applause and several people came down to speak to Tanner. Jason waited until they were finished before he approached.

"Hello again, Jerry."

"Jason." Tanner extended a hand. "I was worried when I didn't see you this morning that you might have said to hell with it. I know you're not exactly an aficionado of psychic archeology."

"I was not a fan of anything when I was trying to get out of Kennedy Airport this morning, and your psychics didn't prevent me from getting stopped by one of your highway policemen on the way here."

"Did you get a ticket?"

"A what?"

"You know...a citation?"

"Oh. No. Just what they call a warning."

"You see. We *did* help."

"Touché again, Jerry. I've got to learn to say little around you. I say, that was quite a show Dhalquist put on, wasn't it?"

"Alas. I shouldn't have answered that way."

"A failing of yours, right?"

"Right. I engaged my mouth before my mind was in gear."

Jason laughed. "Still, I think he would have left in any

event. If you think I'm traditional—"

"Yes, I know. Dhalquist isn't really certain of fire or the wheel yet. Seriously, though, I thank you for coming."

"In one respect, I couldn't resist. First, you paid for the trip, and second, there was that thing in your letter about the artifacts. I guess in the final analysis, that was the real challenge."

"You brought the items with you, then?"

"Of course. I chose them all carefully."

"Excellent. Don't tell me what they are—"

"I don't plan to," Farewey interrupted.

"Good. Why don't you get them, and we'll meet in my office."

"You do live well here, don't you. This psychic business looks profitable." He grinned.

Jerry Tanner folded his arms. "I expect that this ribbing will go on forever, or at least until we get to the experiment." He pointed in the direction of the polished conference table. On it lay a folded, thick, opaque cloth. "Take the artifacts from the bag and place them under the cloth ... that is, after you have unfolded it. Put them in any order you wish, but make sure to space them at least a foot apart."

Jason stared at Jerry. "Nothing personal, but where will *you* be while I'm doing that?"

Jerry laughed as he walked to the far side of the table and turned his back. "Will this position do, or am I going to have to use a blindfold?"

"I didn't mean to—"

"That's all right, Jason. You're a rational skeptic and you are about to see something that will defy your position on things. If you like, I'll leave the room while you place them, and you can call and tell me to come back."

Slightly embarrassed, Jason ran a hand through his hair. "Of course not, Jerry. I'm not Dhalquist, after all."

"No offense taken, Jason. Place the objects. We agreed on five, correct?"

"Yes," Jason said as he started to spread the cloth. "Why is the cloth so heavy, Jerry?"

"It's lined with lead, like an X-ray apron in a dentist's office."

"Is that designed to impress me?"

"Not really, Jason. We use it and a number of other blocking agents and substances in our tests."

It took Jason a few minutes to get the bulky cover unfolded. Then, with care, he placed the artifacts under it.

"You can turn around now, Jerry."

Jerry looked at the table and nodded. "There's one more thing." He went to his desk and took a small cloth bag from the center drawer. "Did you leave room on this end?" he asked Jason as he moved to the now shrouded conference table.

"Yes. That end." Jason gestured.

Without showing Jason the small item that he took from the bag, he slipped it under the cloth. "There. Now, we're ready."

"Is this the time when I get to meet this... superman of yours?"

Jerry smiled. "Not quite a superman, Jason." He moved back to his desk and thumbed an intercom switch. "Send Lupe in, please."

A few moments later the door opened and a petite young woman entered. Jerry crossed the room to her and then turned to Jason.

"Dr. Jason Farewey, this is Miss Lupe Muñoz. Lupe, I've already told you about Dr. Farewey."

"Yes, you have. How do you do, Doctor?"

"Ah, excellent... and, ah... you?"

"Well, thank you, Doctor."

Her dark eyes fixed his with an almost hypnotic pull. Her raven hair framed her face, and her black dress, though demure, revealed a striking figure. She was close to the most beautiful woman he had ever seen. A bachelor and an only partially reformed womanizer, Jason had had few meaningful or lasting amorous relationships. Rather, he had spent months at a time in the field. And, as he assumed that such a practice would continue, he had concluded that his love life would eternally consist of a series of brief trysts and flings.

With a consummate force of will, he pulled his eyes from hers and looked to Jerry. "I must confess, I had conjured up an image of a man in robes and a turban . . . not a young woman."

"There are no clichés among psychics, Doctor," Lupe said, still smiling, though there was a slight edge in her voice.

A sensitive point with her, Jason thought. He decided to stick to business rather than alienate her further with abortive attempts at charm. Still, he found it hard to keep his eyes from her.

"Miss Muñoz is perhaps our most gifted subject," Jerry said, "although I guess I shouldn't call her that. She's been a member of the staff for over six months. I might add that her late grandmother, Maria, was also working with us here until the time of her death, and was also a very successful psychic."

Jason chewed his lip for a second and then turned to Jerry. "Look, you know I'm not very familiar with this field at all. . . ." He turned for a second back to Maria. Again her eyes caught him. "So, there is little that I know that is more than a cliché from popular fiction. But does this have anything to do with what I've heard . . . oh, you know, about psychics running in families?"

"Yes and no, Doctor." It was Lupe who answered as she moved directly across the table with Jason. "You see, assume for a moment that a grandparent demonstrates psychic ability in some form. They might be followed by a parent and then a child, in turn. Hence, the myth—the seventh son of a seventh son, and so on."

"Is that the no or the yes, Miss Muñoz?" Jason smiled, though he could see that Lupe was all business.

"Again, it is both."

"I'm sorry." Jason raised his hands in mock supplication. "All of this sounds like a Zen koan... the sound of one hand clapping and all that."

Lupe laughed. It was a beautiful, deep-throated, sensuous laugh, Jason thought.

"I know it sounds confusing and for many it is," Jerry said. "But to be brief, we contend that all children are born psychic. If the parent has had a successful psychic experience and has felt positive about it, the child has a head start."

"How?" Jason was starting to probe.

Lupe took over. "If the child comes to such a parent with a possible psychic event, say procognition or telepathy, *that* parent is apt to encourage the child, thereby saying that it is correct or proper to have more of them. A superstitious or frightened parent might call a priest or warn the child that such things were evil—"

"Thereby preventing the development of what you say is a latent skill? Is that correct?" Jason asked.

"Exactly," Lupe replied, again flashing a devastating smile.

"Well, shall we get to the demonstration," Jerry suggested as he moved to Lupe's side of the table.

She nodded, sitting quietly in a chair that had been placed there for her.

Jerry looked across the table to Jason. "There are some things that you will have to do."

"Such as?"

"Move a bit away from the table while she works. And ... please don't think that this sounds strange—try not to let your thoughts be skeptical. Stay blank if you can, if you know what I mean."

"Many of my friends contend I've been mentally blank

for years. I'll try. But why?"

"It has to do with something we call observer interference. Negative energy is a simple explanation. Just try to remain mentally neutral for now, okay?"

"I'll do my best."

Lupe's eyes were closed and she seemed to breathe deeply. Jerry leaned down to her and spoke softly.

"Lupe, can you hear me?"

"Yes, Jerry." Jason thought her voice sounded quite clear—not as if she were in a trance.

"There are six objects in front of you. You may take them in any order you wish."

Jason backed away from the table and tried to be mentally impartial. Lupe opened her eyes and got to her feet. She moved slowly, almost as a blind man might while learning the face of a new friend. Her fingertips caressed the air above one of the hidden lumps. Her choice, Jason thought, was random.

After a minute of this motion, her fingertips moved together and her head cocked to the side. There was the barest hint of a smile on her face.

"Bone," she said.

A pause.

"Carved... barbed."

"A fishhook!" It was almost a shout.

Her head slowly turned to Jason. "Eskimo, perhaps from the late nineteenth century."

Jason forced himself to remain poker-faced.

Jerry looked toward him. "Is that right, Jason? It would help if she knew."

"Ah... that's right." Jason was having a hard time gauging his own reactions. He wasn't sure if he was watching a stage mentalist or something totally valid but enigmatic. It was hard to accept the latter, but even harder to accept the former. There was little chance that a man of Jerry Tanner's stature would set up a hoax.

He looked back to Lupe in time to see her move to another object. Her hands moved much more swiftly now than they had before.

"Jade . . . carved . . . a statue . . . Quan Yin, perhaps from the Tang Dynasty."

"Correct."

"A stone . . . very smooth. River bottom. There are circles engraved. It's not very old." She turned to Jason. "Australia?"

It was the first time that she had said anything in the form of a question. Still, Jason was dumbfounded.

"That's correct," he intoned. "Is there anything else about it?"

Again her hands made several delicate passes over the object. "It doesn't seem quite real . . . not like the others."

"Dear God," Jason mumbled. The stone was a mock-up that had been mass produced and sold to tourists in Sydney. He had purchased it there some years earlier. He had slipped it in among the four others as a kind of control. She'd caught him.

She moved on. The next object started to give her some trouble, and after a minute or so she moved past it, shaking her head. Jason could not help but wonder which object it was, then remembered. It was the one Jerry had placed under the lead blanket.

She spoke about the next one almost before her hands were over it. "A ring . . . ivory. It's African." There was an almost childlike excitement in her voice. "Nigeria . . . an Ibo ceremonial ring, less than a century old."

At this point, all Jason could do was nod. Dear God, what is all of this? he thought. He pushed the wonder away and his practical Welsh mind started to roam through the possibilities with the excitement of a born-again Christian discovering faith.

"Long and thin . . . a branch . . . again, carved." She turned to him. Her smile was almost giddy. "A Hopi Indian ceremonial stick about two centuries old. I think they used them for digging datura root."

"Correct again." Jason was finding himself suddenly cheering as she got each right.

She moved to the last one, the one she had passed over earlier. She spent more than five minutes on it. Jason could see the slight glint of perspiration on her forehead.

She turned to Jason and Tanner and then simply sat in the chair, clearly fatigued.

"I don't know. It's ancient... just terribly old. It's also a very heavy metal. But... well, it's going to sound silly, but the feel is almost frightening."

Jason and Jerry came to the table and removed the cover. Lupe looked at the first five objects with a satisfied smile, then looked to the sixth curiously. It was a small gold figurine, carved in the shape of a snake. She picked it up and held it between the palms of her hands, briefly closing her eyes. She opened them and shook her head. "Still nothing more than I got before."

Jason asked to see the object. The serpent was a rattlesnake, carved in gold with incredible detail. It was totally representational, almost photographic. Jason could not understand how Lupe would have said it was so ancient, though after her stupendous success with the other five artifacts, he was not going to question her.

"Where did it come from Jerry and what the hell is it?"

"Jason, we don't quite know what it is. I can tell you that it came from Oaxaca, specifically from our new dig at the Monte Alben Tomb Seven area. It was found at a depth of thirty feet below the level of the oldest tomb."

"Tomb Eight?" Jason quipped.

"Quite possible."

"I think," mused Lupe, "I have dealt with some pieces before, have I not, Jerry?"

"Yes."

She nodded knowingly and turned to Jason. "I had no

luck with any of them, just that feeling of something ancient. A number of times I got the feel of heavy metal ... occasionally I could guess gold. But that was all. It's almost like it was a control in the experiment."

Jason looked at her sheepishly. "I'm afraid that my little Australian stone was the control. I almost regret putting it in there, now ... after that astounding performance. Can I ask how you do it, getting the exact period and all?"

Lupe smiled back. Again he was drawn to the magnetic dark eyes. "The only psychic part is getting the object itself, I must confess to that."

"How do you mean?"

Jerry smiled and folded his arms. "What she means, Jason, is that the location, period, and use come from another part of her background. Lupe holds a Masters in Archeology."

Jason was appropriately impressed. "I see. But the other part, the ... psychic part?"

Lupe looked to Jerry, knowing he could give a more succinct explanation than she.

Jerry took the cue. "We think that objects carry an energy with them. Mesmer called it Animal Magnetism. Some people can focus in on the energy and determine things about the object. One name for it, when an object is held in the hand, is psychometry.

"Is there a range limitation to this?"

"We don't know. Lupe can manage up to, say, five hundred feet."

"More, if the conditions are right," Lupe said. "In the lab, when there are pressures and protocols to observe, the range is shorter."

Again, thinking practically, Jason took the small gold snake in his hand. He examined it closely. "I wish I had a jeweler's loop."

Jerry went back to his desk and got a powerful magnifying glass. He handed it to Jason, who examined the piece with professional scrutiny. Even under the glass the detail was exquisite. Every scale on the snake's back was carefully incised. The mouth open, as if to strike, contained fangs with minute incisions for the venom tubes. Jason looked back to Jerry. "I don't believe it. What could bore such small incisions in the fangs?"

"They are less than a hundredth of an inch across, Jason. That's hard for many industries to manage, even now." Jerry pointed to the piece Jason held. "It was that piece that prompted me to get you here in the first place."

"You mean I've been had?"

"You'll have to tell me that, Jason."

Jason glanced across the table at Lupe and thought, ironically, if not had in one way, I may have been snared in another.

"What I mean, Jason, is you have expertise in tunnel digs and you're one of the best men in the field. I want you to go to Oaxaca and take command of the dig. George Rodgers, who's running it now, is excellent. In fact, he is the one who personally found this piece. He'll be your second in command. In addition, George is rather...colorful."

Jason could feel his antennae go up. He had seen more than one eccentric in archeology; those who sought the Holy Grail and such. He folded his hands carefully on the desk and cocked his head to the side. "How eccentric?"

"Well, perhaps I shouldn't use that term. He's a health and fitness nut. He runs ten miles a day and—"

"At that altitude?"

"Yes."

"That's almost immoral."

Jerry and Lupe laughed.

"And he is a vegetarian, choosing his own from the market in Oaxaca. That's the extent of it. He's not a missionary or anything, if that's what you mean, and he's damn good...." Jerry paused. "And there's another thing."

"What?" Jason somehow suspected that there was some hidden condition.

There was. "I want Lupe to go with you and have free rein on the project. If she asks you to dig in a certain location, you should dig there. Not that she will be in command. I don't intend that. What we're looking for is a full-blown, honest to God field test under normal operating conditions. We will keep a careful record of the successes and failures that Lupe might have and the conditions under which they might occur. And there we are."

Jason paused for a long minute. He looked at the snake again and then at Lupe. Finally, he turned to Jerry.

"When do we leave?"

Jerry and Lupe smiled broadly, as if in relief.

Jerry retrieved a clipboard from his desk and pulled an itinerary sheet from a pad. "Most of what we need is there already. We—"

Suddenly the door opened and all three looked up. The man who stood there held a yellow paper in his hand. His face was pale. Jason recognized the look. It was shock.

Jerry looked at the man quizzically. "What is it, Tom?"

Tom Hughes brought the yellow paper across the office to Jerry as if he were carrying a ticking bomb. "I think you better read this, Jerry. It came in about fifteen minutes ago, and they routed it to me, as you were in conference."

Jerry took the paper and read it. His eyes didn't leave the paper, which Jason recognized as a cable, for a long moment. When he looked up, his face had the same expression as Hughes's. When he spoke, there was a forced, careful calm in his voice.

"Does anyone else know?"

"Not yet. I brought it right here."

"Thank you, Tom. Let me keep this."

Hughes backed away a few steps, then turned awkwardly and left.

Jason watched as Jerry's eyes moved back to the cable. "What is it, Jerry?" he asked tentatively.

Jerry said nothing. His eyes remained glued to the paper. Lupe leaned across the table. "Jerry? Please?"

TOMB SEVEN

He looked up, first to Lupe and then Jason.

"George Rodgers is dead."

Lupe crossed herself. "Sweet God," she intoned.

"How?" Jason asked.

"It says that he was found dead at the bottom of the Tomb Seven tunnel."

Jason, too, now leaned toward Jerry. "How did it happen? Was there a cave-in or something?"

Jerry shook his head. "The doctor says he died of heart failure."

Jason shook his head. "Heart— But didn't you say he was a health nut?"

"He was. But there's more."

"What?" Jason asked.

Jerry's eyes met Jason's. "George Rodgers was only twenty-nine."

2

Oaxaca, Mexico.

The frijoles bubbled and hissed in the pot that hung by the fire, but Xacha was no longer aware that they might burn. It seemed that she had prepared them more than a thousand years ago, before the girl had arrived with the sacred things. Now, everything was different. She tried to tell herself that the arrival of the sacred object was something that she had waited for all of her life. She argued with herself that the arrival of the gold-and-jewel encrusted items was inevitable; something planned for eons before, when an ancestor sat in the crude hut and human flesh hissed and boiled in the pot rather than frijoles. The thought did not help her through the moment. There were things that had to be done. They had to start now.

The hut was in a shantytown that wound its way, snake-like, along the road from the city to the airport. Small gardens produced corn for the tortillas. For other food and income, the Indians—pitiful remnants of the mighty Zapotecs—made themselves fair game for the shutters of the tourists. Few of them could remember their heritage. Xacha served for memory. She told the children the tales of the Great Ones and the battles that they fought until they were overwhelmed by the flesh-eating Aztecs from the north. After that came the Spanish, and the Old Gods had died, replaced by a single new one. He had not helped the harvest and the Indians grew gaunt while His servants fattened in their brown robes. *Los símbolos*—the symbols only survived, and it was Xacha's ancestors who passed them to her. In her youth she had been kept from the government schools and the Spanish spoken there. She was taught in Zapoteco and spoke only that all of her life. As years passed, she became a shaman—a holy woman—and the women of the snakelike pueblo came to her for spells and potions. The farmers sought planting advice. But it was the children she was to teach, and they would have little to do with her. Passing the Learning was something that would end with her—it was foretold, as was the other thing had been foretold.

She shuddered as she thought of it. *Tombo Siete*—they would have found the things in *Tombo Siete*. Tomb Seven. It was the signal. Her role was that of warning only, though she knew that it would be of no avail. That, too, had been foretold. The Other would carry out part of the mission too. The thought terrified her despite her years and her knowledge. The Other would carry out the mission of the Old Ones. Somehow, she was glad she would not see that.

Xacha took her stick from next to the tarpaper door and limped to the kettle that hung above the fire. She took the hissing cauldron from the rack and set it on the floor. Painfully, she crossed the room and opened a large trunk in the corner. She took a cracked and peeling leather sack from it and lovingly caressed it. In the center of the hut she seated herself cross-legged on the floor and stared at the bag. Her grandmother had given it to her, and she was sure that a grandmother before that had done the same.

She untied the string and rattled the contents of the bag, satisfied that everything was there. An owl claw, an eagle feather, and eight bones—human bones of various sizes: Each stood for a charge from the Old Ones. The way they would fall to the floor would tell her to whom and where the warning would be spoken. She let her eyes slit, and saw the light that slipped through cracks in the battered door. As the light turned into dancing figures, she let her eyes slip closed, and breathed deeply. In minutes she was in a deep trance.

She soared with her brother hawks from the floor of the valley, rising on the warm thermals. As she rose, Monte Alban flashed below; a flattened mountaintop monument to the Old Ones. The ten pyramids glistened as they had centuries before, stucco-covered to honor the sun. The pillars before the sunken court rose to the sky again. She turned to the sun and soared into the blazing whiteness.

As Xacha opened her eyes, she could see the pattern of the bones on the floor. She did not remember casting them. She never remembered, for it was not she who really cast them. It was what she had, for an instant, become. But it was her lot to read them.

A mere glance told her that what she had felt had been right. She closed her eyes again, nevertheless. It was something she would have to take a moment to digest, something she'd been prepared for from early childhood. She was the last and she was destined to be the last. It *would* be her warning, and the action and decision of the Other, which would shape the future. There was fear, but there was also pleasure in her—pleasure in the fact that she had remained faithful and carried the secret for all the years. There was much to do, now... much.

Leaving the bones on the floor as she had cast them, she got to her feet and made her way back to the trunk. She stopped and squinted at a small calendar on the wall. There was really no need to do it, no need to look at all. The rising of the moon and the position of the stars had told her. It was the time of *La Guelaguetza*—the summer festival. It was fitting that the warning be given there.

In the bottom of the trunk she found the robes neatly folded. It only took her a few minutes to put them on. The tall, ornate headpiece of the Zapotec priestess was last. She took time with that, carefully folding the scraggles of ebony- and gray-streaked hair beneath it. She touched the bony fingers of her left hand to the embroidered hawk that, as her patron, shouted its power in crimson from the breast of the crimson robe. Her hand moved to the sunburst on the headdress. She touched it reverently before she scanned the room.

Moving with her stick, she managed to upturn the trunk and spill the remaining contents on the floor. She took the small reed mat from the corner of the room and added it to the pile. She gathered up the sacred relics that the girl had left, then pulled the paper drawings from the walls, one by one. She moved in reverse order, taking the bastardized figures of the later Aztecs, followed by the Zapotecs, Mixtecs, and on to the earliest Olmecs. Before that, there were only the nameless ones, and before them, the Old Ones.

All of the drawings were added to the growing pile in the middle of the floor. Staring at the heap of cloth and paper, Xacha was satisfied. She moved to the hearth, and for a second, absently stared at the cooling frijoles. They would be of no use now, she thought. In a matter of minutes all that would be left would be the warning.

Propping herself with the stick in her right hand, she grabbed the hearth shovel and scooped the burning sticks and embers from the bottom of the fireplace. After a second's pause, she flung the burning firebrands across the room. They were starting to smolder when she tossed another spadeful on top of them. The third spadeful of blazing embers was consigned to the pile of cloth and paper on the floor. As the flames flashed to life, she dropped the shovel and limped to the door. She closed it behind her, and as she moved in the direction of the road, could see the first tongues of flame start to lick through to the outside of the tarpaper walls. She stopped only one more time as she hobbled toward the city. She saw the smudge of black smoke that told her the hut was immolated, and smiled a gnarled, toothless smile. There was something satisfying about that... something completed. Now, the real work of her life would be carried out.

3

Oaxaca, Mexico.

Dr. Jorge Lopez muttered to himself as he strode down the hospital hall in the direction of the pathology division. He had not wanted to perform a post mortem today. There was a mammoth pile of unfinished paperwork on his desk, and even José, his meticulous assistant, could not thin it by much. Besides, tonight he had to open the Guelaguetza Festival.

The hospital administrator, Senor Julitora, was pushing for design suggestions about the new pathology facility. It seemed the grant the hospital had searched for had been approved, and now the inflated needs Julitora had postulated to the foundation would have to be justified. Jorge's pathology department was in no need of expansion, but Jorge had to provide some rationale for the money Julitora had garnered for him.

Now the esteemed administrator had called him with another "emergency." The very thought of it infuriated Jorge. The doctor on the scene had evaluated the cause of death as heart failure, without any pathological evaluation. Julitora had then approved a cable to the American institute indicating that heart failure was indeed the cause of death, and now there was a rush to verify it, using the expertise Jorge only could provide. Jorge felt like a fool. God help the prestige of the hospital if there was indeed another cause of death.

He pushed through the swinging doors of the lab anteroom and saw Diego waiting for him, as he always did, with a clipboard in hand. "Well, tell me," he grunted as he started to gown and glove.

Diego, sensing the doctor's mood, looked at the papers and read: "Deceased was a twenty-nine year old Caucasian. Height is one-point-eight-five meters, and weight eighty-six kilos. He was found at the bottom of a shaft in the Monte Alban complex. Initial estimate of cause of death—"

"I know about that."

Diego paused. When the doctor arrived, he was sure that he was in a bad mood. That much was certain from the slamming of the door. But Dr. Lopez rarely interrupted the reading of a clinical work-up. Diego took a deep breath. The old man's mood was really black today. He cleared his throat and went on with the reading.

"As soon as he was discovered, the workers carried him to the surface, where our ambulance arrived. He was dead on arrival at the emergency room and the initial apparent cause was logged as heart failure. An external examination revealed no marks, bruises, abrasions on the body. Eyes were open at the time of death and the facial expression was frozen. It appears to be one of shock or pain." He looked up from the clipboard as Jorge finished gloving. "This *is* consistent with the initial diagnosis of heart failure."

Jorge eyed him icily for a moment before moving in the direction of the examining room. Diego, already gloved and gowned, followed at a discreet distance. Jorge approached the table and threw back the sheet. He reached up and snapped on the mike, starting the tape recording which would later be transcribed into an official report.

"Subject appears externally to be in excellent health. As noted, no marks or scars. Contorted features seem to indicate sudden seizure or fear, though the former is most likely."

Jorge paused and took a scapel from the tray to his side. With a deft motion, he made an incision just below the sternum, and incising about two inches, sliced downward through the multiple layers of the tough rectus abdominus, stopping just above the pubic arch. He removed the scapel, and again raising it, sliced laterally across the serratus anterior, arching upward and intersecting the initial cut. Moving downward, he severed the lower end of the rectus abdominus and intersected the lower end of the initial incision. As he set the scapel back in the tray, he snapped off the microphone and looked to Diego.

"Retract."

Diego nodded and inserted retractors into the incisions. With the skill of a true professional, he used the eight hooks to pull back the layer of muscle, in effect opening the body cavity as one might pull back the covers of a book and reveal an interior page. He looked up at the doctor as he finished applying pressure to the clamps.

They were now able to fully observe the viscera of George Rodgers, a man in the springtime of his life, who had simply died. The doctor was about to snap on the tape recorder, when he looked across to Diego. "There was no history of coronary heart disease?"

Diego shook his head. "We have absolutely nothing. It seems there is some difficulty in finding next of kin. We put in a request to the Moreland Institute for medical information, but thus far there has been no indication of any congenital ailment. The doctor who spoke to the director indicated that the man was a *goc,* and he said he was in perfect condition. I did not know what the term meant, Doctor."

"It is *jock,* Diego. It means athlete." Jorge snapped on the recorder and started his remarks. "The viscera are appropriate in color, shape, and position."

He moved from bottom to top—the genitalia, bladder, kidneys... the peritoneum, the descending, transverse, and ascending colon. He traced the small intestine all the way up to the pyloric valve and found everything normal. Likewise, the spleen, pancreas, liver, gall bladder, and stomach were perfect in color, texture, weight, and size.

"Thorasic saw, Diego."

Diego nodded and reached for the electric saw. He deftly sliced through the sternum and severed the bond that connected the rib cage to itself. He inserted a crank-operated wedge and started to widen the gap in the ribs. What was revealed was again a textbook thorasic. The lungs, bronchii, and esophagus were in perfect condition. Diego noted a slight increase in the lung capacity inferred from the size, and chalked this up to the man's athletic bent. If he was a runner, and from a sea-level area, there was a good chance that the enlargement was a function of exercise. Likewise, the heart was slightly enlarged but there was no external indication of damage to the vena cava or any of the visible coronary arteries. The lungs were severed from the bronchii and removed for weighing. Likewise, the heart was detached from the pulmonary artery and aorta, and removed for weighing.

With the weight noted, Jorge bisected the heart and examined the interior. But the heart was a model of health. The overall texture, chamber walls, and values, were flawless, as far as Jorge could see.

"Close, please, Diego."

"What about the cranium and the brain, Doctor?"

"Remove and send to Dr. DeVega for a brain pathology report."

He turned from the table and moved to the door, pulling his gloves and gown off and tossing them into a bin. He headed in the direction of his office.

As he passed through the outer office, he told Jose to intercept any calls and hold any further business, since he would have to leave early, what with the Guelaguetza beginning so soon after sundown. It was not a lie; not actually. The festival was not something he could avoid, not on such short notice, at any rate.

He pondered the case of Rodgers as he thought of the frozen look of horror and pain on the man's face. There had been no reason for it, and he was sure DeVega would confirm that when he examined the brain microscopically. As he stood at the bottom of the shaft at Tomb Seven, the man's heart had simply stopped and the horror of it had shown on his face. He had a suspicion that when the micropathology of the adrenals came back from the lab, there was a good chance the results would indicate there had been a massive adrenaline spike at the moment of death. That would be accounted for by the expression of the death mask. It would simply lead to one conclusion: the man had been frightened to death. How, was something Jorge could do little more than conjecture. In any event, death by fear was not something that went into a coroner's report.

Heart failure. All deaths could ultimately be described as heart failure. It was the dustbin of medicine.

He sat at his desk and looked out the window to the sunset. It was vivid with purples and pinks swirling through low clouds. The gold strip of twilight spread wider than Jorge remembered across the skyline. *El Chicon*, he thought. Yes, that was it—the volcano and the protracted eruption had added microscopic particles to the atmosphere, and Mexico was to be treated to elegant sunsets for several years to come. He pulled himself from the view and thought again of Rodgers. The principle of Occam's razor occurred to him. The ancient psychological maxim stated that the simplest solution was always the best. But for Rodgers, there was no simple solution. Something stopped the man's heart. It was as simple as that. With an immense effort of will, Jorge pushed the thought aside again. He tried to look ahead to the ceremony.

The Guelaguetza would have dancers from every province of the state of Oaxaca. The dancers and the costumes were as diverse as the conquerors who had trooped across the state. Those from the west coast danced the ceremony of gathering turtle eggs. Others, from farther inland, danced the history of the Mixtec conquest in huge feathered bonnets. That dance amazed Jorge more than any other. The headpieces weighed more than twenty pounds apiece, and all of

TOMB SEVEN

them contained priceless, rare bird plumes. Yet to prevent damage to the plumes, the dancers never managed to collide with one another, or even touch. Jorge knew they practiced nearly all year for the event. Still, he shuddered as he recalled that the gorgeous dance recounted human sacrifice and cannibalism brought from the north.

The last dance was always the Dance of the Virgins. A euphemism, Jorge thought. The original "virgins" were about as virginal as Roman vestals—temple whores, actually. But at the end of the dance, at least in ancient times, the "virgin" was taken to the top of one of the pyramids of Monte Alban, where a priest ripped her heart out. The organ, many times steaming and still beating, was devoured by the faithful in a macabre mummery of the Roman Catholic communion. It was the ultimate sacrifice to the gods of the rain and the sun—those who made the maize grow high. His mind flashed to Rodgers. He chuckled in spite of himself. Perhaps he could put "sacrifice to the gods" on the death certificate. No, he could not. Rodgers was neither a maiden nor a virgin.

The set of Jorge's face became grim. There was no other way... no other. He called José and told him to confirm Rodgers's cause of death as heart failure.

4

Lupe and Jason found conversation easy as they watched the flight wing across the Gulf coast. Though their physical attraction was clear, both kept the chatter on a professional level, especially as Lupe knew a great deal more about the digs of Oaxaca than did Jason. His expertise was Europe and Asia, though there was no question that his qualifications would serve him in good stead at Tomb Seven.

"But how did you do it?" he asked. "You managed to get all of them, except the small serpent."

She smiled a sly, gleaming smile. "I don't really know. That's what the whole MRI project is all about. Jerry Tanner doesn't know either. But we seem to come in varieties. I tend to feel things through psychometry, as you saw in the conference room. Others can see events before they happen. Remember that air crash in Chicago a few years ago? The one where the engine fell off the jet as it was taking off?"

He nodded, curious.

"Well, there were more than forty psychics who called the Federal Aeronautics Administration about the crash, before the fact. All of them had seen it happen, in some detail I might add, and considerably before the fact."

"How did your FAA react?"

"First," she said, tossing her head, "they are not *my* FAA. I am Spanish—third generation, but still Spanish."

"Sorry," he intoned.

"The FAA was cool about it until people started to tell them the time of the year and the make and airline of the plane. That started to get to them."

"But what did they do about it?"

"There was very little that they could do. There was no way to know the exact date of the crash or the airport."

"Why not? Hasn't all of the work that the MRI staff has done over the years taught them anything about that?" His tone was not accusatory. Rather, she recognized the true curiosity of another professional. She swallowed a sarcastic answer and instead spoke with candor.

"It's something we have been working on for some time now. We think that the precognitive part of the brain is the right side. That part can't read, write, or speak. It deals in images only. Just impressions. Dates and places and times would be a function of the left side."

He thought for a second. "Then there are two questions that arise. The first is, what good is the ability? The second, is there a way to train some sort of interface?"

She smiled broadly. "You ask the right questions for a rational skeptic. We have been trying to find some sort of interface for years. An analog-digital computer mix can help with this. The other answer is training. There might be a chance that some people have a natural interface. If we analyze that, then we can train the talent into those who have the basic tendency."

He shook his head and sipped a glass of wine the steward had just brought. "And you find the tendency how? This Rhine card stuff?"

"Partially. There are another series of tests, like you saw me do. But as I said, there are a number of variants of the ability." She smiled. "Did you know that there are several detective agencies in the country that employ psychics? There are also a number of police departments."

"Why don't they publicize that?"

"Many of them keep it secret because they think the

public would simply consider it poor police work. But I can assure you that they exist. I've worked with a number of them."

He nodded. "But there's something else to all of this see-things-in-advance stuff. What about determinism and free will. That debate has been going on for centuries."

"Again, we don't know and neither does our best computer. Perhaps we can change events, perhaps we can't. My grandmother saw her death coming in a crisis. But she told me there was a rightness to it, and I should feel no sorrow."

"Yes," he said dourly. "Jerry told me about that. He said something about blowing up some sort of missile? What variety of . . . ability was that?"

"We call it psychokenesis or telekenesis. It's the rarest of the psi talents and we know nothing about how it works except that it happens under extreme stress, and all of the others happen with the subject totally relaxed. I'm afraid that's one that I don't have, so don't expect that I can move boulders at the dig."

He laughed a broad, genuine, Welsh laugh. "That's what we have diggers for. But what about the dig itself? Have you seen it?"

"Only photos. Jerry wanted to keep it that way. He thought that would be a way to purify the test of the skill. I did a lot of homework, though. There is really very little known about Monte Alban, no matter how much has been published. They think that *Tombo Siete* was built at another time by perhaps an earlier tribe. In the uppermost layers, they found artifacts from different periods of conquest. This is what got us interested in the tomb. As we dug deeper, we found things from other periods. A number of them were Zapoteco, the most indigenous tribe to the region. But there were some others that were total blanks, and they might have been transplanted from the major part of the site."

"The major part?"

"Oh, yes. Tomb Seven is over half a mile north of the mountain platform. It sits opposite a set of ruins called the

Seven Deers area. That also has been barely explored. But it was the Tomb Seven area that started to yield older and older things. Many of them we have no reference to at all. That small artifact that I examined in the office was one that was too old for me even to consider."

"Any guesses?"

"It could be that the little ornament antedates the people who built Monte Alban by centuries. Again, that's left brain information. There's not much more I can say."

"What's all this I hear about observer something or other?" His tone was still professionally skeptical, but Lupe could detect his interest.

"We call it OI, observer interference. Again, it may be the same thing parents do to children. If there is such an axis as positive and negative energy, OI or disbelief is the negative side of that. No one's sure."

"Aren't you afraid that my attitude will hurt what we're trying to do?"

Her dark eyes caught him. "No. You're a professional and you believe in professional results. That's all that's needed... that, and no earthquakes."

"What?" He almost spilled his wineglass on his lap.

"Earthquakes, anything that might collapse the dig. The Cocos Plate and the Caribbean butt up against Mexico. Earthquakes in the past might have been what destroyed a number of the mounds and pyramids at Monte Alban. Other sites like Mitla and the ones in Yucatan were built in less precarious locations. Monte Alban sits quite close to several faults. That's why the dig, which is getting deep now, might need a good archeologist and a not too bad psychic."

They laughed, but there was something in Jason's laugh that was more polite than sincere. "That will mean a lot more shoring, and a slow process."

"That's why I'm here. To tell you where to dig."

"Are there any other surprises?"

"Aside from a dormant volcano or two and a local nuclear plant, nothing."

He said nothing, simply staring at her in his distinctive Welsh way.

"Stewardess," he called out. "A double Scotch, please."

Lupe laughed. "That's something you'll need to take care with—the Scotch, I mean. The higher the altitude, the faster the effect."

"Well, this one will have to be the last until we get back." He paused for a moment as the stewardess brought him the drink. He took a pull at it and looked out the window. They were starting to cross the Mexican coast and he could see the mountain ranges beginning to work their way from the sea. He knew that only a few hundred miles to the south he would meet a strange archeological challenge. He took a long pull at the drink and his eyes moved back to hers. "You haven't wanted a drink."

She shook her head. "It does bad things to psychic ability. Again—"

"No one knows why, right?"

She nodded and laughed.

"There is another thing that troubles me," he said as he methodically swirled the drink. "Rodgers. Is there anything that we know about his death?"

"Nothing at the time we left. If there was, Jerry would have gotten a telex right away. If there's anything more by the time we get to the airport for the connecting flight, he'll let us know."

"I knew Rodgers by reputation. He was young and in the peak of health. There were many good things planned in the field for him. It's something I can't fathom. Someone like that simply doesn't . . . well, die."

"There are many places in the world, Jason, if I may call you that, where such things happen. Remember the Carter excavation in the Valley of the Kings? How many died there? Perhaps a dozen, many of them after the return to England. there are dozens of cases like that. Perhaps that's why I was sent."

"Not to die, certainly... a virgin to the, what, Zapotec gods?"

"I'm afraid I don't qualify."

"Not a virgin?" he asked brazenly, though he realized he'd embarrassed himself.

"Not a Zapotec. My people conquered them. That might be the only trouble. The mestizos or half breeds don't exactly like fair Spaniards, even one as dark as me."

"The class lines are that strong? Christ, sounds like bloody Wales and England."

"It's more so. Did you know that Mexican television still has few if any mestizos, and fewer pure Indians? Sort of like American TV in the early fifties, before blacks started to make inroads. So, you see, you're just a gringo, while I'm the only one they'll really dislike."

He grinned and downed the last of the Scotch. "How could they dislike anyone as attractive as you?"

"Easy. *'Muy fácil,'* as we say." Though she maintained her reserve, there was something in her smile that mesmerized him. It was nothing he could place. He had seen stunning women in all parts of the world. But for the first time in his life, there was something new in the effect her smile had on him.

"You forget that this part of the world was conquered by almost everyone who came from the north, as well as the south. There were Olmecs, Mixtecs, Zapotecs, the Aztecs in a sweep from the north and then, worst of all, the Spaniards."

"Why were they the worst... or should one ask?"

"At least the others brought similar gods—Cojico, Kukuclan, the jaguar gods of Mitla—but the Spanish brought Christianity, and then all of the others went out the window as evil. The missionaries said that the new Christian God would bring rain for the corn and grain. What followed was the worst drought in decades. The old priests tried to rebel and bring back worship of Cojico, the rain god. But the missionaries killed them by order of the Santo Hermanidad—the Inquisition. That left, as you might say, a little bad blood."

"And that's lasted for four centuries."

"Yes, and there was more than a little cause for the bad blood. The Spaniards defiled the tombs and stole every piece of gold they could lay hands on."

"Wasn't there any kind of revolt?"

"There was no way the Indians could combat firearms, especially with the amount of mysticism in their culture. Besides, legend said that ancient gods would come again to Mexico and bring justice. There was a good chance the natives thought that the Spaniards were gods. Montezuma did."

"Oh, that's right," Jason exclaimed. "There was something about a god returning. The day and the place had been foretold, as I remember."

"Exactly. If Cortez had not landed on the exact day of the prophecy and in the right location, and if he did not *look* like Quetzlquatel, there probably would not have been a conquest at all."

"You're saying it scared the ... pants off the emperor?"

"No question. It also drove the Aztecs further south, which is why one layer of Tomb Seven is Aztec. The uppermost level of the dig is six below that, now. Oddly, the depth has nothing to do with the naming of the tomb. It was simply the seventh tomb located in the complex. Excavation has unearthed seven layers. And there is a good chance that there will be more. There is a lot of sorting to do."

"Do you have any information on the situation with the diggers?"

"Not much. All I've been told is that there are enough of them. I don't think they'll be thrilled about Dr. Rodgers's death, but there will be enough of them. They need the money. They're mostly poor Indians and have families to feed. You might have read that Mexico has an inflation problem?"

"I had." He looked to his watch and adjusted it to the local time. "Let's hope we get on the ground in time to make that connecting flight."

5

Jorge looked at himself in the mirror. His pantaloons were yellow and there was heavy embroidery on the silk shirt. His boots were crimson and his tall official hat simply defied description. It was a bright red affair with gold and green feathers. It was meant to be a symbol of Cojico, but it had changed through the centuries. At least it was simpler and lighter. The staff of office was equally ornate, with eagle feathers and other plumes from the various states of Oaxaca. He struck a fierce pose just as his wife Maria came into the bedroom. She laughed, and as he looked back at her, he laughed also.

"Foolish?" he asked tentatively.

"Thank God the Guelaguetza only comes once a year."

"*That* bad?"

"No. No worse than mine." She whirled to reveal her native costume, which, though plumed and festive, was not the match of his.

"Yes, much worse. You look stunning." Though he still stared in the mirror, Maria could detect a change in his expression. Now he wore his professional look.

"What is it, Jorge?"

"Something at the hospital today. I don't like it when I can't find all of the answers."

"Foolish man. Only God knows all of those."

"Yes, but I should at least know a few of them... if nothing else, the medical ones."

Maria, a small, slender woman with strange, penetrating blue eyes which betrayed a Spaniard or a North American in her background, stared carefully at her husband of thirty years. She had married a doctor and mothered four children, three of whom were also doctors. She knew the look. It was something that nagged at him when science would not answer questions. She knew that it would nag for days, especially since she had been read the copy of the cable he'd sent to the North American institute. She thought of asking, and thought better of it. Then she found she could not resist. There were few, if any, things they had not shared in their three decades together.

"It's the death of that man Rodgers, isn't it?"

He looked at her, seemingly insulted for a second. She imagined the rage of a Zapoteco chief staring back at her.

She smiled at him, then started to laugh. "They said that you had left the hospital and the telegram people called here to confirm that your message to the North American institute had been sent. They read it to me on the phone. So, there is no reason for you to be indignant, mighty *jéfe*. Don't you remember that I was a nurse, and that was how we met? How many times was there no apparent cause of death in someone just brought in? All the other doctors did was shrug and say heart failure."

He sat on the edge of the bed, his stern Zapotec pride and the elegance of the regalia suddenly gone. "This one was different." He eyed her carefully. "He was too young. He had been in perfect health. And don't berate me about being a perfectionist. You knew that when you married me. I sent tissue samples north for analysis. They might come up with something."

"Where did he die?"

"*Tombo Siete*. At the bottom of the dig. One of the workmen found him."

Maria chewed her lip for a second. "Gas? Some gas in

the dig? Remember, in the old days, workers used little birds in cages to see if there was gas? If the bird died, then the workers ran?"

He shook his head dourly. "Generally that gas is methane. It has much the same effect as cyanide. His lips would have been blue. There would have been clear evidence in the lungs and in the brain. There was nothing like that here... nothing."

She moved to the dresser, and for a minute straightened things that clearly did not need straightening. Then she turned back to him. He still sat dejectedly on the edge of the bed. "Jorge. Perhaps some other kind of gas. Perhaps one that we know little about?"

He looked up at her and managed a wane smile which was somehow out of keeping with his mood. "That's why I sent the samples—just in case there was something that might be unknown to us."

"Jorge, this is not the first death at Monte Alban and not the first one at *Tombo Siete*. In fact, there have been more at *Siete* than at any other place in the whole complex. They have to go deeper, they say, and after all, it's on the side of the mountain more than on the plateau. Let's not allow this, what do I call it... mystery to ruin tonight. The Guelaguetza is always beautiful. Besides, you get to open it and preside over things."

She offered him a hand from the bed and he rose, an ancient chief given new life.

A line of torches snaked along the winding road that crept up the mountainside. The small hilltop where they had started to cluster was directly across the Oaxaca valley from Monte Alban and had been the traditional site of the gathering from the time of the Spanish conquest. No one was sure why it had been placed exactly there, but one thing was certain to every Oaxacan: the ceremony served a crucial purpose; more than a site for the tourists to spend money; more than a celebration and an excuse to get drunk on mescal. It was a way the Indians during the conquest took something the brown robes considered sinful and turned it into something the Christian priests and the dogs of the Santo Hermanidad thought only frivolous. The most crucial reason for the perpetuation of the event was the continuation of the last shreds of the dying Zapoteco culture and language. Even now, fewer than five percent of the Oaxacans spoke or understood the ancient tongue, and there were fewer every year.

The fairgrounds at dusk were jammed with stalls of Indians selling and hawking goods to the tourists. Most of them knew that the gringos would take the first price offered, and the price tag was inflated accordingly. Oaxacans there to see the festival were not such easy game. They would haggle and barter, as would those who had come from other parts of Mexico for the festivities. The stalls were kept at the fringe of the ceremonial ground, and the local police made sure none was placed too close to the dancing circle and the mock-up of the ceremonial altar. They also set aside a spot for the tents of the dancers. Since many of the costumes were embossed with silver, gold, and precious stones which were three and four centuries old, this area was the most closely guarded.

Around the dancing circle, tall, portable stands had been erected for the spectators, who would pay almost three hundred pesos for the privilege of watching. The security and the finances fell under the jurisdiction of Jorge's nephew Sergio, who, like his uncle, held a most prestigious position in the city and in the entire state of Oaxaca. As a justice of the Supreme Court, he yearly assumed the responsibility for the Guelaguetza. The preparations were always monumental and precise, but Sergio always volunteered and was always equal to the task. The profits from the licenses of the vendors and the tickets would be tallied against the expenses of preparation and transportation for the dancers from all parts of the state. Each year Sergio had run things, the festival had turned a decent profit for the state. Since he was the descendant of the Zapotecs and wanted to maintain the heritage of his people, this year was most pleasing to the slight man in the three-piece business suit. His uncle would open and preside. Sergio had a strong sense of family pride, and this year it would be even more inflated.

He moved from the stalls to the edges of the stands, carefully surveying the restraining ropes that would separate those who paid for seats from those who would simply mill in the crowd and try to see what transpired. There were few he allowed to pass to the seats without tickets. These were the orders he had given the well-trained security force. A few were beggars, and some were cripples. To be sure, there were not to be too many. If there were, two disastrous things would happen. The first, and less important, was that the profit margin would be cut. The second, and most crucial, might be a riot. But none of this had happened in the five years Sergio had been managing things. He had ensured that the chief of police had trained the force of guards well. It was made clear that the chief would be out of a job, as would many of the officers, if anything went awry.

He watched as the walkers came up the winding road with their torches, remembering that fire on the mountain in early summer could be catastrophic. He reminded himself to check the guards who were supposed to extinguish all fires at the entrance. He stopped himself and folded his arms. That was the chief's job. Sergio tried to laugh to himself. He was almost as much of a workaholic as his uncle. Perhaps it ran in the family.

Suddenly, he looked down the long winding road and recognized the old Chevrolet that Jorge drove. He would be glad to see him. It would mean the festival would get under way on time, which would obviate a large number of difficulties. Among them would be crowd control and fires. He waved to the guards who would greet the car, and they ran in the direction of the arrival site.

"Jorge," he called.

TOMB SEVEN

"Sergio," was the return.

As the older man came from the car, they hugged. Sergio cared deeply for his uncle, who was somewhat reserved. There was something distant about Jorge, something Sergio couldn't grasp... a depth of feeling about the past. It annoyed Sergio, though he would never admit it. Was the old man more Zapoteco than him? Foolishness! He still loved him.

He led him to the grandstand with words of love. "Uncle, you look like one of the Old Ones."

"I feel like one of them after the day at the hospital that I've had."

There was a look of concern on Sergio's face. "A very bad day?"

"Bad enough. There is a post mortem that I cannot figure out, and you know how it is when there is something I cannot explain."

"Yes. You give Maria and everyone else in sight fits. What was it?"

"A gringo in the dig at *Tombo Siete*. I can't for my soul find a cause of death."

Sergio looked at Jorge and admired the costume. "Well, tonight you are *jéfe* for the ceremony, and I forbid you to think of it. Understand?"

He made Jorge smile. "Careful nephew or I'll call down the wrath of the gods on you."

Sergio eyed the growing crowd and the crush of people whom his men had to control. "I wish that the gods could help me handle the crowd. You know how Chief Alvarez is about these things. Unless I'm there all the time, he lets everyone and everything into the seats, and the first thing that happens is a riot for seats or a rage of pickpockets. So, I wander and look. That keeps the rest of them on their toes, and there are no relatives or friends who get preferential treatment in any of it."

Jorge extended his arms, the large impressive staff raised

in the air. "If there is any trouble, I will call the wrath of the gods down on the malfactors. Lightning... or something else."

Both men laughed as Sergio seated his uncle and the silently trailing Maria at the head of the canopied platform that was the traditional seat of the *jefe*. Sergio's greeting to his aunt had been a mere nod of the head and a smile. It was a part of the culture that the North Americans would have never understood. There was little recognition of women in the rural areas of Mexico, even in a city of Oaxaca's size. Wives served dinner for their husbands and in many places did not even eat with them, dining rather in the *cocina* with the hired help. This was especially true when there were male guests in the house.

Maria sat demurely behind Jorge in her plumed regalia and waited for the festival to begin.

It was more than an hour into the evening before the dancers and the crowds had managed to settle down sufficiently for Jorge to start the Guelaguetza. He looked to the stage manager, who glanced furtively at a clipboard and then back to Jorge. It was clear in the man's nod that he was tense.

Jorge managed to get to his feet in the strange costume. He had practiced at home and there was little sense in the *jéfe* falling ass backward at the start of things.

He took several steps forward and raised the staff. At the far end of the dancing circle there was the blast of a strange horn which sounded Oriental and Mexican at the same time. It was a buglelike contraption the original Zapotecos had used at the beginning of such ceremonies. In a matter of seconds all of the electrical lighting was extinguished. The torchlight flickered and turned the circle on the mountainside into a strange charade of the past. High above, an Aero-Mexico jet roared in the direction of the nearby airport. It created a bizarre incongruity, an anachronism. Jorge waited, as did the others, for the plane to pass.

Holding the staff of the *jéfe* high above him, he paused dramatically. Maria always said that with his sense of the dramatic, he should have been an actor.

"Silence!" he roared as loud as he could. As there was already silence in the wake of the passing jet, the command was more ceremonial than anything else.

"The gods of our fathers demand silence as we honor them here in this sacred place. We shall celebrate the rain that grows the corn and the great blessing of Cojico who brings it. We shall honor the sun that warms us and Tantixa who sends it to us daily. We shall honor many things, and more than anything else, we shall honor the fact that we are Zapoteco. We shall remember that our land has been taken and retaken from us many times and that we still remain as our ancestors... we endure... we prosper, and we never fail to forget the Old Ones and the old ways that were once mighty and must always remain alive in our memories."

He switched from Spanish to carefully practiced Zapoteco.

"Bring us the revelers. Let them honor the gods."

He waved the staff across the circle and more torches flared, right on cue.

The first of the team of dancers swirled onto the arena floor. They were all men, sixteen of them, and they immediately formed ranks of four. They stood rock still until Jorge thumped the staff to the floor of the platform, then they started to swirl into rhythmic patterns of the traditional dance.

The dancers intertwined and spun expertly, obviously proud of their skill.

Jorge and Maria watched serenely from the platform.

Meanwhile, there was a rumble in the distance which got closer.

In a flurry of swirls and spins, the dancers finished the first performance of the evening. Unlike the way they had entered, they scurried to all sides of the stage and started to throw small candies and other trinkets to the spectators. This resulted in a chorus of oohs and aahs which culminated in a burst of applause. In a matter of minutes the feathered dancers seemed to evaporate into the nether reaches of the grandstands.

Jorge glanced at the program. The next group was from Puerta Escondido, girls who would dance the history of the collection of sacred turtle eggs from the shores of the Pacific. The food was still considered a delicacy by the natives of the coastal area of Oaxaca. Jorge had eaten them and shuddered at the thought, remembering the bitterness of the greenish yolks. Still, he knew that the natives of the coast sucked them from the shells raw, and the young males considered them a source of sexual potency. Jorge had always considered it more than a bit Freudian that maidens danced the history of the eggs. Ova and sperm joining—Freudian frippery, he thought.

What followed happened so quickly that Jorge wasn't sure if it was a part of the program, which he had barely perused, or something unplanned.

There was a brief moment when the dancing circle was bare and lit only by the flicker of the torches. Then the lights came on, as planned, to allow the placement of the egg props by costumed stage hands. As the blast of light flashed through the dimness, and before the placement of the eggs began, Jorge saw an old woman standing in the middle of the circle. She was in a ragged Zapotec costume, one which designated her as a priestess or a shaman. She held a gnarled staff, seemingly a mock caricature of Jorge's.

Her stooped shoulders straightened and she raised the staff.

No. It was not in the program, though he was sure the rest of the audience did not know that.

On the far side of the stage, Sergio did not have to look at his program. He knew the woman should not be there, having committed the entire schedule for the evening to his almost perfect memory. A second after the lights came up he was grabbing for the UHF set and stabbing at the *Press to Talk* button.

"Alvarez? What the hell—"

"I don't know..." There was a hiss of static followed by yet another rumble of thunder from the end of the valley, closer now.

"Get her the hell off of the stage."

"Right."

Sergio could see from the far side of the circle the tan-uniformed police starting to move in the direction of the woman.

Another clap of thunder.

There was a murmur from the crowd. Now they weren't sure if the woman was a part of things or an interloper.

"Get her out fast!" Sergio snapped into the mike.

"Inmediatamente." There was both confusion and fear in Alvarez's voice.

Sergio was more concerned about the former than the latter.

"Gently, Alvarez. Don't have them hit her or anything. Make it gentle, otherwise the crowd will riot and jump to her defense." As he'd said the words, he thought of an earlier conversation with the chief of police and wondered if this was the same woman who had been mentioned then. *Dios mio,* he thought.

The police had started to move in on her when the woman pointed the staff in the direction of the stand where Jorge presided.

"There has been death," she shrieked, speaking not in Spanish but rather in fluent Zapotec. "There has been a death and there will be more of them."

Jorge was stunned. Had the woman read his mind? He managed to get to his feet despite the awkwardness of the costume, then stopped to think. What could he say? Yes, there had been a death, and indeed, perhaps it was the one that he could not explain, but—

"The Old Ones are offended. Their sacred place has been

desecrated. They will no longer tolerate it. There will be more...."

There was a close-in thunderclap following a flash of forked lightning. Much of what the old woman was saying was washed away by the peal. Part of the crowd started to look to the sky as another part looked at the hag before them. After all, she was speaking in a language few of them understood. Less than one in twenty could speak or understand Zapoteco in the twentieth century.

"... if *Tombo Siete* is violated further. All will die. *All Will Die.*" Her voice was now the shriek of the hungry condor and seemed to even overpower the guards moving in on her. She suddenly dug the staff into the ground and wavered. Pulling herself up straight again, she shrieked.

"Tomb Seven is death to all who come near!"

Her head turned to the crowd and she switched to Spanish, repeating what she had said.

"Alvarez, get her the hell out of there, the crowd is sure that she's a crackpot now. Move in."

Another flash of lightning, now dangerously close to the mountainside, and some of the crowd started to get to their feet. All Sergio could hear was static from the radio held by Alvarez. But it was clear that he had gotten the message. The police started to move in on the woman. The bulk of the crowd, except for some of the gringo *turistas*, now understood.

Xacha screamed a few more words in a language neither Zapoteco nor Spanish but one that had not been used for thousands of years. There would have been no one in the crowd who could have understood, not even the finest Mexican historian or antiquarian.

She stumbled forward as the police converged on her, and with a final scream punctuated by a lightning flash and a thunderclap, she pitched forward to the dirt of the dancing circle.

The police ran to encircle her as the first drops of chilly rain started to fall. There was a mad scramble in the stands—

just what Sergio had hoped to prevent. But there was little he could do about it except to try to raise Alvarez on the UHF and tell him to get more men to the exit routes, so that no one fell off a cliff or started a panic.

At one end of the grandstands a light tower with clearly poor insulation flashed and sputtered, showering sparks before it died.

Someone stumbled into someone else in the grandstands and the rest went like dominoes.

Jorge hiked up the gown, and leaving Maria in the relative safety of the canopied podium, dashed to the center of the circle and pushed his way through the cordon of police gawking at the woman on the ground.

"Out of the way," he bellowed as the rain increased in intensity. The thunder and lightning were almost constant now.

As he leaned over the woman, he recognized her. Though he couldn't remember her name, he had examined her in the free clinic only a month before.

He put his head to her chest and grabbed her wrist to feel for a pulse. There was nothing to be found in either place. He smashed a fist into her sternum and balled one fist covering it with a palm. He started the careful rhythmic pressure of CPR. There was a strange feel to her chest.

"You!" he yelled at an inert policeman staring at him. "Get an ambulance. See if the first-aid tent has an oxygen bottle."

It was obvious that in a few minutes something more than CPR would be needed. It was also obvious that in a few minutes the old hag lying in the muddying dancing circle would be dead.

It was less than twenty minutes from the time Xacha stumbled into the center of the circle that Jorge pronounced her dead. By that time the dancing circle was a sea of mud and the stands empty. Another light stanchion flickered and flared into sparks before giving up the ghost. Sergio ran to the middle of the circle.

"Uncle, you will have to get to the first-aid tent. There are others that need your attention. There have been falls and many injuries."

"Have there been any deaths?" Jorge asked.

"No, *gracias a Dios*. Just sprains and cuts and bruises as far as I can see, but there is a need for you there. There might be things that the assistants and I cannot see."

"Well, there has been a death here." He pointed to the now mud-soaked form of Xacha. "This one. She was perhaps dead before she hit the ground. I'm afraid that there was nothing I could do. I don't think there was anything anyone could do."

"Did you understand the last of what she said?"

All Jorge could do was shake his head. He had a strange feeling that the unintelligible words were the reiteration of something very ancient.

Perhaps a curse?

It was less than twelve hours later when Jorge went carefully over the old woman's body on the dissection table at the hospital. There was no question that she had been in perfect health for her age. There was an occasional thickening of an artery and some other anomalies attributable to old age. But there was no cause of death, aside from the fact that the old woman's heart stopped beating. *Heart failure*. The words haunted him when he thought of the shattered viscera of Rodgers and the conclusions he had to submit about it. At least this cause of death would be completely accurate.

Jorge paused above the body. Her heart was in fine shape. It had simply *stopped*. While he had heard of Indian yogis who had been able to stop their hearts, he was relatively sure that the old woman had not undergone such training. He could only wonder: *Had she . . . or something else stopped it?*

6

The hacienda was vast, more than ten thousand hectares. There were fifty in staff and the central complex itself had over forty rooms. It was twenty kilometers distant from the center of the city. Guards patrolled the outer perimeter, and at night dogs were unleashed to prowl the grounds. The meticulously trained Dobermans would rip the throat from anyone except their handlers, and there was not a chance that an interloper, even managing to get over the high, broken-glass encrusted wall, would get more than a few meters in the direction of the central complex. All of the defenses were carefully planned over a number of years under the direction of the multi-millionaire owner of the complex. It was not that he was a hermit. Rather, he required the privacy due to the nature of his business. Diego Quintos Herrerra was a powerful man, more powerful than even his colleagues knew. And, above all, he sought even more power. Power was bought with money obtained from many sources.

Just now, Diego gazed down the long conference table in the hacienda's large meeting room and pondered the thought of gold and the stupendous amount that could be made from it. The renegotiation of interest payments for Argentina and Brazil had made large investors wary of the American dollar. Gold and the peso were twin kings in the international money marketplace. He marveled at how the peso, once the weak sister of the America's financial community, could have raised itself from near oblivion at the time of devaluation to such a position of international power. However, Diego's concern not one of pride or patriotism. Rather, it was one of clear, simple, vested self-interest. The peso was a tool, and just now, a strong tool. There was no way, in the foreseeable future, that the bottom was going to collapse on the price of gold. A monumental windfall in the finest quality pure-gold find in a thousand years would reap the seller an astronomical profit on the international gold market. But there was a hitch: the sale itself would deflate the price of gold and bring the dollar back into a strong position against the peso. And with Diego's holdings heavy in pesos, the result of the quick profit scheme could devastate long-held investments. He had pondered the dilemma for some time until a solution suddenly arose in the form of a new financial partner.

The operatives who approached him were prepared to support his current project and buy the acquired gold at peak prices. For a time this proposition confused even Diego's quick financial mind, then his operatives discovered the ultimate goal of the partnership. Their private acquisition of the gold would allow them to buy weak American dollars for strong gold. With the dollar strengthened, they could buy more foreign products with it. There was no question about what products were involved—American grain.

The only risk was getting the gold and spiriting it out of the country. That would be the job of the six men whom Diego faced at the conference table.

He raised his hands from the table and brushed his carefully manicured fingertips through salt and pepper gray hair. Placing his hands back on the table, his dark eyes traversed the six men. Their names were never mentioned in a meeting, they were simply called "One through Six." Diego had set things up that way. He wanted them to act as a military staff might, each specializing in one area crucial to whatever operation was at hand. He would demand the staff work of them and they would provide it. He would coordinate, and of course, make all of the policy decisions.

"The Oaxaca matter," was all that he said before he looked at the man closest to him at the table. "Senor Uno?"

The man looked at a small sheet of notes in front of him for a brief second. His eyes moved to Diego. "We have managed to infiltrate eleven trusted men into the digging crew. All of them have worked with us before and their reputations with this kind of operation are above reproach."

Diego's dark eyes probed those of Senor Uno. "And what of our chief operative?"

"He managed to obtain the artifacts, which of course you have seen. He has been instrumental in getting the men on the project. As the number of finds increase, as he is sure that they will, he will start to set a time frame, an estimate really, for when we should start the second phase of the operation."

"Your estimate of manpower requirements?"

"Forty, perhaps forty-five."

Diego nodded ever so slightly. His expression did not change. "Are you certain of that number? Would they be additional to those who are already there?"

Senor Uno stared at him for a second. There was the barest flicker of anger in Uno's eyes. After a brief second, he calmed, but not before Diego caught the reaction. He was sure that it would be there. He was probing, as he always did with Uno. There was something about the man that irked Diego, perhaps the vagueness of his reports. Diego could not be certain, but there was *something!*

"Additional, of course, Don Diego. We must not compromise those already on the dig. We, after all, might have to use them again."

Diego suddenly looked away from him to another man farther down the table. "Quatro, how many helicopters and how will they be procured?"

Quatro did not have to consult his notes at all. "We estimate that five of the newest U.S. SH-94 machines would be sufficient, unless the entire mountain is made of gold. Between them, they can carry more than forty tons of cargo round trip from Monte Alban to our loading sites. Ah..." Quatro paused and fidgeted for a second. "I have to add, sir, that there has been considerable difficulty in managing to procure these machines from the American producer. It seems that there is an exclusive government contract on them, and we are on the verge of looking elsewhere to find a similar helicopter with the lift capability as well as the range that can allow a round trip without refueling."

Everyone in the room expected there would be a scathing retort from Diego. It might even mean that Quatro would no longer appear at staff meetings, and in a matter of a few weeks there would be a report of his mysterious demise by heart attack or auto accident. They were wrong. Diego simply smiled and nodded ever so slightly. He took from his jacket pocket a small folded slip of paper and passed it down the table to Quatro.

"It was clear some time ago that the heavy-lift machines would not be available in time. Call that number and arrange with the man who answers the exact deployment of the machines. They will be in place at the time we need them."

Quatro nodded as he picked up the piece of paper. There was more fidgeting as he formed his next question. He had already been humiliated in front of his peers and now he was going to have to risk a second humiliation. He felt like a schoolboy who, when confronted by a stern nun, had failed to produce his homework.

"Sir, ah... I will have to know the type machine. We will have to have the pilots checked out in them—"

"You will not need pilots, Quatro. They will be waiting with the aircraft. For your information, the helicopters will be Tupolov 210. There will be five of them. They will carry the load to the destination."

Quatro's humiliation was complete. The only blessing

was that Diego hastily turned to the next member of the staff.

"Tres? Deployment and operations?"

The man who looked up from the other side of the table was darker in complexion than the others—a Mestizo, part Indian. He stood in a slightly lower social class than the others due to his complexion, as all of the others were descendants of the conquistadors themselves. For a second Senor Tres thought of the irony of that. His eyes moved to Diego's cold, penetrating stare. He spoke before the question was asked; normally a cardinal sin for one of the staff. But Tres was brilliant at operations planning and execution. He knew it, as did Diego. He enjoyed preempting *El Excelso*, a pure Spaniard. Diego tolerated it.

"The access will be from locations A, B, and C. All will allow round-trips without refueling. The aircraft will move back out under radar coverage altitude to sites D, E, and F. The cargo will move to Yucatan at the site we have called Plata y Oro. From there the transfer to the ship will be made."

"Dos? Intelligence and security?"

The second man up at the table to Diego's right was short, fat, bald, and bespectacled. He removed his thick glasses and picked up a series of computer printouts.

"The Moreland Research Institute is quite preoccupied with parapsychology. Channing Moreland, its founder, who once shared a Nobel prize with a Russian counterpart, seemed totally fixated by the notion of para this and that. His successor, a Dr. Jerald Tanner, was his protégé and carried on the tradition. They are funding the new dig on two notions: The new artifacts unearthed indicate a more ancient culture than Monte Alban One and Pre-Olmec. Secondly, an experiment in the use of psychics in archeology. Perhaps those should be reordered. I am certain that the second reason is foremost for Senor Tanner."

"What of this Welshman? This new man?"

Senor Dos consulted another page of printout and looked

to Diego. "His name is Jason Farewey. He has quite a reputation. He was the youngest Ph.D. in archeology ever to graduate from Swansea University in Wales. He almost did not get his degree. While others chose to specialize, he is much more of a generalist. By that I mean his focus covers a number of time periods and geographical locations."

"Is he one of these parapsychologists?"

"Oddly, no. From what we have gathered, he is totally traditional."

"Is he a close friend of this Dr. Tanner?"

"This is uncertain, Don Diego. We know from computer records that he had a passing acquaintance with Tanner. But there is no computer that can tell us the depth of the relationship. All my staff can surmise is that he is taking all of this as a challenge. It is my guess, and you understand this is only a guess..." Senor Dos stopped to replace the thick glasses and adjust them so he could get better eye contact with his superior. "...that he is being paid a very large sum for the expedition. On Tanner's side, Farewey was probably chosen for his sheer brilliance in the field. He also carries a large number of undergraduate credits in engineering, specifically mine engineering. This, of course, gives him magnificent preparations for underground digs such as those in Egypt, and most especially the Monte Alban Tomb Seven operation. As you know, they had to sink a shaft after the initial finds, and as the shaft deepens there will be a greater danger of collapse, ventilation problems, and numerous things that only a good engineer could wrestle with. In short, he is perfect for the project."

"Can he be...persuaded to..." Don Diego drummed the fingers of his right hand on the polished tabletop. "...shall I say, see things from our perspective?"

"This seems impossible. Dedication and professionalism seem to rule him far more than greed. This stems from his professional record and from his family situation."

"Single? Married?"

TOMB SEVEN

"The former, though what I meant is that he is independently, though moderately, wealthy. His family in Wales owns a number of lucrative coal mining operations. This might also account for the academic emphasis on mine engineering. I assume he was supposed to take over the family business. Both parents are dead and Farewey is an only child. He is something of an absentee landlord for Farewey Ltd. The company is managed quite well by a man we believe to be a college friend of Dr. Farewey."

Senor Dos stopped, seemingly pleased with himself. Diego's expression did not change, though he indeed was pleased with the thoroughness of the report.

"Who, then, *is* this psychic? Or would there be more than one?"

This time Senor Dos did not have to look at the printout.

"Her name is Lupe Muñoz. She comes from a family that is half Castillian and half Puertoricano."

"Tell me more. I know little of these psychics."

Senor Dos looked across the table to a tall slender man in his fifties. There was a certain air of the academic about him.

"Perhaps Senor Cinco can illuminate you more about that, sir. I only have data about the woman herself."

Diego frowned, just a flicker. He should not have asked the last question of Dos. It was clearly *not* his domain. He became fleetingly angry with himself for the slip in management procedure, and a tiny bit irked at Dos for exposing it. His eyes moved back to the academic.

"Tell me about the woman, then."

Dos glanced at his printouts for a long minute.

"She is far more American than Spanish, in all respects. Her family, specifically her grandmother, was a psychic of great repute with the Moreland operation. Lupe has a graduate degree in archeology. She is twenty-six and single."

Diego looked across to the academic-looking Senor Cinco. "What about all of this psychic business, and how does it connect with the gold to be found in the dig?"

Cinco explained psychometry and various other psi phenomenon as briefly as possible. All Diego could do was shake his head.

"I see little connection with her and the project. I am prone to say that all of this psi business is foolishness. At any rate, I see her as no threat to the project. She speaks Spanish, I assume?"

Cinco nodded and Diego looked back across to Dos.

"The operatives have been warned about idle chatter?"

"Absolutely, sir."

"Good." Diego looked back at Cinco. "Is there anything to indicate that . . . what do you call it? Parapsychology will speed anything?"

"That is hard to say, Don Diego. Treasure has been found with the aid of psychics, or at least there have been claims of this written about in a number of articles and books. Tanner at Moreland Research has published a great deal of material, as have the Russians in Leningrad. . . ."

He paused for a second and tried to think of a name. Diego always considered such pauses as interruptions to the meetings, but the man was a walking encyclopedia when it came to such things. Perhaps he overresearched, but that was something Diego did not mind. Planning was the key to success, and there was no such thing as too much planning. He waited, but only for the short few seconds it took for Cinco to flash through his mental inventory. Actually, there was little need to know the name of the Russian researcher. However, the name itself might kick something else loose from Cinco's mental file drawer. *That* was important. It had been the key to success many times in the past. He owed much to Cinco's think-tank mind.

"Yes. Sholodkin. Dr. Sholodkin. His first name escapes me. But at any rate, he also has written about such experiments. I must confess that my first reaction was similar to yours. He thought that it was all foolishness. There is little known, and much more to research in the area. But for our purposes I can say that from the reading that I've done, there is a good chance that with the Muñoz woman on the project the location of the gold might well come faster than by the use of traditional techniques alone. This, of course, will have a considerable impact on the speed of operations that Senor Tres can develop. We"—he gestured to the others at the table—"all know that the operation will have to be completed before the Federales are on the scene." He glanced at Senor Seis at the far end of the table. "Pardon me, Senor. I impinge on your domain."

Seis, dark and dapper in a three-piece suit, was slender and quiet. His thin mustache was perfectly trimmed and his eyes small, giving him a vaguely sinister look. Seis first glanced at Cinco and smiled with a slight nod of his head— it was obvious he was not offended—then his eyes moved slowly back to Don Diego. Cinco was certain that the man was going to call on Seis next in any event, and also sure that there was no offense in that quarter. There was little more that he could add to what he had already said. Actually, he felt, all that he had done was to lead the way for the rest of the report. As Diego started to speak Cinco realized he had been correct in his estimate.

"Perhaps that should be the next topic of conversation. What of federal intervention in the matter, Seis?"

Seis shook his head slightly. "I cannot see that there will be any that might interfere with the operation. The Federales, as my learned colleague prefers to call them, will be delayed until after the operation is completed."

"How?"

Seis' eyes narrowed even farther. He was more than a bit insulted. His methods had never been in question in the past. All that Diego was interested in was results, and he knew that. The real names of the men who sat at the meeting might be violated if there was too much information divulged about methods. Still, if Diego asked, he would have to answer. The question indicated the amount of money and power the operation would yield.

"Our chief operative on the scene is a man who is the

official government liaison for such digs in the state of Oaxaca. He is prestigious and well placed in the local government structure. The federal government listens to him and he will simply delay telling them until we have learned of large finds and carried out the operation. It is as simple as that."

"Will there be any suspicion here?"

Seis assumed that Diego meant in the federal government. "I can assure you that there will be none at all. The operative in Oaxaca is absolutely above reproach."

He said nothing more. But it was clear to Deigo from a quick glance at the man's eyes that his ego had been bruised. This did not bother Diego. The staff were going to make more than each might make in a lifetime from the operation, and the past operations of this nature had made them wealthy men. He had brought it all together. He had carefully researched all of them and assembled them as his private think tank. He could afford to bruise an ego or two.

"Very well. As we have discussed, speed will be the key to the operation. The Oaxaca operative says that he thinks from the artifacts already found, there might be large catches of treasure. These will be assembled at the site and at that time we will move swiftly. This meeting is adjourned. I remind you to leave in the reverse order of arrival. The cabs will come at ten-minute intervals to the side gate. Thank you gentlemen."

He got to his feet and the others followed suit. When they had moved through the huge doors and out into the anteroom, Diego returned to the chair and mused. All of them would carry out the operation efficiently. He knew that he had complete control as far as his six colleagues were concerned. It was his newly acquired partners who most concerned him. They did not have a track record of flawless business dealings in the international community. But, he thought, perhaps their desperate need in this situation would force them to deal in good faith.

He moved from the conference room to the adjoining

inner office, unlocked a desk drawer and removed a phone. He punched in a number and the call was answered on the first ring.

"Yes?"

"The Oaxaca Project is under way."

"The dates and times are exactly as discussed?"

"Of course. What of the people you have on the site?"

"They are legitimate, at least they think they are. Were you concerned about our coordination of the operation, Comrade Diego?"

"No. I was just checking, and do not refer to me as comrade."

7

The Mexicana 727 circled the Oaxaca airport near dusk. The Oaxacan pilot could not resist announcing the local features to the passengers. He dipped the wing of the jet so that the tourists could see the impressive mountain complex of Monte Alban.

Staring out the window, Jason realized that pictures of the place did it little justice. Even from five thousand feet above the flattened mountaintop, the sheer enormity of the undertaking astounded him. There was not a site in Wales or in all of Europe that could have been built with such engineering skill. Without even the wheel, he thought. Without even the wheel.

Lupe turned from the view, her face close to his. "Also, there was no water."

"What?" Jason asked. The two were eye to eye and only inches apart.

"I said there was no water. All of it had to be carried up from the valley."

Jason fumbled, looking for words. "B-but . . . you don't understand. About the wheel . . . I . . . I *thought* that. I didn't say it. I . . ."

She smiled wryly and he could smell the barest hint of delicate perfume.

"I *know* you thought it."

He tried to look away but could not. Her dark eyes held

him. After a few seconds he shook his head and ran a hand through his hair. "Well... another demonstration?"

Her smiled turned coquettish. "I have my good days."

He smiled too. "Does this mean we are soul mates or something?"

"No. I just have my good days." She turned back to the window. "Look, there's Tomb Seven."

He forced his eyes away from hers and peered again through the window. He should have seen it at first glance. It had all of the earmarks of a dig; a reinforced causeway entering at a downward angle, a series of carefully separate piles of red clay, a hand crane rigged to draw earth from the bottom of the dig and deposit the dirt in one of the segregated piles. Though he couldn't see them, he was sure there were digging tools and screen boxes, designed to sort the earth from even the smallest artifacts.

He turned to see Lupe still looking at him. "Ah... interesting that the tomb is so distant from the rest of the complex." He tried to sound nonchalant, though her eyes were making him feel like a naked man at Buckingham Palace. Had she really read my mind? he wondered.

"Many of the tombs here are distant from the rest of the complex. The thinking is that while the Egyptians used pitfalls and other traps to elude grave robbers, whoever built these used distance and secrecy. Tomb Seven is one of the few we have found that has been multilayered. And, of course, as the dig gets deeper, there seems to be more to be found, like the small serpent you saw in Jerry's office. There is a lot to be learned from the dig, but there are other mysteries about the complex too."

"Oh?" He still couldn't let go of the phrase she'd picked from his mind. Coincidence?

"The Seven Deers area. See it?"

In the fading light he could see a small oval at the far end of the carved plateau. Piles of rock and demolished buildings were barely visible.

He turned back to her. There was the barest hint of a

smile on her face, but he could see that she maintained her professional distance. "The area is named for an engraving of seven deer on one of the lintels of a structure. The odd thing about it is that the artifacts in the S.D. area are newer than those found in the main complex. Still, the architecture of the main site is much more sophisticated. For example, the door arches of S.D. are only about five feet high while the older area has arches, peaked at that, with heights of more than eight feet. Since doorways are functional—"

"The newer buildings had to be considerably shorter than their ancestors, and that defies genetic logic," he said, flashing his own version of a wry smile. He had written a paper some five years earlier about mound design in Wales. While he had mentioned the phenomenon in the paper, he had little if any grasp of the apparent paradox.

"Have you—"

"Yes," she grinned. "I read your paper."

Suddenly, he looked wary. "Did you anticipate me or did you slip into my head again?"

"The former, I assure you. And I don't just slip into people's heads. I don't yet have that kind of control. Besides, there is the right to privacy. And no, reading your paper was a part of one of my own research projects. I'm not an archeological groupie."

Now it was his turn to probe. "What was the subject of your paper?"

"Catastrophism." She tossed the phrase off lightly, though her eyes were riveted to his.

"Not all of that Edgar Cayce and Velikovski stuff?"

Her glance grew chilly. "Part of it, yes. That *stuff*. The theory is supported, among other things, by the two sites you just saw down there."

"Yes, but don't you think that there would have been more tangible evidence of higher civilizations left in situ?"

"Perhaps you do not fully understand the underlying hypothesis. If the basic idea is correct, early civilizations, which are now little more than the making of legend and science fiction, would have been utterly devastated by a geological cataclysm. There is precedent in Pompeii, the Saint Pierre disaster in 1902, and others. What of the explosion of Mount Saint Helens? What if there was a thriving, vastly advanced civilization inhabiting the area of Spirit Lake, some six miles from the northside blowout? There would be nothing to find. Suppose there was an Atlantis and it was destroyed in the same way, falling into the Mid-Atlantic Rift? How much could we see at such a depth, and indeed, why would we bother to look?" She stopped, suddenly realizing that she'd been lecturing. She looked down. "I'm sorry, I—"

"No, not at all." Jason could see the slightest touch of a little girl in her. It was well worth the beginnings of a lecture, though he could not accept the subject of the hypothetical lecture. "You are obviously well versed in this area, and there always is the possibility that I am far too conservative. But forgive me if my skepticism makes me say that I'd have to see a great deal more tangible evidence before I embrace your theory."

She looked at him intently for a long moment. There was something he had not seen before. It was a distant look, as if part of her was probing inside of him, and at the same time, another part was in its own world, perhaps the psychic world that had so shocked him only moments before. It disturbed him, and he was glad to see the look slip away in a few seconds.

"Perhaps, Jason"—it was the first time she'd used his given name, and there was a warmth in her voice that was more than inviting—"perhaps you will find the evidence that you seek on this dig."

For a split second he could again see the distant look, and then it was gone. Jason pondered, his thoughts scattered and muted. Had she seen something? What was she thinking? There was only one answer to the question and that was to question. "That look you just had... ah, how do I put it? Did you *see* something?"

She tossed her head back and laughed. "You are learning, aren't you? No. I'm not laughing at you or probing inside your psyche. There was a slight feeling that I cannot explain, but it has been there before. It is light...a light breeze across moist skin in the summer. Subtle...indefinable. There was something there and I was not probing you. But you put the question the same way that Jerry Tanner did after I was at the Institute for a while. The problem with whatever psi is, is the subtlety of it. There are times when I am sure that I am seeing something, and there are times when the symbol in the feeling is so delicate that I can't catch it before it vanishes somewhere back in here." She gestured to the right rear portion of her head.

"Jerry thinks that this is the area where the psi ability rests. The right occiped. It can't read, write, or speak. All that it can do is cough up imagery. The rest is up to us. Perhaps I saw that you would see things the way I do before we finish our business here. But then again, there is always the chance that I was simply wanting you to see things my way, and what I felt was not precognition at all but something like wish fulfillment. At the same time, I felt something else...." She stopped and there was a long pause as Jason waited for her to continue.

"What was it?" he finally blurted.

Again she smiled. "Let's let that one remain my secret for a time, shall we?"

The landing was smooth, and as they crossed the tarmac, heading toward the small Oaxaca terminal, Jason was surprised at the strong cool breeze that made the Mexican summer seem like Wales in May.

"I thought it would be much hotter."

Lupe nodded as she tossed her head, letting her raven hair be sifted by the wind. He found himself thinking how her hair would look splayed across white pillow sheets in the cool dawn. He pushed the thought away, afraid for a second that she might be reading his mind again.

"So did I. But it's the altitude, I guess."

"Hmm? Oh, yes... I guess it is."

They stepped into the waiting room and toted their carry-on luggage to the center of the room while the rest of the passengers waited for bags to be unloaded from the bowels of the 727. Going from one remote location to another in the last decade, he had made it a habit to travel light. He was glad to see Lupe thought the same way he did. Not only did it prevent the possibility of the bags getting on the wrong plane, but it also let him get through customs and airport lobbies like... he tried to think of the name of the American football player he had seen on television commercials and could not remember it.

Through the crowd Jason could see a man approaching them, and knew instantly that he was the one whom they were expecting. He was large—a bear of a man, with thick shoulders and a broad chest. His tan was deep and leathered. He moved in long slow strides that gave him the appearance of catlike ability. Jason would have known in an instant that the man was an archeologist or perhaps a digger, but the man's bearing said more of the former.

"Dr. Farewey? Senorita Muñoz?"

"I'm Farewey," Jason said as Lupe turned to look at the man.

"Welcome to Oaxaca. I'm Ugo Caldera, chief digger at the project. Can I help with your bags?"

"Yes, thank you." Jason and Lupe almost said the words in unison. Jason was surprised at the flawless command of English that Caldera had. There were few native diggers in his experience who could speak without the hint of an accent from their native land.

"Please come this way. I have a car waiting outside."

While Ugo carried Lupe's soft leather suitcases, she and Jason followed him to the main entrance of the terminal.

The narrow strip of the Pan American Highway took them along a stream dotted with shacks. One of them appeared to have had a recent fire. The shack was nothing more than a burned-out black patch on the ground. Jason could see the major portion of the city in the distance. His curiosity overcame his natural hesitance to speak in a strange situation.

"Mr. Caldera—"

"Please..." Caldera glanced at Jason for a split second before his eyes returned to the road. "Please, call me Ugo. Everyone does."

"Thank you, Ugo. I was going to remark that your English was flawless. Are you from Oaxaca?"

"No, Doctor. I am from Mexico City. The Department of Antiquities in the Office of the Secretary of the Interior sent me to Dr. Rodgers some months ago, when your foundation was starting to negotiate the reopening of the dig with our government. As for my English, I studied at the University of Texas for a year and then at the University of Colorado for another."

"Major?"

"Mine engineering and archeology. Just like your degree, Doctor. Except you finished yours, and I ran out of funds."

"Your background seems excellent."

"Thank you. Dr. Rodgers seemed pleased with it. Things were progressing very well. It was a shock to all of us... his death, I mean. He seemed to be in perfect health and was very, very excited about the finds in the lower levels of the dig. A great many of the diggers were... what is the term? Spooked by it?"

Jason smiled. "That's an American term, and I'm afraid that I'm a Welshman. What does it mean?"

Ugo's eyebrows furrowed as he peered at the oncoming traffic. "There is a great deal of superstition about the mountain and the Zapotecs, as well as the ones who might have been there before them. Just last night an old woman, a shaman from the shacks..." He pointed in the direction of the hovels across the small stream. "She turned up at the Guelaguetza and cursed all those who worked on the Tomb Seven project."

"And?" Lupe leaned forward from the rear seat at the mention of the word shaman—one who holds power, like the medicine man or the witch doctor, but Lupe knew it meant far more than that.

"And the woman died right there, in the dancing circle. No one knows what she died of yet. But she was apparently quite old. They say that she was speaking Zapoteco when she died."

"You mentioned the guya... what?"

"Oh, I'm sorry. It is pronounced 'Guyagetcha' and it is an ancient ceremony held at the beginning of the summer. We think that the Zapotecs started it but we cannot be sure of it. The best thinking is that it was a ceremony to honor the ancient gods. It contained a great deal of ritual, and culminated in a human sacrifice."

"What about, ah, this... spooking of the diggers?"

"Most of them are local and know all about the Guelaguetza and the legends that surround Monte Alban. It had been considered sacred for centuries. They are simply afraid of the curse. In addition, it was not the fact that the woman spoke the curse, but that she died on the spot, and as she died, the rains came. The festival has not been interrupted by rain for decades. Less than a third of the men were at the dig this morning. I am going to have to recruit some more as soon as possible, and the chances are that additional men are going to dent the budget the government has allotted for the project."

"I'm sure MRI will take up the slack," Lupe said with assurance.

"I hope so," Ugo muttered in a worried tone. "Getting them is hard because of what the government pays. But with inflation what it is, and unemployment high, the chances are that I can get the men I need. The only rub is training them on the job. Many of them are construction men who don't know that you must walk on your toes in a dig. Many are used to heavy equipment and the like. Hand shoveling and sifting through screen boxes is not exactly what they are used to. But we have not stopped digging. Before the end of the week, chances are we will be up to strength. I think I can assure you of that."

"That's good to hear," Lupe said. Jason looked back at her and for a long second could see that her eyes were lost again, distant as they were in the plane. Momentarily, her eyes were drawn to his and the look vanished. He inclined his head as if to ask her what had happened. She shook her head and said nothing.

Despite all of the logic and history that had been drummed into him in the years of college and in the field—years that had made him a clear-thinking logician who should have been disturbed by such indefinable frippery as psychic this and psychic that—Jason was not disturbed. Rather, and much to his dismay, he was finding himself fascinated by this stunning woman and her remarkable, inexplicable ability.

As they moved from the outskirts of Oaxaca into the city proper, Jason could see that this was indeed a city and not the small dusty town his imaginings had led him to picture.

"Ugo?"

"Yes, Doctor?" Again the digger's eyes flashed to him for a second before they moved to the congested traffic on the main street.

"What's the population of the city?"

"Close to two hundred thousand, and that does not count the tourists. Many of them come for the Guelaguetza." He shook his head and pointed to the dark line of clouds over the mountains in the distance. "But it looks like tonight might be the same as last night. It will be hard for the vendors and the artists to sell their work." Ugo's tone was glum.

"Perhaps we can recruit some of them for the dig?" Jason quipped, seeing the concern in Ugo's face.

The burly driver shook his head disdainfully. "No, Doctor, there is no chance of that. Most of them would need an ambulance after a half a day on the mountain in the sun.

No, though the population is large, there is a select group from which I would choose. If I did not, we would be wasting my country's money and that of your institute. But don't worry. We will get the skilled ones we need."

Jason eyed the mountains and the hovering dark clouds that skirted them. "Does it normally rain here at this time of year?"

"A bit... in the afternoon, normally."

"Not in the evening?"

Ugo shook his head. "If you are asking whether the torrent that washed out the ceremony last night was normal, it was not. At this time of year there is a shower in the late afternoon. Perhaps it might last until sundown. But a cloudburst such as we had last night is unprecedented. That is what started the exodus and all of the rumors that are about the city today."

"Are that many people believers?" Lupe asked.

"Enough of them are, Senorita. Enough in the ranks of those from whom I would chose diggers. But, as I said, I will find them."

"Actually, Ugo," Jason said, "there was another reason for the question. What about the drainage in the dig if this kind of evening rain becomes, how shall I say it... a habit?"

"There is little to worry about, Doctor. The red clay of the mountaintop itself provides good drainage. We are two thousand meters above the water table in the valley. We have also, under the direction of the late Dr. Rodgers, built drainage ditches and a pool for collection of the water. We have a gasoline-powered pump if we need to drain the pool."

"Is the water screened before it enters the collecting pool?" Jason asked.

"Absolutely, Doctor. Dr. Rodgers was very careful about that. We have covered the routes of egress with sixteenth-inch wire mesh. I'm afraid that anything smaller would cause a silt and clay buildup that would clog the entire system. I told him that it did not rain that hard at this time of year, but he insisted. I am glad he did, after last night."

"What about shoring?" Jason could start to feel himself getting into gear. He was anxious to get to the dig. There was only one thing that disturbed him, and that was the lack of time he had to prepare for the dig. Normally, he would spend months researching the area to be explored. This time, there had only been a few days, due to the untimely death of Rodgers. He was going to have to rely on the historical expertise of Lupe and Ugo, as well as the former's strange talents.

Ugo pulled up at the front entrance of the Presidente Hotel, which he assured both of them was the finest hotel in the city. As Jason helped Lupe from the backseat, he noticed that the hotel looked like a fortress from the outside. There were few exterior windows, and high walls bordered the block-long exterior of the building. Across the street, another hotel had the same countenance. As his eyes moved farther up the road, he saw identical architecture. Barren, scrubbed exteriors faced him. There was no trash in the streets and no visible garbage cans. *Clean desolation* were the words that came to him as he looked at the scene.

The view led him to momentarily ponder the psychological makeup of the Oaxacans and the Mexicans in general. Though different in specifics, the character of the architecture was similar to others he had both seen and studied in books. Japan and ancient Rome bore similarities to what he saw here on a Mexican street. Xenophobia—unreasoning fear of anything unfamiliar. It had caused Japan to be closed to the rest of the world for centuries, and Roman patricians to build huge walls surrounding their homes and estates. It was this very act of turning inward that might have led to the fall of Rome, and certainly shattered a great deal of the traditions of Japan with the arrival of Perry and the advent of American technology. Here, the xenophobic syndrome would force many of the citizens, no matter how much they embraced the customs of their North American cousins, to believe the ancient legends that surrounded Monte Alban, Mitla, and the extensive ruins to the south.

TOMB SEVEN

"Jason? Shall we go inside?"

"Oh... yes, of course." He had lost himself in thought again. It was a long-term habit when he was starting a dig. At first, he had consciously tried to grasp every nuance of the local culture in the hope that current tradition, superstition, and even fad might aid him in the development of a reconstruction of what had thrived in the past. For this, many of his colleagues thought him a snob. But they could not deny his results. However sensitive to their attitudes, Jason tried carefully to make his mental sojourns brief when he was in their company. He disliked being caught drifting.

"Did you have a nice trip?"

"What?"

"Wherever you were for a few minutes."

"Oh." He laughed. "Sorry. I was concentrating on the architecture."

They entered the lobby and headed in the direction of the registration desk. Ugo deposited their bags with a bellhop and they found that their rooms were adjoining on the third floor.

"Perhaps, Doctor, you would like to spend some time this afternoon looking through the city. There is much to see, many sales and exhibits from the Guelaguetza, despite the rain last night."

"Well, I'd rather change and get to the dig, actually."

"There will be nothing going on at the dig, Doctor, not at this time of the day. It is siesta. There will be more work tomorrow, but all that will be happening now is sleep and preparations for tomorrow. You might as well enjoy the city."

Jason still wanted to visit the dig, but a look at Lupe told him that a tour of the city with her might be of much greater interest just now. "Perhaps you are right, Ugo," he said. "A tour of the city might be interesting."

"Very well, then. I will pick you up in the morning. Say ...six?"

Jason swallowed hard. It had been some time since he

had been on a dig, and every one of them started when the local customs dictated that diggers should get to work. Apparently the Mexicans started things early to compensate for the siesta in the heat of the afternoon.

"That will be fine, Ugo, just fine."

"Oh, there is another thing, Doctor."

"Yes?"

"I have taken the liberty of making an appointment for you to speak with Dr. Martin Caranza. He is the head of the department of antiquities at Santo Domingo Museum. He has been very helpful to us at the dig and it was he who sent the samples to your institute. Dr. Rodgers worked closely with him. Ah... is the time all right with you? It is at one, tomorrow, when the diggers stop for siesta."

Jason looked to Lupe. She shrugged. "You're the archeologist."

"The time is fine, Ugo. We can drive right in from the dig."

"Very well, Doctor. Until tomorrow morning, then. Senorita." He bowed slightly to Lupe, turned and left the lobby.

Jason got to his room, unpacked his all-purpose suitcase, and stepped out on the tiny balcony. Below, the courtyard was ablaze with dozens of varieties of exotic flowers. In the distance, through a Moorish arcade, he could see another courtyard and yet another garden. "His" garden tended to have hot colors, and the piece of the one that he could see in the distance seemed to emphasize cool colors. He suspected that there were at least four such varieties of color in the rest of the interior courtyard.

He thought again of xenophobia and how that would have been acquired by the Oaxacans from something other than their ancestors. Otherwise the ancients would have built temples surrounded by walls and shelters to protect them from the view of outsiders. Rome and Japan had been consistent for centuries, even eons. But Oaxaca and the other architectural sites had not been so influenced. Rather, they had gone in the opposite direction from their ancestors. As he looked at the garden, he wondered if the Spanish had brought the tradition with them, and if it had overcome the traditional outwardness of the ancients. Lost in thought, he almost missed the gentle knock at the door.

"Oh. Come in." He turned to the door as he spoke.

The door opened and Lupe stood for a long moment, framed in the doorway. She wore slacks and a light summer top. The sensuous curve of breast and hip struck him immediately. He caught himself staring.

"Ah... well, come in. You look like a native rather than a tourist." Inwardly he cringed at the lack of wit or tact the remark showed. But caught off guard by her, he could find no other words.

"Well," she said, cocking a fist on her hip, "I can't say the same of you. If you want to buy anything in the marketplace, you'd better let me do the haggling. With blue eyes and that hair of yours, you would be fair game for any sharp vendor."

"Touché. Have you seen the garden?" He gestured in the direction of the balcony.

"Yes. Who could miss it?"

He paused for a long moment, painfully pulling his glance from her and moving it to the garden. "It's stunning. Did the Spanish bring this architecture in the conquest?"

She shook her head. "I'm not sure, but there is a great deal of this kind of design in Spain. Then, we have to wonder if the Moors brought it there. It's kind of like chasing your tail."

He repressed a grin. *Chasing tail, huh!* "Well, if we're tourists," he quipped, "where should we go first?"

"The bellboy mentioned Avenida Morales. He said it leads to the largest park in the city and that's where they are having an art exhibit today. He also said there were bargains for the shopper, but I doubt the latter. It's not too far to walk. But he warned me to take it slow until we got used to the altitude."

Jason glanced at the sky through the window. "If we're

going, we'd better go. I'm not sure how long the weather will hold. Do you want to take a jacket?"

She shook her head and her hair caught the light haloing her for a second in a strange blend of ebony and gold. "Mmm ... no! It won't rain!"

"Is that a hunch, a prediction or something, ah... psychic."

"None of them. My big toe tells me it will not rain."

They laughed and left the room, heading down the hall in the direction of the elevators.

As they walked, Jason could feel the effect of the altitude. It was slight but evident. He was clearly expending more energy than he would at sea level. The dig would be two thousand feet higher still, and he mentally reminded himself to gauge his energy output until his system adjusted to the height. If Lupe was affected in the same way, she did not show it. Jason pondered for a second the possibility of asking her, but thought better of it. With the things she already told him, there was a chance she was reading his thoughts as he spoke. There was something uncanny about her. But for the first time since he could remember, he was not repelled by talk of psychic things. He was seeing demonstration after demonstration of an ability that the majority of the scientific community utterly dismissed. But in her it was something natural and beautiful.

Half lost in his thoughts, his eyes absently scanned the far side of the street. He stopped suddenly and Lupe, surprised, cocked her head to the side as she spoke to him.

"Forget something?"

He shook his head while his eyes remained on the far side of the narrow tourist-filled street. "Yuri?" he said to himself.

"Who?"

"Yes, it's Yuri. Come on." He took her hand and led her through the stream of traffic. "Yuri!" he yelled.

On the far side of the street a small, dark, rotund man

in a pale blue summer suit stopped suddenly, his head turning from side to side, looking for the source of the voice.

Jason waved and the small man saw him. For a second, he smiled, and then the smile evaporated, replaced by a diplomatic mask.

"Yuri, what a surprise. What are you doing here?" Jason paused, and remembering Lupe, introduced the two.

"Lupe, this is Yuri Kurtzov from the Hermitage. We worked together in Tibet, how long ago was it? Four years?"

"Five. But you have developed prettier colleagues than you had then, Jason."

Lupe smiled, but Jason could see it was a different smile than the one he had seen on the plane or at the hotel. It was an artificial smile.

"I hear that you are working with MRI?"

"That's right. The money's better." Again there were smiles, and Jason wondered how Yuri knew so quickly about the MRI expedition and his affiliation with it. And what the bloody hell was a Hermitage team doing in Mexico without *his* knowing about it! He decided to be direct.

"Since when has the Hermitage sent its top oriental specialist to the other side of the world?"

"Since funds became tight. I think they expect that if you can lead a cost-effective dig in one part of the world, you can do it anywhere. It's the same thing as... what did you call it once? Oh, yes. The British government theory?"

Both men broke into laughter and Jason glanced at Lupe, whose eyes still betrayed the artificiality of her smile. "Lupe, the theory says that the government believes that if one woman can have a baby in nine months then there is a good chance that nine women can have a baby in one month."

She nodded but there was no change in the smile or the eyes.

"Where have they got you working, Yuri?"

"Mitla, just now. But there is little more there that can

be unearthed. I am sure of it. They do not tell me directly, but they have just gotten government approval for a new dig in the Seven Deers area of Monte Alban. We are setting up there now."

"We'll be neighbors, then. We're at Tomb Seven."

"This I had heard just yesterday. I also heard about Dr. Rodgers. Terrible thing. I never met him. How did it happen?"

"They say it was a heart attack. Might have something to do with the altitude. He was a runner."

"Still, a terrible thing. I—" Yuri stopped in midphrase as a young, slender man turned from a shop window a few feet away and joined the group. "Oh, let me introduce a... learned young colleague, Georgi Valarin." He finished the introductions and quickly extended a hand to Jason. "I'm afraid we'll have to be going. Nice to see you again, Jason, and to meet you, ah... Senorita. Perhaps we can get a chance to see you at your part of the dig?"

"That would be wonderful, Yuri. I look forward to it."

Jason and Lupe parted company with the two Russians and headed off onto the narrow side street that led to the Avenida Morales. After a few moments they both walked wrapped in silent thought. Lupe looked up to him. "Jason?"

"Hmm?"

"The man who joined your friend?"

"What about him?"

"I think he was a... policeman."

"I know."

"You *know*? How?"

Jason smiled broadly. "No, I didn't beat you at that psychic game you play so well. It was the way Yuri introduced him. Calling him 'learned colleague.' It was a term he used when he spoke of the watchdog they placed on him in Nepal."

"Watchdog?"

"A personal watchdog supplied by the KGB, or whatever they're calling the secret police now. The Russians don't let leading scientists out of the country without them. Occasionally they are actual archeologists or other scientists working for the KGB, but that made Yuri furious. So they decided to stop the pretense and send a real policeman."

"He doesn't mind?"

"He has no choice, not if he wants to remain a member of the Soviet Academy of Sciences. That is, as Americans say, the way the game is played. I still don't understand why they'd send Yuri here."

"Is it that odd?"

"Yuri is an expert on deep excavation digs. He knows at least as much as I do about them, perhaps more. But he doesn't know an Aztec artifact from a Mayan one. Why send him?"

"Is there anything else that he has an expertise in that might offset that?"

"There is. He is an expert in the evaluation of precious artifacts."

The Avenida Morales led them to the Parque Central, which was jammed with small booths and stalls. At the far end of the park there was a huge open-air art show. They ambled from booth to booth. At one that purported to sell antiques, Jason stopped to pick up a small black clay replica of Cojico, the rain god.

He turned and handed it to Lupe. "Aren't you afraid you will offend him by predicting sun for this afternoon?"

She grinned and handed it back to him. "Not in the least. My big toe never lies."

He looked closely at the small flat engraving before he turned to the toothless Indian woman who ran the stall. He noticed that her eyes lit up as she anticipated getting a good price from the gringo for the trinket.

"Es un artículo antiguo?" he said carefully, trying to remember his equally ancient Spanish.

She nodded vigorously. *"Si, Senor. Es una antigualla verdadera."*

"Cuanto?"

The old woman eyed Jason, taking careful notice of his

dress and the fact that he was clearly a tourist.

"Tres-cientos pesos, Senor."

He shook his head and turned to Lupe. "Cow dung!"

"Is that an observation or an editorial opinion?"

He shook his head and laughed. "They age the clay in cow dung. I would guess that this piece is less than a few weeks old."

"I thought you said that *I* was the one who was to be the guide?"

"I have to confess that I read the guide book in the hotel room."

He turned to the woman and handed back the piece with a smile.

As they moved away from the booth, Jason could hear the woman lowering the asking price and then calling to them. He was not sure what the last thing that she said was, but as he looked to Lupe he could see that her face was red and she had broken into a grin.

"What did she say?"

"She said something about your parents being unmarried. That was followed with a clinical expression of what she considered to be your sexual preferences."

He smiled. "Oh, was that all?"

"I'm sure that if she had been given time, she could have come up with something better. But that was on the spur of the moment."

"Well, I guess that makes me the ugly Welshman."

They moved to the art show, where every style and medium was available to them. They wove through the rows of stalls and booths and Jason marveled at the number of Oaxacan artists. An hour and a half later, they both admitted to a severe case of sensory overload, deciding to go back to the hotel.

They were moving slowly to the edge of the park when Lupe suddenly stopped. Through the still air both of them could feel a sudden ripple. The tree to Jason's right weaved and creaked slightly, as if caught by a sudden zephyr. Both of them could hear an eerie, low moan which came from no particular direction. Across the street several dogs, tied outside a store, started to keen and wail. Jason could feel a slight vibration under his feet.

Lupe stopped a passerby, who seemed to be oblivious to what they were feeling.

"Perdóneme, Senor. Qué es esto?"

The middle-aged man shrugged. *"Pequeño terremoto,"* he said without breaking stride.

Jason watched the man for a second before turning to Lupe. "What did he say?"

"Terremoto. He said it was a slight earthquake."

8

As they arrived at the hotel reception desk, the clerk looked at the pair and he moved in the direction of the key slots. He returned with a small slip of paper.

"Dr. Farewey? There is a message for you." He handed the paper to Jason, who in turn passed it to Lupe, since it was written in Spanish.

She read it and looked up to him. "It's from Dr. Caranza, the one who Ugo mentioned. He says he has been forced to cancel tomorrow's meeting and asks if we can see him this afternoon at the Santo Domingo Cathedral. He mentions four or four thirty."

Jason looked at his watch. It was almost four. "How far is the cathedral?"

The answer came from the room clerk, who had been overhearing the conversation. "It is only a few blocks, to the other side of the park on the Avenida. You could walk in a few minutes."

Jason looked to Lupe. "Shall we, or are you tired?"

"Let's go. I get the feeling that once you're at the dig, you are going to want to stay there."

The cathedral-museum complex was immense and packed with tourists. They asked directions of a guard and were sent through a labyrinth of artifact-filled corridors to the office of the director on the top floor. They opened the door and were greeted by a slight dapper man in his fifties. He approached and offered a hand.

"Dr. Farewey and Senorita Muñoz. What a pleasure. I am Martin Caranza. I hope you have not been too inconvenienced by the rescheduling of our meeting. I'm afraid there was something that came up and tomorrow became impossible."

"Not at all, Doctor. We were seeing some of the sights. That was all."

"Well, won't you sit down." Jason noted that there was a touch of King's English in the man's speech. There was a chance he had been educated in England, or perhaps learned English from an Englishman rather than an American.

Caranza went to the side of the office, returning with a carafe and three glasses. "Perhaps you would care for a sherry? I recommend it. It's quite good."

They accepted the hospitality and the sherry. As they sipped, Caranza explained how he came to get involved in the project. He said he had studied Monte Alban for a long time and was pleased to see the government and the Americans were expressing fresh interest in new excavation.

"As you might know, there is much of Monte Alban still to be unearthed," he added soberly.

"Yes." Jason nodded. "Miss Muñoz mentioned that there was more than ninety percent of the dig still unexcavated. How is that?"

Caranza nodded and folded his arms as he leaned back in his easy chair. "It all boils down to funds. So much of archeology does these days. When the government first did the excavation, pre-war, there was an abundance of foreign funds from foundations all over the world. As the Second World War started, these dried up. Many of the foundations were in Europe and there was little interest in financing when the countries were occupied by the Nazis. Likewise, much of the money the American government had put into the dig went into the war effort. After the war there were other projects that became more attractive. So, Monte Alban was left half done."

"How is it that you seemed to have...how shall I say it...kept the faith, Dr. Caranza?"

Caranza smiled winningly. "I really can't say. There has always been a fascination about Monte Alban for me. I have walked the ruins hundreds of times. Each time I see a partially unearthed structure, I am clutched by incredible curiosity. I want to see more. Perhaps it has become an obsession. When Ugo Caldera approached me about reopening the dig with your late Dr. Rodgers, I couldn't help being enthusiastic." He got to his feet and gestured to the door. "Perhaps I could show you some of the museum. You will have a great deal of time later to see the rest of it, but the Monte Alban area will give you a bit of background."

They moved from the office and into a gallery that wove its way around all four sides of yet another walled garden. Jason was put in mind of the hotel and xenophobia. The Monte Alban exhibit was vast and carefully designed to move the viewer from the very ancient artifacts to those that were post-conquest and carried the influence of Christianity and Spain. Caranza moved them through the halls in the opposite direction of the intended flow. They saw the latest first and the most ancient last. Caranza, Jason thought, was clearly an expert at this. He knew every nuance of not only the site but of each of the cultures that had lived there.

"Many of the earliest artifacts date to the time of pre-Homeric Greece." Caranza pointed to a case with jewelry. "But there will, I am sure, be others found deeper."

"Why are you sure, Doctor?" Jason asked.

"These"—he pointed to a case which contained bones and some terra cotta figurines—"were found at a shallow level of the dig. It is likely, more than likely in light of the recent dig, that there are more ancient artifacts deeper. I have always thought that, and now it is starting to prove true."

Lupe and Jason looked through cases of exhibits, each

taking them further back into the history of Monte Alban. They moved through the post-conquest artifacts, which stood in sharp contrast to their precursors. The Spaniards demanded that Christianity be represented in all of the carvings and paintings the Indian underlings created. It was thought, Caranza told them, that the representation of Christ in all art was demanded by the feared and hated Santo Hermanidad back in Spain. It was that sainted, sacred brotherhood that, together with the Jesuits, ran the terrifying Inquisition. Officers of the brotherhood arrived in the new world with the Franciscans to do God's bloody work. This consisted, Caranza contended, of either converting or killing the subjugated peoples of every conquered region. There had been little choice for the Zapotecs, especially after the fall of the mighty Aztecs to the north. Vast numbers and razor-sharp obsidian swords meant little when pitted against the cannon and almost mythological muskets of the Spaniards. As their armies fell, so did their art.

Jason found himself attracted to a case containing several skulls. He noticed that two of them had no rear occipid portion, as if the back of the head had been cut away or bashed in. It put him in mind of several similar artifact skulls he had seen in the East Indies.

"Cannibalism?" he wondered aloud.

"Perhaps," Caranza answered. "Or perhaps there was combat involved and the rear of the skull was crushed. I would have to look it up by number. It would depend on the location and the shards that might have been found around the skull, as I'm sure you know, Doctor."

"Certainly."

"A large number of skulls were found in various parts of Monte Alban, and the condition in which they were found, as well as the location, seems to indicate that the Zapotecs and their predecessors had a rather advanced knowledge of medicine."

"At what level?" Jason responded.

"At many. Anatomical and vivisectional stele abound at

the site. You will observe that when you go there. In addition, there was a great degree of sophistication in dentistry, and eventually there was a great deal of success in cranial trepanation."

"Trepanation?" Jason said.

"Look here." Caranza pointed in the direction of the lighted case next to the one that Jason peered into. Jason walked the few feet to the next case where there were about a dozen skulls on display.

"Look at the three on the right," Caranza directed.

Looking, Jason could see that the holes on the skulls were clearly not the result of a skull-crushing blow with a club or obsidian sword. Rather, they were perfectly round incisions clearly indicating that there had been several years of recalcification which partially closed the trepanning site. A second, smaller skull displayed double trepanning. It seemed that this patient had not survived, since the perforation was perfectly round and had little or no calcification connected to it. Yet the perforation on the other side of the skull was almost perfectly healed, as if the surgery took place at widely separated times. The first might have been when the patient was a child, while the second could have been at middle age.

"How could they have known where to trepan? We would need X rays now to determine the location of perhaps a tumor."

"We are not sure. We think that there was a good percentage of hereditary hydrocephalisis, and in that case there would have been little need for location. Any occiped area would have released the pressure."

Jason pointed in the direction of the third skull. "But that one has frontal trepanning incisions. That would hardly be for water on the brain. Correct?"

Caranza looked at the skull and at the number. Jason could almost see the man going through a mental checklist.

"I think, that the incision was determined to have happened due to a tumor. So, in that respect, your question about locating the tumor is quite valid. All that we can conjecture is that the ancients had something like acupuncture. Except, for these ancients, acupuncture was diagnostic rather than curative. For the cure, surgery was used as well as a large array of native medicines. They had categorized, according to the first missionaries, more than twelve hundred plants and their uses in medicine. Many of them were the precursors of modern medicines. But I am sure that you have seen this in other places in the world, Doctor. Didn't the Roman legions use moldy bread poultices to heal infections? And if I remember European history, Purple Foxglove was distilled and given to those who had weak hearts. It was a natural source of digitalis. But as far as this is concerned," his arms spread, seemingly embracing the entire exhibit, "a man might spend a lifetime and not begin to penetrate what there is to find, let alone explain."

Jason could see why Caranza had devoted so many years to the study of a single dig. He had seen others do the same. They were men obsessed, devoted to love affairs with a single project. The field study simply called them regional experts. He thought of Carnovan, Maria Reich, and others who had done the same. He had to admire them, but he could never be one of them. He moved from area to area and sought new challenges. This made some of his colleagues consider him a dilettante, while he liked to classify himself as a generalist.

After moving through the exhibit to the earliest phases of Monte Alban and Mitla, Dr. Caranza took them back to the office and offered them more wine. Lupe accepted, though Jason, heeding her warning about the altitudes and alcohol, politely refused.

Caranza moved from the desk to the cabinet on the wall, then twirled the combination on a safe that lay within. In a few minutes he came back to the desk with a large string-tied velvet bag.

"I think that this might be of interest to you. It was brought to the museum some six months ago and it was what spurred the renewed interest in excavation." He poured the contents of the bag onto the desk blotter and arranged the artifacts carefully for viewing. There were six articles in all: two eagles, each the exact replica of the other; two dragons, a cougar, and what seemed to be a dove. Digging into his desk, Caranza retrieved a jeweler's eye and passed it to Jason.

"Take a close look at the workmanship, Doctor."

Jason placed the band of the magnifying eye on the back of his head and picked up the nearest statuette.

The small cougar was clearly pure gold, with tiny green stone flakes carefully inset to represent eyes. Under the glass Jason could see that the musculature of the animal rivaled the best sketches of Da Vinci or Audubon, and that the pure skill of workmanship was incredible. Details almost invisible to the unaided eye stood out in bold relief under the glass.

"Doctor."

Jason looked up. "Yes?"

"There are further and more minute details that can only be seen with the aid of a fifty-power microscope."

Jason looked again at the piece before he carefully placed it back on the desk. "Did these 'ancients,' as you call them, have anything resembling magnification? Did they know anything about the use of lenses?"

"We have never found an artifact that would indicate that. In addition, let me pose the question that I thought of when these pieces first came to be. Of what value is microscopic detail, no matter how precisely done, if it cannot be seen with the naked eye?"

"Might I see them, Doctor?" Lupe asked.

She had said little during the tour, and Jason suddenly realized that Caranza had been directing his attention far more to him than to her. The attitude, even in an educated man, was clearly indicative of Mexican, and certainly Oaxacan, social mores. The fact that she was a woman made her less important than a man. Jason wondered what Caranza would think when he was confronted with the fact that Lupe was more than another archeologist.

"But certainly, Senorita. Forgive me."

She moved her chair in the direction of the desk and got comfortable. She passed up the magnifying glass and took the cougar piece in her hand as she had done with the piece in Jerry Tanner's office. She closed her eyes and took a series of deep breaths. As she started to probe the object, Jason studied Caranza. The archeologist's expression was polite, but there was no question he was baffled. After a few minutes she placed the artifact back on the table and sat quietly. Jason could see Caranza's bafflement had turned to uneasiness, especially after Lupe had offered no comment.

Jason wondered why she had done it that way. He decided to wait. His experience with her as well as his growing respect for her told him that she knew what she was doing. On the other hand, he wondered if her liberationist dander was up at having been ignored by Caranza. She sat, creating a long, uncomfortable silence. After she was sure that Caranza was twitching inside, she looked to Jason.

"The same as back in Jerry's office."

"I see," Jason responded. "Everything is the same?"

"Quite."

"Ah..." It was clear Caranza wanted to interrupt but did not know what to say.

"Dr. Caranza." Jason broke the awkward silence as he turned to the curator. "Miss Muñoz is a rather skilled..." He paused, wondering at the ease with which he was forming the word. "...psychic, as well as being an excellent archeologist. She gets impressions from artifacts that tell her things that many of the traditional methods do not."

Caranza smiled winningly. "Do you characterize that as psychometry or retrocognition, Senorita?"

Jason was taken aback, though he could see that Lupe's expression betrayed nothing. He began to wonder if he was the last one in the field to know about psychics.

"Mostly psychometry, but occasionally there are unverified instances of retro flashes. You seem to know about the field."

Caranza shrugged in a gesture that Jason thought falsely modest. "I have read many of the papers produced by Moreland Research and the Leningrad Institute for Brain Research. I believe the late Dr. Moreland was connected with a Soviet researcher in some way?"

"Yes. He also did some experiments with my grandmother, and that seemed to get him interested in using psychic skills as adjuncts to archeology. Whatever... skill I might have, comes from her, whether it is genetic or learned."

"I have not seen the skill in use in the field. Would you mind if I watched on occasion when you get to the site?"

"Not at all, Doctor. All I ask is that what I am doing not be advertised to the public at large or to the crew of the dig. As Mr. Caldera seemed to indicate, there was a lot of superstition surrounding the excavation. The last thing that I want to do is for the local workman to think there is a witch in the crew at the dig. I'm sure you understand."

"Certainly. And that reminds me, I have to mention something that is perhaps distasteful to you, and I hope it is not insulting."

"I'm sure that it won't be either," Jason said.

"Thank you. I hope so too. All of the diggers at the site are going to have to be apprised of the procedure for registering artifacts. As you know, for some time now the central government has been more than protective about the objects that have been unearthed. They are considered national property as soon as they are out of the ground. While every effort will be made to get desired pieces sent to Moreland Research for investigation, they will remain the property of the government of Mexico. That, in itself, is no problem. You and the organization you represent are professional or there would be no dig taking place at this time. What I refer to is the digger himself. There are pieces, these among them, that are more than figurative gold mines for the field. They are literal gold mines." He gestured in the direction of the pieces on the desk. "Each of these has been metalurgically analyzed. They are almost pure gold. The odd thing about it is that to get nearly pure gold is to possess very advanced smelting skills."

"But doesn't gold melt at a relatively low temperature?" Jason asked, realizing that his question sounded dense.

"True. However, separation from base elements is the hard thing. To do that, heat must be controlled at several stages of the process. Nowadays, South African mining operations as well as others use computers to get the exact temperature needed. These"—again he gestured to the pieces on the table—"are of that quality. The complicating factor is that pure gold, in order not to be malleable and to retain its shape, needs a minute quantity of foreign alloy. The analysis done in the capital indicates that there is such an alloy in these."

"What did they use? Could the composition be determined?"

"That was the easy part, Dr. Farewey. It was what they found that was astounding. The bonding material was titanium."

The three sat quietly for a moment, as if to absorb the notion. Jason found himself talking before he even knew it.

"Spacecraft and jets. How could they?"

"There is always the chance that they came on it by accident," Caranza said as he saw the wonder in Jason's eyes.

"Perhaps . . . a happy accident. Still, it's amazing," Jason said, shaking his head.

"Well, the alloy selection is not the point that I wanted to make. While there was always the danger of theft in earlier times, the escalating price of gold in recent years, combined with the devastating inflation that has hit the United States in the last few years, has made the theft of gold by workmen much more of a temptation than before.

There is little chance that we can impose the same restrictions the South Africans impose on their black mine workers. That is little short of slavery. The only option is that we screen the workers before we hire. The government has an agency in the capital for just that purpose. I have taken the liberty of contacting them in this matter. In fact, as soon as I obtained these, I started to make arrangements with them, in anticipation of the reopening of the dig. I have been working with Ugo Caldera on that. We think that together we can provide a crew of workers who are not only responsible, but trustworthy. The temporary workers we have on the scene will be slowly replaced with others more qualified under these criteria. The replacement process should not take more than a few weeks."

Jason caught something that Caranza mentioned. It had been something that nagged him for some time. He thought it might be the right time to broach the subject: "You mentioned acquiring these artifacts, Doctor. That was, of course, done prior to the initiation of the dig. How did you come to lay hands on them?"

Caranza swept a hand through his hair and smiled. "It was more than fortuitous, and quite by chance. There was an immense rainstorm several months ago, and the valley was battered with almost ten inches of rain in less than two days. At the tomb side, despite the fact that the drainage is excellent, there was a washout. Part of the older dig washed down the hill and with it went several pieces. These," he gestured at the items on the desk, "were among them."

"Then why the dig at all? Why didn't Rodgers simply follow the path of the washout to the source of these?"

"It is quite and aggravatingly simple, Doctor. The upper levels of the tomb settled into the gap, and there was no source left. The dig now in progress will keep as much of the remaining structure intact as possible. But I am sure that Ugo Caldera will be able to explain that more expertly than I. In addition, the government has required that we keep intact as much as we can. They send inspectors at least once a month and they establish guidelines."

"Well..."

"Forgive me, Doctor. There is no *well* or *what* or *how* about the visit. The guidelines they set are not at all breakable. If they are transgressed, the chances are that the central government will remove the permit to dig. It's as simple as that."

"I was not going to argue with that," Jason replied. "I have been thoroughly briefed on the stringent policies of the government. What I was going to ask is how these articles, specifically, were found. Perhaps there is a chance that Miss Muñoz could speak to the person who found them. Then she might be able to put her unusual talents to work."

He looked at Lupe with a smile of admiration. "I have seen her operate, and the thought just occurred to me that meeting the finder could help."

Lupe smiled at Jason's voice of confidence. "Perhaps there could be something there," she said.

Caranza's smile was one of pique mixed with confusion. Jason reasoned that the pique was a throwback to the fact that a woman might actually have talent in the area. He assumed the confusion he saw came from his lack of understanding of things psychic. Jason had to commiserate. The chances were that if he had never seen Lupe in action, he would have been more than confused too.

"Of course. You will forgive me, but despite the fact that I have read much about psychics and what they can do, I have never been honored by the presence of one in my office or on a dig. Especially one as charming as the Senorita.

"At any rate, they were found by a young woman, Anna Marcos. My secretary told me that she came to the office while I was not here, demanding an appointment. She said it was urgent. I managed to see her the next day. She poured these things on the desk saying that she had been on the mountain for an outing and had found them on the hillside. I had them tested, and then on behalf of the government, I bought them from her. She was paid quite well. It was not actually a purchase. It was more of a finder's fee. She left the office with the money and has not come back. I have her address and phone number if you need them. Getting them was part of the paperwork required to release the funds."

"She was excited?"

"Senor, she was, how do you say it? Ecstatic. She almost ran from the office. She said that she had to see someone."

Anna slipped quietly into the room and glanced around, looking for the old woman. She smiled as she saw the bent figure at the small stewpot.

"Vieja?"

Xacha turned from the fireplace with a look of surprise.

"You startled me, child. You were so quiet." She looked through the open door to see where the sun sat in relationship to the mountains. She did it with the same nonchalance that someone might look at a watch. A look of curiosity came across her face. "Why are you here? Shouldn't you be at your job?"

Anna came across the room to her and hugged Xacha. She had grown up in the small shantytown and known the old woman all of her life. She had become like a daughter to her after her parents had been killed in a fire that gutted their shack. Despite the fact that Anna had managed to move into the city, she always managed to visit Xacha a few times a week, bringing her food and gifts, and listening as she had in childhood to tales of the ancients and magic.

Holding the old woman's frail shoulders, she smiled. "I have a surprise for you, Vieja."

Xacha cocked her head to the side. A slight flicker of concern crossed her face. "What is it?" she asked in measured tones.

Anna reached into her purse and took out a handful of

peso notes. She handed them to Xacha. "These are for you. You are the one who really made me go up there. After all of the stories you told me, I've been going up every few weeks just to explore. I never dreamed what I would find after the storm. Here. Take it." She extended the bills toward Xacha, but the old woman did not take them. The curious look was on her face again, more intense than it had been before.

"Where had you been going?"

"Monte Alban, of course. After all of the tales of the Old Ones and everything else that you've told me over the years, I've been making regular journeys, up to the mountain just to see it in the way that you do. It's magnificent."

"What has that got to do with the money?"

"Oh. Well, I went up there with Carlos one day right after the flood. You remember when that was?"

Xacha nodded impatiently.

"We went up with a small picnic. Everything was so clean and wonderful after the rain. We did not know that there had been any damage at all, not until we found the washout near Tombo Siete...."

Xacha's eyes narrowed. "And?"

"The sun reflected from something on the slope, and it caught my eye. I walked over and picked up some tiny pieces of jewelry and took them to Carlos. He said that he thought they were made of gold. He told me that I should take them to the museum, and when I took them, the curator gave me money for them. I had to share it with you. After all, Vieja, you were the one who is really responsible for my going there."

Now, there was a look of alarm on Xacha's face. "What you found—the gold—what did the pieces look like?"

Anna reached into her purse and searched. "I did not give them all of the pieces. There was one that I kept... for you." She pulled out a small lump of tissue and gave it to the old woman. "Open it. I did not have time to properly wrap it. I hope you don't mind."

Xacha opened the wrap and her eyes went wide as she stared at what was in her hand. It was a small, delicately fashioned cougar. "Aieeee," *she gasped, closing her hand around the piece and taking an involuntary step backward.*

Anna reached out to her. "What is it? Are you displeased?"

Xacha's eyes met the young woman's. She shook her head slowly. There was no way the young one would ever know. She sighed to herself. *So it has come and from such a strange source,* she thought. *Now the events will fall like autumn leaves. The sacrifice ... the discovery ... and then ... She* shuddered as she thought about it. The pendulum had come full swing. It would all happen again as it had before. She felt suddenly relaxed. There was a rightness to it. It was as if it had been written. She thanked Anna and shooed her back to her job. When the girl was gone, Xacha sat quietly on the floor and stared at the small object.

"I'm not sure why she left in such a hurry but, she was obviously happy about the money. I—"

There was a knock at the door that stopped Caranza in midsentence. He looked to them. "Forgive me. I gave instructions that I was not to be disturbed. Yes?"

The door opened and a small, harried-looking Mexican guard entered. He crossed the room, glancing awkwardly at Jason and Lupe, aware that orders had been given about interruptions. He handed a paper to Caranza and beat a hasty retreat to the door, closing it silently behind him.

Caranza opened the folded paper, read it, then looked at Jason with a disturbed expression. "It is from Ugo. He tried to get you at the hotel but you had left. He says ..." Caranza paused for a second, translating the note in his mind. "There has been a cave-in at the mine. It came at the same time as the tremor this afternoon. He says that there are perhaps ten men trapped in the shaft. He asks that you come out at once."

Jason and Lupe got to their feet and looked for a second

at one another. Lupe nodded. "We will both go. Is that all right?"

Jason nodded curtly. "Is the man still here—the one who brought the message?"

"No, Doctor. It was phoned to the hotel and then phoned here. I will arrange for a car to take you to the mountain. The driver will be instructed to wait for you. If there is anything you need..." Caranza pulled a pen from his jacket pocket and scribbled on a pad. He tore the sheet from the pad and passed it to Jason. "This is my home number. Call me and I will get right to work. Or, if you wish, I could join you at the dig a bit later?"

"No. I'll call if we need help. If the cave-in was serious enough to trap men, there is a chance we will need heavy equipment. We'd better go."

Caranza watched as Jason and Lupe left the office. He had told them to head back toward the main entrance and that a car would be waiting for them there. He called the garage and sent his driver with a museum car to the front ramp. He hung up the phone and looked around the office, his glance finally settling on the gold objects on the desk. He toyed with several of them. A slight smile crossed his face. He reached for the phone, dialed, and waited for an answer.

In his hacienda outside Mexico City, Diego answered the private line. "Yes?"

"This is Ocho. We have managed to turn nature to our advantage."

Diego made an impatient gesture. He never liked playing cat and mouse. "What is it?"

"There was a tremor here this afternoon. Some of the workmen were trapped at the site... deep in the dig."

"And?"

"And now I can get digging equipment and men on the site without any suspicion. Can you get me perhaps thirty men through Uno?"

"It can be done. When?"

"Perhaps tomorrow."

"I'll check. Is there anything else?"

"Yes. We will need a core drill and a great deal of lumber for shoring. Is there a chance that we can get it by helicopter? That way, when the helicopters arrive for the mission, they will be an accustomed sight."

"I see no problem. I will contact Quatro. Is there more?"

There was a pause, and in Oaxaca, Caranza doodled on a pad in the same way Diego had weeks earlier. "Yes. It would be best, for the time being, that I be placed in operational control. I can coordinate everything here."

"We had not discussed that." Diego managed to disguise the irritation in his voice.

"I know we had not, but it is what I need and what you need if we are going to succeed. I am close to the dig at all times. I will manage to get closer to the operation by using the ploy of the new diggers and the machinery."

"I'll consider it and call you tonight." Diego stabbed his cigarette out in the silver ashtray a few inches from his hand. "Is that all?"

"No. My share of the proceeds will have to be raised ten percent. I am taking a larger risk than I did before. I think that you will agree, considering how much there is for everyone involved."

So that was it, Diego thought. He had suspected it. There had been something in the man's manner the first time they'd met that told him there would be problems with money. It seemed that all he wanted was to carry out the current project and get out. Caranza did not know that to ally himself with Diego meant a lifelong agreement.

"Very well, Caranza. It seems reasonable. I will send Alfredo down to speak to you about it. I must go now." He hung up without waiting for an answer from Caranza. He waited a second and picked up the phone again.

"Get me José," he said.

In a matter of minutes he was talking to another underling: "There is something that you will have to do for me."

There was a pause while the voice on the other end made an inquiry.

"Yes. In Oaxaca—tonight, if possible. I will give you a number to call for more information about the man."

9

The small Ford sped through the center of the city, and the tires squealed as it turned on the Calle Trujano, heading out of town. The turn pitched Lupe across half of the back seat and into Jason's arms. She looked at him as if to apologize, but as their eyes met she knew there would be no need to. There was a flicker of excitement in the piercing glance he shot her. They both paused a second, then she righted herself and moved back to the other side.

The car drove into the suburbs, then on in the direction of the northwest mountain range. The sun was starting to set in the distance and the flat plateau of Monte Alban stood out in stark relief. The driver maneuvered the car through the switchbacks up the ever-increasing slope of the mountain road. Jason noted there was a series of small hovel clusters on the road to the top. Part of his mind wondered if the tiny hamlets were a function of the topography or there before the road was finished. The slender power line that paralleled the road baffled him even more. What did electric power have to do with all of this? He tucked the thought in the back of his mind as the car took another curve.

The road was steep, more so than he'd expected. It made him wonder all the more about how the megaliths of Monte Alban had been built. He had not seen them on the ground. From the air they had resembled the toys of a giant, scattered fortuitously on the top of a leveled mountain. As they passed the museum and the foot-traffic access road, the car sped into the center of the complex before braking.

Jason was numb. The sight from the air was nothing compared to what he was seeing now, from the car. The plateau was vast. He looked around at the other peaks. They were conical, or as conical as erosion would allow—perhaps the product of volcanos in ancient times. He was put in mind of the first time he saw the pyramids, especially the great structure of Kuphu at Giza. He knew from his reading that there were more than twenty structures, not including tombs, that had been erected here for a period of more than a millennium.

He got out of the car with Lupe and looked at the panorama. They did not speak. There seemed something that prevented speech in the face of a ruin so vast. For a second Jason wondered why he had spent so much time in Welsh bogs and heaths. That was clearly Neolithic, and this... there were no words. He and Lupe stood in the center of the great plaza and looked at the structures in total silence. As he tried to assimilate the sight a thought occurred to him. The Monte Alban ruins encompassed more than fifteen square miles. Sweet Jesus! That much? Why would any culture drag stones to a mountaintop without water at the top? He tried to push the thought from his mind as he considered the structure of Stonehenge. It took more than two millennia to finish, and the inner-structure blue stones had to have been carried from Wales across numerous rivers and mountain ranges—they had been more than a ton. How had this been constructed? When? He had no idea.

He considered the vastness of the endeavor and the complexity the engineers found in the execution. His trained eye scanned the structures and the parallel lines they seemed to inscribe. He took a small pocket compass from his pocket, looked to it, then to the pyramids and other buildings. Yes. They were aligned perfectly north and south, as he had read. Again he thought of Giza and Stonehenge. He tried to encompass the mathematics of the ancients and the engineering difficulties they might have faced. As he scanned the plateau in terms of symmetry, he saw the observatory.

It was aligned in a clear forty-degree differential from the nearby south platform, and all of the other structures. Stellar observations, he recalled, were available to the priests by sighting through holes in the surface at various angles. He remembered one scholar had written that these alignments were viewable in the daytime as well as the dark. Looking through them must have been like looking up from a well in the middle of the day to see a stellar constellation. The mathematics required would have necessitated pi and other geometric theorems. But these people did not have the wheel.

"Jason?"

His head snapped to the right. Lupe was looking at the south platform. She seemed in a trance as Jason turned to her. Suddenly there was a rush of emotion in him, something he could not fully understand. He turned to her and stepped between her and the view of the platform, reaching out and grabbing her by the shoulders. He wasn't sure what he was doing. It was as if she were in a dream.

"What is it?"

In a fraction of a second her left hand swept across his chest to his right side and, with a single blow, she moved the arm right and swept him off his feet.

He tumbled to the red clay of the plateau, rolled to his feet, and stared at her. She had had the strength of five men. Or had he been off balance? He could not be sure.

"Lupe?"

There was no answer. If there was a reaction to sweeping him from his feet, he had not seen it.

"Lupe?"

Again, there was no answer.

He stepped in front of her, this time prepared for a possible blow. She blinked.

"Lupe?"

Her eyes seemed to look through him. "I died here."

Gingerly, he took her by the shoulders, prepared this time for a blow. There was none. Rather, her eyes closed and she slumped into his arms. As he held her, he could feel her pulse racing. There *had* been something there and now it was gone. All he could see of the event was the remainder; the exhausted Lupe in his arms. He found himself confused and fascinated at the same time. What had Conrad said? "Fascination of the Abomination." And yet there was no abomination here. There was something else . . . something that he could not define and he was sure she could not define yet, either.

"Doctor? Doctor?"

His head snapped in the direction of the voice. He could see a figure dashing toward him in the twilight.

"Ugo. We're here."

He watched as the head digger ran across the plateau in their direction. Jason was still involved with what Lupe had intoned and the almost superhuman strength of her blow. What was it? He was clearly over his head when it came to a rational explanation. He looked down at her. Her eyes were glassy, but as he watched, they blinked and moved up to his. He could feel her push herself from his grasp and regain her feet. They stood eye to eye for a long second before his eyes darted to the dashing Ugo and then back to her.

"Are you all right?"

She nodded, still seemingly drained. Her eyes followed his to Ugo and she pushed herself away from him. "I'm fine."

"Senor." Ugo was only feet from them now.

"Yes."

"Thank God you got my message. I am not sure how to start this operation."

Ugo ground to a halt almost nose to nose with Jason. He was dust-covered and obviously harassed, his shirt torn from the rescue operation. Jason knew the questions to ask.

"How far down are they?"

"Nearly ninety feet. There are two rockslides between them and the shaft."

"What about the shoring?"

"There was none."

"You mentioned shoring when we met."

"No. I mean yes. What I mean, Doctor, is that they were digging ahead of the shoring, before it could be put in. We were going to get it in tomorrow morning with the help of a full crew. Many of the men have left. I told you that." There was an edge to his voice. The last thing Jason wanted was recriminations. He knew Ugo was working shorthanded, and a shoring crew would have required more men with more skill than ordinary diggers. He tried to focus on the problem.

"Let's get over there and try to sketch a cross section of the dig and where they are. When we are sure of the depth and angle and the amount of positive shoring above them, we can get a plan started. Lupe?" He looked to her. For a second her eyes darted to Ugo and then back to Jason. It was as if nothing had happened, but Jason had seen her in operation before. This was no momentary aberration—it was something of importance, something he would have to pursue after the immediate crisis was terminated.

"Lupe?"

"We'd best get over there." She nodded to him with a smile.

They headed in the direction of the dig, traversing the plateau, passing the huge central building complex. They wove their way around the adoritorio and the ball court, and skirted the mammoth central court. They passed Building X and started the slight downhill trek past the bus parking lot and the small tombs that led to the spotlit area of *Tombo Siete*. As Jason first saw the sight, it looked common enough: pillars, a three-sided wall, two sets of steps, and a small entrance below. But below the entrance there was a wide shaft descending into gloom at the bottom. The tomb entrance had not been discovered until 1932 by Dr. Alfonso

TOMB SEVEN

Caso. It had been an accident. Then the excavation revealed that there were Mixtec and Olmec artifacts in the tomb, as well as those of the Zapotecs. Why had more than one civilization used the same area as a tomb? It was a natural question for archeologists. It was not until more than half a century later that Anna Marcos had found the figurines that indicated there was more deeper.

They stopped at an awning-covered desk which was surrounded by workmen. In the distance there were two ambulances and several litters. Apparently there had been a number of workers on the near side of the cave-in who had been hurt and were being evacuated.

Jason pointed to the litters. "How many were on the near side?"

Ugo turned from the scene to him. "There were four on the near side and ten on the far side. When it happened there was no warning, only the falling of the earth. When—"

"What was the exact depth?" Jason interrupted.

"Ninety-two feet."

"Get me a sketch. Make one if you have to."

"There is no need, Doctor. I have prepared one." He moved to the table at the center of the canopied, makeshift headquarters and gathered up a rolled piece of engineering sketch paper. As he unrolled it for Jason, the problem became clear. There was a good portion of the plateau between the surface and the other side of the cave-in. Jason was not concerned about the thickness of the slide and how many diggers it would take to get through to the trapped men. Rather, it was the amount of earth over the heads of the diggers that concerned him. As he looked at the sketch, he tried to measure the angle of attack of the fallen tunnel and balance that against the depth to the surface. He reached into his pocket and pulled out a small calculator. After a few stabs at the buttons, he had calculated the potential of the overhead weight and the amount of counter-shoring necessary to dig through the fallen red clay. It was too much. There was no chance of success. Ugo had been right to pause before anything started. He would have put a crew of fifty men down in the pit digging, and as soon as someone sneezed, the plateau would have sluiced laterally and filled the gap, trapping the rescuers. Another approach was necessary. He explained it to Ugo.

"Is there a chance that we can get a wide-core drill and another generator?"

"Yes. There is a core drill on order now. I took the liberty. They will have it here in perhaps two hours."

Jason felt relieved. The digger, he remembered, had been an engineering student. He had momentarily underestimated Ugo. It was a mistake he would not make again.

"Of course. You were right to do it. What about the placement of the escape shaft? Have you any ideas?"

"Of that I cannot be sure, Doctor. The rock of the hillside is of the same density and texture as that above the fall. But for the angle, I think we might need a survey team. Unless you are sure of where to dig."

The decision rested on Jason, and he fathomed the immensity of it instantly. To dig in the wrong place was to ensure that there would be another cave-in. To ensure they hit the enclosed pocket shaft required a survey team that could give the exact azimuth to the correct angle of the dig. All of that would take too long.

"Ugo, have you ordered a compressor and an air insertion tube?"

The digger nodded, and Jason wanted to hug him. He had anticipated a great deal but he could understand the man's bewilderment at exactly where and what angle to dig. Even if there were the possibility of the insertion of an air tube to the trapped men, the odds on hitting them would be greater than those against hitting an inch-wide stake in an acre field—blind. A survey team would be there too late. Jason paced from the table. There had to be—He stopped in his tracks.

Lupe!

He turned on his heel and strode back to the table where she was looking at the hastily made sketch. As he remembered again the incident in the field, he slowed. He did not know what he was dealing with, only that it was both powerful and accurate. It was the same feeling of helplessness that had overcome him on the plane. But there was no time for tact.

"Can you help us?" he asked.

She did not answer, but simply stared at the sketch.

"Ah . . . Lupe?"

Still no answer.

He waited, and after a few seconds she turned to him. The look was in her eyes again. Unsure of what to say, he remained silent.

"There is a way," she said. She paused and looked back at the sketch. She regarded it for a long moment before she turned back to him. "You cannot go directly in, can you?"

He shook his head.

"Dig the shaft here." She pointed to a spot on the map. "The angle will be twelve degrees downward from the horizontal, and thirty degrees west of north."

Jason stood silently for a long moment. If she were off by a single degree in either direction, chances were the tunnel would collapse a large portion of the mountain on the diggers or that the trapped men would be bypassed completely. While it was something he had to consider, he could not do so rationally. There was too much certitude in her statement, too much precision. Knowing the risks, he made the decision almost immediately.

"Ugo, we will dig at this point. Make sure that the core drill and an air compressor are there when we are ready to start. Also, get shoring for a dig of one-hundred-forty feet, and the rest of the equipment that we will need."

"It will be done," Ugo replied, and ran off yelling to his diggers.

Jason moved closer to Lupe. He gently placed his hand on her shoulder. "What happened out there, and what happened here?"

"I just knew where to dig . . . here. Out there . . . I don't know. I hit you?" He nodded. "I'm sorry. At the moment I was . . . not quite there. I've felt many things, but never anything like that."

"Do you . . . feel that there is a chance we'll get the men out?"

She nodded. "I'm hopeful we will. The position is correct. I cannot say if they will be alive when we get there, though. That's not what concerns me."

"What then?"

"I'm not sure. But I have the feeling that I've been here before."

"Déjà vu?"

"No, something more than that. I've experienced déjà vu. This is . . ." She shrugged and shook her head. "I don't know. There is a chance that I will know more later."

Jason was frustrated by a thousand questions but knew there was no sense in asking any of them. The method by which she derived where and how to dig eluded him as much as the meaning of the episode on the plateau. There was no time for any of it.

"Ugo?"

"Yes, Doctor?"

"You mentioned that there was a generator on order and that the lead time is two hours. What about the compressor and an air tube? Are they locally available too?"

"No. I was going to say that before. The closest equipment of that kind can be found only in Mexico City. Without it, we will have to tunnel by hand. It will add a factor of five to the time."

Jason thought for a moment. The answer was so obvious he almost missed it. He dashed from the makeshift emergency headquarters to the vast open field. Unsure of what was going on, Ugo followed a few steps behind. In the distance Jason could see a string of worklights in the Seven Deers area. The light was sufficient to indicate that there was something there, but was clearly not bright enough to betray a night dig. But knowing the Russians, there was a good chance they had the compressor and the core bit he needed.

"What is it, Doctor?"

"The Russians have a dig over there in the Seven Deers. I

TOMB SEVEN

met the archeologist in charge. I've worked with him before. I know how they operate. They will have far more equipment than they need. I'm certain they'll have what we're looking for. Is there a way to get there from here?"

"Only a footpath. There is no road that will take a jeep. Seven Deers was barely touched when the government stopped exploring years ago."

"Let's get over there."

"Ah, Doctor . . . they do not like visitors. I went over a few days ago and was very quickly asked to leave."

"I might have a better chance. Let's go."

They started across the plaza with Ugo's flashlight illuminating their way. They were only a few feet from the halo of their own dig's searchlights when a voice behind them stopped them.

"Don't go."

Both men turned to the sound of the voice, and Ugo played the flashlight toward it. Lupe stood in the eerie light. For a split second Jason thought she was in the same kind of spell or seizure that had gripped her when they arrived. As he took a few steps in her direction, he could see a look of concern on her face and he felt relieved. It was better than the look he had seen when he knocked her to the ground. He stopped a few feet from her, and looking down, could see how the soft, distant lights seemed to halo her. "That's Yuri's dig over there in the Seven Deers, and I'm sure they have diggers and equipment. There's a good chance we can borrow it."

She shook her head absently, seemingly in another place or lost in another thought. "It's not good that you go there, Jason. It's not good for you to get involved with them."

"Why?"

"I . . . I don't know, but please don't do it."

Jason looked back at the distant glow of the Seven Deers area and then down to Lupe's sincerely concerned face. "You have to be able to tell me why, Lupe. There are too many lives at stake. Is it one of those . . . feelings that you have?"

She nodded.

"Well, there's an unwritten law in operations such as this. We diggers help one another. Nationality doesn't matter, not a bit. I have seen Greeks help Turks and Americans help Russians on digs when there were lives at stake. There are lives down there in that dig and the time it will take to get them out can be shortened by getting help from Yuri and his group. I'm going to have to overrule you on this one."

She stared up at him for a long moment before she spoke. "Well, there *is* the chance that I am wrong." She looked down. Jason knew from her tone that she was sure, very sure, of what she was feeling. But he was equally sure he could speed the rescue with equipment and experienced hands.

She reached up and touched his arm. "Don't tell them any more than you have to, and get them away from here as soon as you can."

He nodded. "You'll stay here?"

"Of course."

Gesturing to Ugo, he headed back toward the Seven Deers.

The path was narrow and washouts impeded their progress. To the right, huge shapes of unearthed pyramids and temples heavily overgrown with vegetation loomed in the darkness. Ahead was the small circular string of lights and the muffled drone of a portable generator. The small, flat open area was the tail of the plateau. It was undeveloped and mostly unexcavated, and the ruins there seemed to have been destroyed more by invaders than by time and the elements. The name had come from the carving of seven deers found on the door of one of the shattered stone huts. Jason wondered that Yuri would devote his time and energy to such an unappetizing area. But, he thought, the chances were that the Mexican government had thought the same thing, as had all of the other excavators of the Monte Alban area. It was possible that tradition and oversight mixed with inconvenience had kept serious diggers from a valuable find. He conjectured that might be the reason for the Russian expedition, though there was still no way he could account for Yuri's presence. But as he and Ugo trudged to the lights, he

TOMB SEVEN

thanked the pure coincidence that allowed him to meet Yuri on the Oaxacan street.

"Alto!"

The voice was ominous and unseen, the accent strange. Ugo stopped in his tracks and Jason followed suit. They stood still for five seconds and were greeted with silence. Ugo did not try to play the light into the darkness to look for the source of the voice. He seemed to know something Jason did not. Impatient, Jason took a few more steps.

"We are trying to find academician Yuri Kurtzov. This is an emergency."

"Alto. Silencio."

Ignoring the voice, Jason took another step in its direction.

"Cuidado!" The voice was stern, and the single word punctuated with the clashing sound of metal on metal. There was no question that it was the bolt of an automatic weapon being thrown. Jason froze.

"Do you speak English? *Habla usted ingles?*"

"Momento."

There was a long period of silence. Jason wanted to speak to Ugo, but after the sound of the weapon being cocked, he dared not say anything.

Then there was a second voice, higher pitched, slightly farther away. For a second Jason thought he could make out a form against the glow of the perimeter lights.

"I speak English . . . a little. What is your purpose here?"

"Ah, there has been an accident at the Tomb Seven dig. There is some equipment we desperately need to dig out some men. We came to find out if you might have what we need. We would pay to rent it."

"You mentioned academician Kurtzov. Do you know him?"

"Yes. We worked on a dig together. I'm Dr. Jason Farewey. Tell him. He can identify me."

"That won't be necessary." Suddenly a bright light played across both Jason and Ugo, blinding them for a second. "Yes. I remember meeting you." The voice seemed to come closer, and after a second, the light was turned in the other direction.

Jason recognized the "learned colleague" Yuri had introduced him to in the street. What was the man's name? Yes. It was Valarin.

"You are Valarin?" The man was now close enough to see. He extended a hand to Jason.

"Welcome to the dig, Doctor. I'm sorry about the security but we like to make sure that valuable equipment does not vanish. I'm sure you know what I mean. Come." He led the two of them toward the lights and called in Russian to an unseen presence. The voice that responded with a grunted Russian comment was the same one that had stopped them, and Jason presumed the same one who had cocked the gun.

They entered the perimeter and Jason was surprised to see trailers near the digging sites. They were far smaller than the standard boxcar type, but they looked sturdy and very practical.

"How did you manage to get these in here?"

"Helicopter. They were designed to be brought into inaccessible areas for a number of purposes. Archeology is one of them."

Jason watched as Yuri Kurtzov came from one of the trailors, buttoning a shirt and smoothing back his few thin strands of hair.

"Trouble, Jason?"

"A great deal. Let me explain."

Jason told him of the situation, and in less than an hour a team of Soviet and Mexican diggers were at Tomb Seven with all of the rescue gear needed for the operation. Jason could not help but notice that Valarin went with them, observing and not commenting on what he saw. The man reminded Jason of a human camera—all he did was record. He did not seem to have a play-back function. Throughout their arrival, Jason noticed that Lupe said nothing about her earlier remarks.

The position of the escape tunnel had been laid out with engineer tape on the ground. It moved at ghostly right angles from its point of origin to the hypothetical place where Lupe estimated the diggers to be. Despite the faith he had in her, Jason felt a number of qualms. A miss would literally be as good as a mile, and there would be no time for a correction of the shaft—not if the trapped diggers were suffocated corpses when they were found. As huge floodlights brought from the valley lit the area, he waved to the crew and they started digging. The core drill they used was not unlike those Jason had seen used in Welsh mining rescue operations, though in the latter, such a drill bit straight into level earth parallel with an existing mine shaft. When the correct depth was reached, a lateral tunnel was cut through to the caved-in chamber. That was standard procedure. It was something else to work on the slope of a hill where the angle was based on the feel of a psychic and the earth to be moved was red clay. All they could do was pray that everything was correct.

The entire operation was slow and laborious. Initially, the slow four-foot diameter core drill led the way, followed by diggers with hand tools pulling out the loose dirt. Following them were the more professional diggers, many of them just arrived from the capital, pulling the fill, establishing the shoring points, and positioning the uprights. Jason established the rate of the dig at twenty feet an hour. In the middle of the sixth hour he decided to get to the bottom of the dig personally and see where they had gone. The angle of attack was more than accurate and the depth approached perfect, but he had to get his hands on the cutting edge of things to understand them.

The dig entrance was eerie, lit with halogen lights and headlights of the workmen. He donned a hard hat and started down the incline.

"Jason."

He stopped in his tracks. "Yes?"

Lupe had come in behind him and stood at his shoulder. There was something in the tone of her voice that reminded him of the episode in the Grand Plaza—something both ominous and mystic, that made him feel a slight chill. He knew only that if there was something she wanted, he was going to have to listen and do what he was told. Somehow it bothered him more in this setting than it might have in Jerry Tanner's conference room. He was working now in the field, in his element. It was like a layman—even a talented one—interrupting a brain surgeon while in the operating room. Still, he had seen her do too many things to do anything but listen.

He turned to her as she spoke. Her dark eyes flashed eerily in the halogen lights haloed by rock dust. He had come to know the look. "Is there a chance that we can split the shaft?" she said. "I mean, I don't know of such things, but can we take a small part of the shaft off to the left?"

He stared at her for a long minute while part of his mind ran through the engineering requirements and the digging angles, not to mention the time factor in getting to the trapped diggers while they were more than corpses.

"Where and how far, Lupe? That much I would have to know. I need at least an estimate."

She screwed up her nose in a way he had not seen before. Oddly, in the midst of the current crisis, he found the gesture attractive. It seemed to give her the look of a vulnerable little girl, lost in a maze. But the professional scientist in him—the one who had seen her in operation as a psychic—told him that it meant something far more than that.

She pointed to the shaft. "Down at the bottom. It's to the left of the shaft... just a few feet, I think."

Jason was pondering his next question. He knew he should not ask it but something inside him forced him to.

"What will we find?"

"I don't know."

"Stupid question, right?"

She smiled slightly. "No. You just don't know psychics well enough yet. It's not empiric, remember?"

He nodded.

He looked back up the shaft through the miasma of rock dust.

"Ugo?" he bellowed.

TOMB SEVEN

"Si." The digger was stumbling down the freshly dug incline.

"No. I'll come up." He met Ugo and took him back to the awninged headquarters area.

"We have a slight change in plan."

Ugo placed his hands on the hips of grimy dungarees. *"Dios mio,"* he intoned. Jason caught the remark. He knew just how the man felt. *What next?* Though he could share the sentiment, he did not choose to mention it to Ugo.

"Your pardon, Doctor, I—"

"It's nothing, Ugo. I've been on digs where I said it a thousand times, except I said it in Welsh."

"Gracias, Doctor. What is the change?"

Jason sketched it as best he could, as an overlay to the earlier plan.

"What do you estimate the time factor to be?"

Ugo scratched his head, knowing the question was really threefold. Initially there was the time factor to reach the trapped men. Ugo would know that best, being most familiar with the dig. Second, he would know the manpower needs for the extra project, and third, he would know about the soil texture and composition, therefore the tools needed.

"Perhaps an extra... how do you say it... small hour?"

"Half hour?"

"Yes. Half hour. And three men with hand picks. I do not see that it will effect the primary shaft dig time."

Jason could have hugged the man if it had not been for the immense traditions of machismo in both cultures. "Thank you, Ugo. Start as soon as possible."

Ugo simply nodded and took off at a trot to start organizing.

The time line had been right. The second shaft was finished by grumbling workers in the predicted "small hour."

Jason and Lupe moved to the bottom of the shaft and gingerly looked at the mole hole that extended from the main tunnel. She stared at it for a long time before she turned to Jason and gestured outwardly with her hands.

"It is only perhaps a foot more. Could we take it out with our hands?"

Inwardly, Jason grimaced. A mole hole it indeed was. Even moving through it would be hazardous. There was no shoring, and a cave-in could place them in the same situation as the trapped men.

"I suppose we can but—"

"Please don't spare me, Jason. I think I know that there is danger. But it is important."

After a long second he simply nodded, and slipping to his knees, moved into the dark, tiny abyss. She followed a few feet behind, seemingly knowing that only one could dig.

They were in the cramped space only a few minutes when Lupe felt a slight breeze on her face.

"Son of a bitch." Jason's voice reverberated in the tiny space and Lupe could almost feel him thrashing ahead.

Moments later, they were on their feet. It was a chamber, one never excavated, never found. Dimly lit by their hat lights, it seemed some forty feet by twenty and perhaps twenty feet high. Jason was amazed that the upper layers of earth could support such an arched chamber. Then he saw the buttresses. It was not a buried pocket. It had been dug and made to last. He looked to Lupe.

"What—"

"I knew it was here. I wasn't sure what. I knew something."

"Do you know anything more?"

Her face shimmered in his light. "I'm not certain."

They started to move through the chamber, slowly, their footfalls raising clouds of dust. Jason stifled his excitement and tried vainly for professional detachment. They would have to get light into the chamber, and more air. He wondered how the ancients ventilated it. He reasoned that if they had done it, there might be a way their method could be found and utilized without bringing a compressor in.

As he scanned the chamber, he could not fully make sense of it. The high ceiling was cross-hatched with buttresses in a spider web pattern Jason had seen before, though he could not remember where or when. But there was little question that the structure was aboveground. It was not something unearthed at the ninth level of a dig, as Schliemann had discovered Troy. It was meant to be buried, meant not to be entered. Why? He played his light to the walls and to the ceiling and tried to think as the ocher dust and grit started to settle. Slowly, frighteningly, he started to feel something creep into his thoughts. It pried open the back of his mind and settled in, moving closer to the thinking part which was refusing subconsciously to admit it.

Jason was a child again, walking slowly into the gloomy darkness of a Welsh coal shaft. The shaft had taken a turn and he was far ahead of his father and the shift manager. Glowing niter dripped from the walls and there were no workers about, and something crept into his child's mind. Fear. Not a fear of anything, just fear—something inescapable and as relentless as the tides that swept across the Welsh coast. It pushed him forward and pulled him back at the same time. The tiny Jason turned to see the light of his father's hat come into view, and the fear retreated.

As he peered into the chamber, there was a part of him that wanted to feel the safety of his father's light in the distance. His hands were cold, and strangely, his forehead was dripping with perspiration. He shook his head to clear it and still the feeling was there. He had been in a hundred strange digs in his career and there had never been *this*. It was not just fear, nor childhood. It was something else... something he did not believe in... something he could not accept. It was power... *evil*.

Suddenly Jason could feel a small hand on his shoulder. Lupe swung around to face him. The fear retreated, but there was something in her face... something...

"Can you—"

She cut his words off with a nod. "Yes, I feel it. I'm frightened."

Suddenly he turned. Behind them, back past the access tunnel, there were shouts.

He started to speak but Lupe cut him off. "It's the workmen. They got them out alive."

Jason knew better than to check. They simply took the few minutes they had alone in the chamber to stare at it and gently explore.

They were halfway down the length of the room when Lupe stopped in her tracks. Dutifully, as if another hunting dog honoring the point of the leader, Jason stopped too. She looked around the chamber in a strange way. She took a few steps to her left and reached gently down into the dust. Grasping something, she stood erect and turned to Jason. She handed it to Jason and he tried to focus his hat light on it.

Tiny . . . gold . . . a bottle-nosed dolphin with emerald eyes.

"Sweet Jesus."

Lupe said nothing. There was no need. Jason's mind raced. The workmanship was the same as he'd seen at Santo Domingo. But the dolphin! These were inland people who would never have seen the dolphin, and the eyes, the fucking eyes . . . !

Emeralds. God, emeralds. There were no emeralds in Mexico. At least not unless they were imported. Russia—Siberia actually—and Colombia were the only two places in the world where there were emeralds in any quantity. How the hell did perfectly worked emeralds get here?

He turned it over and over in his hand, buffing and cleaning the dust of centuries. He didn't notice that Lupe had moved away.

Lights playing behind him and the sound of voices made him spin in the direction of the entrance tunnel. The sudden movement swept up a cloud of dust and swirls of grit that made him cough and gag. The lights in the tunnel became

TOMB SEVEN

eerie, dusty lasers seeking a target. After a moment two clay-smudged men emerged from the tunnel. Through the dust Jason could see that they were Kurtzov and Valarin.

"Jason?" Kurtzov called, not yet able to see him in the ocher gloom.

"Here, Yuri."

Noticing the plumes of dust swirling, Yuri moved in Jason's direction cautiously. "The diggers are safe. There are a few minor injuries and there is an ambulance about to take them to the hospital. Your head man, Ugo, is it? He's going to go with them." He paused and looked around. "I see now why you branched the tunnel off. This appears to be an undisturbed find."

"I'm sure it is," Jason intoned, not wanting to mention the reason for the diversion. He was sure that Yuri would not believe him. "Or we wouldn't have found this." He held out the small bottle-nosed dolphin figurine.

Yuri took it and played the light across it. "Emeralds? Well-cut ones too. Strange. And the gold, Jason. I would have to test it, but it looks purer than any I have ever seen."

"It is beautiful," Valarin said as he approached and played his light across the figurine. "You found it here? In the dust?"

Jason nodded. "That's why I'm sure the find is undisturbed."

Valarin said nothing more, but Jason noted that the man's eyes did not leave the small gold trinket. There was a flicker of joy or excitement in his eyes, the first time he had seen any emotional reaction from the man he had considered a tape recorder.

Suddenly there was a scream in the distance. Lupe!

Jason turned his light in the direction of the echoing sound and dashed toward the figure at the far end of the chamber. Kurtzov and Valarin followed.

Trembling, she turned to him, leaned against his chest, and broke into racking sobs. He could feel her body quivering against him. They stood for a long moment in the dim light and amidst the dust before she pushed him away, holding him at arm's length for a few seconds. She pointed in the distance to something Jason could not quite see.

"G-go. Look . . . there."

There was a part of him that didn't want to leave her, and another part that resented the presence of the Russians. Somehow, he did not want anyone else to see her so vulnerable. At the same time, he *had* to see what was there. He shuffled ahead like a man in a foggy dream. In a few seconds his light revealed what had made her scream.

A perfectly intact skeleton. He had seen hundreds, perhaps even thousands, in his career. He moved closer, played his light on it, and he knew why she had screamed.

The skeleton was nearly eight feet tall.

10

"Holy shit."

"I'm serious, Jerry," Jason said. "It seems to be well over two meters tall and perfectly intact. I've cleared it with this local official, Caranza, and we're shipping it to you today. If you don't get it back intact in a matter of a week, I'll be in an Oaxaca jail cell forever. So for God's sake, be careful."

"Jason, I'm trying not to lose my lunch. How...? I mean the size. Are you sure that this isn't another Cardiff giant? You know what I mean."

"Absolutely. If there's any comfort in it for you, Lupe led me to it and there was absolutely no way it could have been planted there. I can attest to that. I'm sending the artifact, too, and with the same restrictions."

"Emeralds?"

"Correct. Have your people check, but I don't think that they are indigenous to Mexico at all. I would say a microscopic analysis is in order there. It seems to have something of the flavor of the pieces we've seen down here, and it's similar to the piece Lupe couldn't identify back in your office.

"I think you're going to have to send a letter of thanks to the Hermitage people in Leningrad about this. Yuri Kurtzov is here and his team helped to get those diggers out from the cave-in. There is a good chance that the diggers would have died if the Russians didn't have the equipment here. I—"

"What Russians?"

"A Russian team. They're working in the Seven Deers area, not too far from the tomb."

"When the hell did they get there?"

"Not long ago. I would say they were here only a few days before we got to the dig. Say a week at the most."

"They would have arrived at the time George died?"

"Around that time, but what has that got to do with anything?"

"It has nothing to do with anything, Jason. I'm still boggled about the find."

"We're going over the chamber carefully now. If there's anything else, I'll—"

"Jason?" Tanner waited, and all he could hear on the phone was a series of whizzes and clicks. Phone service in Mexico, Tanner knew, was fragmentary at best. He tried to reestablish the connection but it was fruitless.

He hung up the phone and stabbed at the intercom buttons. He was going to put what he liked to call his "battle staff" on alert for the arrival of what might be the greatest archeological-paleontological find of the last five centuries. He made a special mental note of the fact that Lupe had been instrumental in the find. That, after all, was what she had been sent there to do. He tried to form a mental outline of the publication the Institute would develop about the role of psychics in archeology. He thought briefly about old Dhalquist and his fit of pique at the conference, and he determined that, no matter what the publication, he would send a copy to the old man.

The following afternoon, with considerable expense and the genius of Jason speeding the careful packing and crating, the specimen arrived at the Moreland Research Institute. Dr. Chet Kumasaka, resident medical and paleoresearch specialist, as well as Rosemary McGee, computer analysis expert—took delivery like obstetricians lovingly preparing to assist in a delivery. They moved the crate to a clean room prepared for the arrival, and the tedious job of unpacking began. First, the outer wooden crate was stripped away. Following that, they carefully sliced away the inner bubble pack. It was much like unwrapping a mummy. Aggravation was the operative word. They had to exert extreme care so none of the bones that were semiconnected were left intact. The worst of it was that there was such a short time frame for the operation. Normally such a procedure would have taken months to complete. They had perhaps a week, two at best, if the Mexican government would allow it. However, Jerry warned them at the outset that an extension could not be considered. He had worked with the Mexicans before and knew exactly how well they guarded their artifacts, skeletal and otherwise.

Once unwrapped, the remains were photographed from every possible angle. As the table on which the bones were placed was plexiglass, its bottom side could be shot without moving or displacing.

Chet waited impatiently for the process to be complete so that his team could start their investigation. He approached the remains with the tenderness of a lover approaching a mistress, took a careful look at the skeleton, and just tried to absorb the impression. If the five-feet-two Japanese who could have passed for a mini-sumo wrestler had ever been awed by anything in his life, this was it. He knew that the pictures would yield the measurements to the fraction of a centimeter when Rosemary fed them into the imager attached to DANIEL. The computer was perhaps the most expensive toy in the institute. Digital Analog Integrated Logic System, or DANIEL, could do just about anything. It had been programmed with what Chet thought might have been everything in the world, everything from astrology to Zen, with side trips into world history, philosophy, and just about everything else. Rosemary played DANIEL like a piano. Chet was sure she would get every shred of information about the technical areas, as well as extrapolation on origins. This allowed Chet time to make specific observations and fill in the gaps.

"State of preservation is fantastic," he read into his tape. "Knee ligament shards still exist. This is perhaps a function of the low humidity at the area of the find. Cranial shape is..." He paused as he looked at the skull and pondered. He knew every possible skull shape from Australopithicus through all of the homonids, and yet he had never seen one with quite this shape, not even to mention the size. He stared at the grinning skull for perhaps five minutes, carefully analyzing each skull plate and the curvatures and fissure points. He made a few more comments into the tape machine before using forceps to gently pry open the mandibular from the upper part of the jaw.

A loose tooth clattered from the bottom jaw onto the cool plexiglass.

"Shit," he hissed, then remembered he would have to erase the expletive from the tape.

He picked up the tooth with tweezers and examined it carefully, reasoning that he could always epoxy it back in before the remains were returned to Mexico. He used a magnifying glass to check the detail. Son of a bitch sure had good teeth, he thought. *Jesus Christ!*

It took him more than a few minutes to regain his composure.

"Note to Rosemary McGee. I want a complete series of detail shots of the second lower molar of the specimen."

If Chet Kumasaka, MD, Ph.D., foremost scholar in his field, was the kind of man who could have lost his bowels on the spot, he would have.

It was five days later when a haggard and exhausted group of staff heads met with Jerry in the conference room. There were piles of note paper and typed observations everywhere. Styrofoam coffee cups seemed to have been showered on the table. Tanner sat at one end of the table and gulped the last of a cold, bitter cup of greasy coffee. He had several days worth of stubble, as did some of the other men. The few women were frazzled. But they had managed the monumental task of extracting all of the possible data from the bones and the small gold dolphin, as well as the hurried but thorough sketches and observations Jason had managed to send.

"Okay, troops. Let's try to put it together."

"I wish we could find 'gether,'" Rosemary quipped through a yawn.

"Come on, Rosie. We have to sum up before we all have to take speed to stay awake. What have you got on the dolphin?"

Rosemary shrugged her shoulders. They ached from hours and even days sitting at a computer console. "Well, first, it's very pure gold. Chem department says that it is the purest they have ever—"

"Wait," Jerry interrupted. "Wouldn't pure gold, I mean gold *that* pure, simply not hold shape?"

"That's right," Rosemary said, again trying to stifle a yawn. "Chem says it would just be like putty. They did spectroanalysis on it and said it was put together with an alloy when it was smelted, much as we do today. That was what allowed the artisans, whoever they were, to shape it and carve."

"What was the alloy?" It was Jerry's turn to shift in his chair and yawn.

Rosemary stared at him for a long minute, as if trying to find the words and to form a reasonable answer.

"Jerry, they don't know."

Tanner cocked his head to the side. "They what?"

"They don't know, and neither does DANIEL. What I mean, I think, is that the alloy that they could separate from the piece and run through the spectro tests—and they ran every one in the book—was one no one has ever seen. It's a heavy metal."

"That's all they know?"

She nodded and held up a huge pile of computer paper.

"Jerry, this is three days with DANIEL, and he says the same thing. Don't think that wasn't frustrating."

The other department heads, despite their fatigue, stirred.

"Is there any chance that—"

"I'm sorry, Jerry," Rosemary said, anticipating him. There was a slight edge in her voice. "There is no way past it. This stuff, whatever it is, doesn't exist. Or it does, but we've never seen it before. It's as simple as that."

Jerry sat back and ran his hands through his hair. After a second, he leaned forward again. "Well, I guess that's that. Looks like we add a new element to the periodic table." He turned to Chet, then suddenly back to Rosemary. "What about the engravings and the emeralds?"

She took a quick glance at her notes. "The anatomical rendering of the dolphin is perfect. It's as if a Harvard ichthyologist did them. There are even tiny stryations in the blowhole. DANIEL had a field day with them. It seems that they're almost microscopic, and perfectly symmetrical. There are very few tools even today that could carve them, and I'm talking microsurgery stuff. As far as the jewels are concerned, DANIEL tells us that the best sources for them are Colombia and the Orient. There might be some mined in Mexico, but the chances are these weren't. The quality is just too good. Also, they were carved from much larger pieces. The workmanship was something just short of genius, as were the settings. That's about all we have."

Tanner now looked to the man at the far end of the table. He was Evan Walters, a staff cultural anthropologist.

Walters looked more like an accountant than a scientist. He was in his fifties and dapper in a business executive sort of way. It always amazed Jerry that he had spent half of his life in places like New Guinea's Owen Stanley mountain range and the villages of Nepal.

"Evan? What about the chances of the designers knowing about dolphins?"

Walters pursed his lips. "Well, not to be sarcastic, obviously, they did because we have the artifact. Beyond that, if you want to construct a theory based on time of origin vis-à-vis culture, it seems to me that there is little chance the creators of the little critter could have really seen one. That does not mean dolphins are not in adjacent waters. They are. But the Oaxaca Valley is some distance inland, and depending on the time of the origin, I would tend to think there was little chance they could have seen one. Now, remember, we have not set the time of origin, and there is always the chance that there might have been trading which brought the artifact to situ."

Jerry shook his head. "No, Evan. I doubt it. This thing was buried very deeply, and besides, we have to consider the emeralds. Also, if what Chem says is right, then the creators of the artifact might have been trading with spacemen or something. Come to think of it ... well, anything's possible, but there seem to be too many unknowns."

Walters gestured. "Jerry, there are many anomalies such as this, you know that. The Plains of Naszca, Easter Island, those Peruvian figurines that look like modern jets ... Machu Picchu. You know that the list goes on. We might just have to add this to that list. Offhand, I would say the chances are that any of the *known* peoples of the Oaxaca Valley would not know of dolphins in such detail, if at all. I can say little more than that."

Jerry thought that Evan, as usual, had used many words to say little. But he could not really fault the man. There was something of an enigma on their hands, and little any of them could conclude, at least thus far.

"Chet, you're up."

The Japanese, as tired as any of them, didn't show it. Jerry always ribbed him about it. Chet argued that it was from his long hours of conditioning as an intern. Jerry counterargued that he was taking speed from his own medical supplies.

"Jerry, I still have a reading coming in. I took a tiny bone sample. Don't worry. The chances are that the Mexican government won't ever find where from. That's what I'm waiting for—the carbon results. But meanwhile, our tall friend blew my mind."

There was a titter around the table. Chet never used phrases like that.

"Sorry." Chet realized he had destroyed any fragment of the image of oriental inscrutability that might have been there. "Actually, there is a great deal of information we do have while we're waiting. I don't know where to start. The odds are that our friend was not an oddity—a hyperpituitary case. From the bone structure, which is perfectly proportioned, it would seem he was a normal specimen of a larger—no pun intended—group. Something like the Masai or other tribes, that are just genetically tall. Beyond that, there are a number of things that are more than exceptional. First, there is the curvature of the skull plates." He stopped for a second and looked around the table. "I'm sorry. For those of us whose specialities are non-medical—the skull of homo sapiens is not solid, but made up of plates that come together as we grow and are cross-hatched by fissures. The angularity I speak of is the way the fissures come together, forming the overall shape of the skull.

"Therefore, we can see the evolution of the species from the size and shape of the skull. Generally speaking, our ancestors were smaller than we and had far less forehead. Several hundred thousand years ago, there was a considerable shift in the skull. Essentially, it marked the shift from Neanderthal to Cro-Magnon. We call this the cortex explosion."

Jerry could see that Chet was starting to warm himself into a lecture, and decided to do something about it. "Chet?"

"Oh . . . yes, Jerry?"

"Could we just essentialize the data?"

"Of course." Chet paused a moment and Jerry could see he had caught the point. More than that, he could see in Chet's expression that there was no offense taken. They had worked together too long for that to happen.

"Well, when that shift happened, Man started to reason. At least that's what we think. Our friend has a fully developed forehead and the skull circumference is... well, enormous. A hundred forty centimeters to be exact."

"Chet?" Walters was gesturing as he usually did.

"Yes?"

"What's normal?"

"Well, there is no normal. But for an adult..." He gestured in an uncertain way. "Say fifty-five centimeters. But, as I say, there is no average... yet you can see what I mean about our friend. But let me get to the most important part.

"There was a tooth that fell from the skull as I examined it. I determined that I would replace the tooth before we sent it back... of course. But there is something staggering about this tooth. Once it had fallen, I examined it closely. I asked Rosemary to get the data and run it through DANIEL. Friends, the tooth has had a root canal done."

"Ridiculous." It was Evan again.

This time, Chet reddened. "Evan, don't be an ass. I know what I'm saying. I had it checked and rechecked. It is a root canal on the buckle root of a second lower molar, and I know what I'm talking about."

There was silence for a long second. Evan was not accustomed to such an outburst, and certainly no one at the table had never seen Chet behave this way.

"Sorry, Chet." Evan tried to look contrite. Indeed, he was. He had overstepped himself and he knew it.

"Very well. There is more, much more. The pin that is used to fill the bored canal is made of titanium."

No one spoke or even moved at the table. It was as if a single frame had been culled from a film. What Chet had said was clearly impossible, and yet it was there.

"Given this, there was little I could do but have the tooth dissected by the medical department. Again, I say we will replace it for shipment. But even if we didn't, the find is just too important. The titanium point was perfectly set at the root tip. I have more information coming along with the carbon-date data on the bone sample, but this was just too meaningful for me to hold back. I—"

Evan, almost cringing, had to interrupt again.

"Pardon me, Chet. I really must make one point."

"Yes?" Chet was impassive again.

"Dental work in ancient times *was* used and *was* sophisticated. We know that in Mexico, it went back as far as several thousand B.C. I would say that the portion of the information that is most germaine is the material. But the odds are that the material for the canal would have been available."

"Evan..." Chet was starting to redden again. "I am talking about the workmanship, not even the titanium. The setting of the point on the canal is something that would have required X rays. There is no other way that the... dentist would have been able to get in exactly to the root tip. To go too far would be to pierce the mandibular nerve. If too short, then the tooth would have rotted from possible seepage of bacteria from the vacant space. God, man, don't you see? It's like Jerry"—he pointed at the end of the table without actually looking at Jerry —"and all of his study of Stonehenge and astronomy. Someone, I think it was Hawkins, once said that there had to be a Neolithic Newton or Einstein out there on the Salisbury Plain. This is the same thing. The technology for root canals has been sorely recent in development.

"Can you all see what I mean? Rosemary? Will we have that data from DANIEL?"

Rosemary looked at her watch. "I hope quite soon, Chet. Even Big D takes some time with things. We'll have the sample data too." She got to her feet with a quick glance at Jerry. "Let me check on it. It should only take a minute."

Jerry nodded. He was not one to stand on protocol in meetings, especially when something like this was being discussed. Rosemary slipped from the conference room and headed hurriedly in the direction of the computer center, where she could see the state of the printout. DANIEL took his good time with things, but usually—damn near always—his data were perfect.

In the conference room, Jerry had put Chet on hold and started on the analysis of the site of the find.

"You all know that my real field is parapsychology, but allow me to just add a few things gleaned from Jason's sketches and notes about the situ of the dig. As you know, Lupe Muñoz was instrumental in the find and there seems to be a connection at least between her direction of Jason and some psychic connection she seems to have to the whole Monte Alban area. I won't get into reincarnation or collective unconscious. I know a number of you are queasy about such things. But about the dig itself—the positioning of the chamber in which the artifacts were found seems to indicate that it was built. It is not just a cranny or cave. Jason says there are buttresses and that the chamber support structure seems to be—and I don't quite know how you'll take this—like a geodesic dome."

Jerry paused as he watched George Kasolski, a staff engineer, drop his head into his hands.

"I know, George. Fuller invented it. Or did he reinvent it? Who knows? All I can say is what Jason wrote. There will be photos soon, and you will have plenty of time to look at them. The vault, if I can call it that, was never aboveground, like the rest of the Alban complex. Also, Jason's hurried notes indicate that the support structure appears to have been designed to support more weight than is there now, by a considerable factor. Sort of using an airplane jack to support a sheet of plywood. None of this jibes in the sightest with the Alban system. The conclusion at this point is that the vault at Tomb Seven is considerably older than the rest of the dig."

"Dammit, Jerry." Again it was a flushed Chet who spoke. "How could it be even older than that place and have people doing perfect root canals?"

"Chet." Jerry smiled an exhausted smile. "I didn't say

we had any of the answers. We don't even know the questions to ask. We're ten blind men trying to describe an elephant. Remember the Indian story? One says it's like a rope and another like a wall and on and on. We don't know enough. But let me say one thing, ladies and gentlemen. That is the purpose of this institute. It was when Channing Moreland was alive, and it is now. We probe the unknown. We search, and if need be, we say to hell with conventional science. With apologies to all here." Jerry stopped. He realized that with the excitement of the moment and the information he had heard, he'd started to preach.

"I'm sorry, all. The soapbox goes back in the closet. More about the structure. George? Is there a chance that we can pry you from the other things you are doing, so you can get down there in the chamber and really eyeball the thing?"

George smiled at Jerry. "I'd walk . . . naked."

There was an explosion of laughter around the table, and Jerry knew that a good deal of it was nervous laughter from the pressures of the last days.

"All right then—" Jerry stopped in midphrase as the door opened and Rosemary came in carrying a sheaf of computer paper.

She moved slowly, like a woman in a dream, in the direction of the conference table, where she deposited the paper. There was a wild look in her eyes, one that Jerry had never before seen. She slowly decollated two sheets of paper from the rest and stared at them. She looked up and down the table and then back to the paper. She said nothing. Jerry's background in psychology told him what he was seeing. He was looking at someone on the edge of something—collapse, tears, psychosis?

"Rosemary?"

She said nothing.

"Rosy?" he said gently.

It seemed to snap her from the far-off place where she had been. "Yes?"

Her voice seemed tiny and frail, not that of the crack professional and good friend he and Eve Tanner had known for so many years.

"Rosy? Have we got the data?"

All she could do was nod and look back to the papers.

"Would you read it to us?"

Her mouth opened and shut several times, as if she could not get out the words.

Jerry quietly got to his feet and moved down the table in her direction. Everyone present simply watched. The silence was maddening. He reached her, took the papers from her hand, and tenderly sat her down. He returned to the head of the table and sat before he glanced at the papers. It took him a few moments to read the top sheet. He shook his head slightly and looked up at the faces at the table. He cleared his throat.

"Friends... it seems that DANIEL says that the root canal in the tooth that Chet spoke of was drilled... by a laser."

Silence and more silence. No one moved.

Jerry moved to the second sheet.

He could feel a knot of steel start to build in his stomach as he read the findings of DANIEL. He had never known the computer to be wrong. Rosy McGee was too damn good for that. And yet... Sweet Mother of Mercy, he thought. It took several moments before he could bring himself to look at the staff and several more before he could find the words.

"Ah... about the bone sample... and from what I read, the findings have been cross-checked and verified. Ah... yes... the bone sample. It seems that it is two hundred thousand years old."

11

The rear of the tiny cab cramped Jason's already sore muscles. He had spent the better part of the last week in the dig, crawling to each of its deepest recesses. In the full light of the man-made day that had been brought to the chamber, Jason confirmed his theory that the shape of the vault had been something on the order of a geodesic dome, and the expert from MRI confirmed it. He was as perplexed as he was excited. There were so many things he could not explain that he could not even consider them. He had to force himself not to make judgments about age or origin, and simply concentrate on his strength, which was the supervision of each facet of the dig.

The dawn trip to town had been unexpected and more than irksome. He looked to Lupe, who sat to his right. He was going to need her more than ever in this sudden crisis. The Mexican government had officially demanded return of the artifacts. There was no reason stated, though Jerry Tanner had indicated in a wire—phone communications being abandoned—that the demand had something to do with an organization called InterHelp. This group, it seemed, championed the cause of keeping all of the artifacts under Mexican control. It appeared they had considerable influence with the government. Caranza had been contacted by phone and had confirmed the power of InterHelp to both Lupe and Jason. He had indicated, though, that there was a strong chance that the enormity of the find and the possible implications could be wedges to allow the American institute to keep the remains for the alloted week, and perhaps even longer. Jason was irate at the demand of the government and InterHelp, since it defied all of the known conventions of archeological practice. Countries *did* assist one another in such things, except perhaps those which were diametrically opposed to each other ideologically. He turned to Lupe.

"What did Caranza say when you got him on the phone last night?"

Lupe shook her head as she looked at him. Her eyes were tired and he knew he had been pushing her too hard, though not for psychic data. There was nothing he could do to push or prod that. Rather, he had been using her as an archeological assistant, something that she was fully qualified to do, considering her advanced degrees. She was about to help create an argument that Caranza could use as something to lubricate InterHelp's wheels and give Tanner every possible minute with the remains and the artifact.

"I never got him, remember?"

Jason cursed to himself in Welsh. "I'm sorry. We're both tired. What was it the maid said?"

"Basically that he had gone to the museum to do some night work, and that it was not unusual for him not to return until midmorning. She said he liked to work in the lab there because the phone system was shut down at night and he could get peace and quiet if he was working on a project. I'm just hoping we can catch him before he gets home. How urgent was the wire from Jerry?"

Strange, Jason thought. Why did he resent the fact that she called Tanner by his first name? He pushed the thought aside. "Tanner said the government telex was sent to the State Department at the same time it went to MRI, and that this InterGroup had been mentioned . . . or at least your State Department, in the form of one of the officials Tanner knows, alluded to InterHelp. The second wire—the one he got last night—didn't request, it *demanded*. Jerry was frightened that we were going to start an international incident with all of this. Thank God that in that earlier conversation you had with Caranza, he said he had some considerable influence with this pressure group."

Lupe's head snapped to the driver, then back to the surroundings. *"Senor!"* she snapped. *Derecho, por favor . . . rapidamente."*

"What . . . ?" Jason was lost.

"He was taking us the long way, a ploy to increase the fare. This is no time for that. Typical tourist stuff down here—a tour of the town to go three blocks, if you know what I mean. I told him to take a right. That will get us to the cathedral faster."

"Oh." Again she had amazed Jason.

There was a time he might have said Lupe worked with the strength of a man. The Mexicans, as much victims of a machismo tradition as the Welsh, would have said the same thing. Now he could only say that this was the normal thing Lupe did. She was fantastic—Strong, quick, intelligent, and then there was that wild talent of hers, the one he could not fathom. He respected it and also knew he feared it. There was something about the way she had swept him aside in the plaza, and been so sure that the chamber would be right where it was, that astounded him. He would never have believed back in Tanner's office that this dark-eyed, raven-haired slip of a girl could do the things she had done, or touch his emotions as deeply. He could feel his stomach churn and his loins stir just to look at her, despite the grime that covered her, despite the broken fingernails and the circles that days in the dig had wrought under her eyes. Yes, this was one hell of a woman. A special woman. He had only begun to plumb the depths of just *how* special she was becoming to him.

There had been other women, of course. Jason tried to think of them. Graduate students asking coyly, "Doctor Tanner? Can I get some one-to-one help with my project?" There had been the women on the staffs of a dozen museums in the world who had somehow been moved to passion by talent mixed with masculinity. Jason could fathom little of it. After the death of his parents, with the tail end of school and all the exigencies of putting the family business in order, he had had little time for anything but the sojourns to digs in many parts of the world. The women he'd thought of earlier had all pulled from him, drawn from him, drained him and replaced little. Fireworks in the rain, he thought. And then there had been the demand for commitment—the subtle web spun carefully with sex and conversation. He had run from it. Spending his life in one dig after another was no way for a married man to devote time to a wife and family. His father had proved that, giving his life to the mine office and the boardroom.

Jason reasoned that that was the reason he ran. But he also knew there was something else buried inside him. It might be fear—he couldn't be sure. He had always postured as his father had, the image of the self-assured, confident Welshman. He was Shakespeare's Owen Glendower blustering over the coming battle with Harry Hotspur. It was an image stamped on him, branded on him, and he was certain in a tiny corner of his soul that it was not true. He knew that deep inside there was still the small boy, wanting to play on the great slag heaps of Wales rather than to examine their density and determine profits from the black stones that came from his father's holes in the ground. In the end there was a shyness that he managed to cover with the Glendower brashness. All of this he knew.

But here was a woman he did not fear, one he began to feel he would rather die for than run from. There was something in her smile. God, he wished he knew what it was. And there were the things she had said on the plane, things that had pierced his armor like a Saxon lance might have rent the glistening crest of a Welsh knight.

"Lupe . . . I—"

"We're here." She looked from him to the driver and Jason realized she had been staring at him as he thought.

For the briefest second he wondered how much of his thinking she had "overheard", but there was nothing threatening about it. He had long since accepted that.

She told him how much to pay the cab driver then they got out and stood looking for a long minute at the magnificent twin towers of the Santo Domingo. The towers were starting to catch the morning sun, and the facets of the domes seemed to flicker ever so slightly. The long open plaza was the same one where Franciscans had stood to tell the ragged Indians about the god who did not demand sacrifice, the god who would bring plenty. Most of the Indians simply nodded, with more than terror in their hearts. It was not a fear of the new god that the brown robes had thrust upon them. They knew that Cojico and the others of the hierarchy of their gods could sweep the newcomers from the land when they wished. Part of the fear had been that Cojico might have forsaken them or might be punishing them for their transgressions. The greater part of the fear, though, was that of the jackals—the men in black with the red dagger crosses on their chests—the serpents of the new god who rent bodies apart with their four-footed beasts and nailed Indian children to the crossed boards because they might be seen placing an offering of corn at the altar of Cojico. Part of this Jason could feel.

Lupe looked up to him and faintly smiled. Again he could not be sure what was going on inside her, but he noticed that as she turned in the direction of the huge oak doors of the cathedral, he could see the barest flicker of change in her otherwise drawn and exhausted expression. For a split second he thought the expression might be fear.

"I hope we can find a guard to open or at least to call," she said, somewhat under her breath. "They're usually pretty bureaucratic down here about such things. Like opening a bank on time in the U.S. They're never excited about altering the routine. Maybe, together, we can scare someone."

Suddenly she took Jason by the hand and led him in the

direction of the doors. Was she leading or relying? Somehow, it didn't seem to matter.

The doors, as she had half predicted, were locked. Apparently, no one prayed early in the morning. Jason thought it odd, as in this part of the Catholic world, there had to be masses going on somewhere. After all, these people prayed all the time, didn't they? He wondered if he was thinking in clichés again. But as the doors were locked, despite the fact that the cathedral was a working church as well as a museum, they were going to have to find another way to get into the place.

"If I remember, the museum entrance proper is off here to the left," he mused.

They moved to the left, walking faster as they fleetingly saw a guard come from a door, spit on the cobblestones, and return. At least there was someone whom they might badger. All Jason could do was glare, but he knew that the verbal part of things would be handled by Lupe in truly intimidating fashion.

She called to the man, who was about to start back into the building, and he turned to them suddenly, not expecting anyone to even be near the museum entrance this early, considering that the massive, multilayered edifice would not open for more than three and a half hours.

Jason waved to the man as Lupe called to him in Spanish again. The guard, or perhaps he was a watchman, looked at them long and hard. He turned to the door, then back to them, then simply looked back at the door again, apparently certain that the tranquility of his morning café con leche had been utterly lost.

They approached him and Lupe unleashed a barrage of Spanish at the man. Ruffled at being so accosted by a woman, he stiffened and looked at his watch. Jason did his best to look authoritative during the exchange, but he had his misgivings. Both of them looked as if they had spent the night, and possibly a number of days, rolling in the red mud of the hillsides or plying the Indian huts on the road to the airport. Several times Jason heard himself referred to as doctor, and he thought this might be one of Lupe's ploys. If it was, it succeeded. After a few minutes the guard shrugged and admitted them through the door of the museum. He headed for a phone, obviously to call Caranza, wherever he might be, while they headed off to his office.

There was no question of knowing the way. The office occupied the most prominent spot in the museum and was the only place in the complex that seemed to have outside windows. The rest of the walls had been classically Spanish. Jason remembered thinking of them as xenophobic. When was that? Perhaps it was a century ago, he thought, though he knew it had been little more than a week. The dig and the amazing discoveries had stretched time as a film director might, telescoping shots and splicing them together.

It was only a matter of a few moments until they reached the second-floor office. The door, as expected, was closed, and Jason was starting to have second thoughts about disturbing the man at such an ungodly hour. After all, they had come for help. The chances were that this visit, with the sun barely over the mountaintops, could turn him against the very thing they sought, the very organization he could sway. And then there was the specter of an international incident. Well, he thought as he knocked firmly on the door, the die was cast. There was no turning back.

There was no answer. Jason felt a tightening in his stomach. He knocked again, harder.

Nothing.

He decided to try the door, and to his surprise and Lupe's, found that it was open. Apparently, once inside the massive complex with its seven-feet-thick walls, there was no need for locked doors.

As they entered, Jason could see that Caranza had turned his chair to face the window and the superb morning view it offered. Jason strode around the desk and came face to face with the director, trying to form his opening gambit as he moved.

Caranza was seated bolt upright in the chair—wide eyed, grimacing, dead.

"Lupe. Stay there."

"What . . . ?" she said as she, too, rounded the desk.

Her scream echoed through the entire complex echoing, from four-hundred-year-old walls. She turned away, burying her head in Jason's chest.

"Jesus Christ," Jason whispered. He had seen dead men before. There were always accidents in digs, though he had been spared the formal horror of seeing dead men in war. He had seen enough to know. There was something about the face, something akin to abject, total horror. In his shock and fear, he thought fleetingly that the face looked like one of the local gods grimacing, or grinning, he could not be sure.

Jason could feel Lupe's sobs against his chest. Her hands were drawn into balled fists on each side of her head. She was shutting it all out, and he wished he could too. He held her for a while slowly moving her away from the rigid corpse and sitting her in a chair where she could not see the glazed eyes and bizarre grin.

Once he was sure she wouldn't faint, and that she was not totally catatonic, he looked to the phone. The police would have to be called. He made sure not to touch anything in the room that did not have to be touched, but that was only something he had remembered from detective films. He picked up the phone and dialed the operator.

"Si?"

He stopped, words choked off. He didn't know the language.

"Si?"

He turned to Lupe, then back to the phone. There was no way she could help him with this one—he didn't want her to move or speak. She looked like a Dresden figurine teetering on a cliff in a windstorm.

"Si?"

He took a deep breath and said, "Do you speak English? Ah... *palabra*... ah, *Ingles?*"

"Momento, por favor." There was silence on the phone for a long minute. All Jason could hope was that the stab at the language had hit home.

"Yes?" came back a heavily accented voice.

"The police, please?"

"You wish to make a report?"

"Yes."

"One moment."

It seemed that a century passed before another voice came on the line.

The police officer, apparently some sort of desk type, also did not speak English, and Jason had to go through the routine again. This time the wait was not quite as long.

"Guevera. You wish to make a report?"

"Yes, this is Dr. Jason Farewey and I'm at the office of Dr. Caranza in the Santo Domingo Museum."

"Yes, Senor. And the report?"

"I... I am afraid we just came into the office and found Dr. Caranza... dead."

There was no passion in the voice that came back, no calculation. There was, indeed, nothing... nothing but pure professionalism. "I see. You said *we?* There is someone with you?"

"Ah, yes. A... colleague. She and I had an early morning meeting with the doctor and we came in and he was dead. I'm afraid that my colleague, Senorita Muñoz, might need medical attention."

"Why?" the voice on the other end snapped. Even through his own shock, Jason could understand the question. The officer's job was to probe, even at the first moments of a phoned report.

"I think that she's in shock... seeing the corpse and all."

"Very well. We will send an ambulance along with the

officers. I ask that you touch as little as possible there. You said that you and the late doctor are in the office?"

"That's correct. His personal office... it's the one with the windows."

"Very well, ah... Doctor, we will be there immediately. Our headquarters is only a few blocks from you."

The voice on the other end simply stopped, and there was a click followed by a dial tone.

Jason gently hung the phone back in the cradle. He looked back to Lupe, who sat with her arms folded tightly against her breasts. She stared ahead, seemingly seeing nothing. In an instant Jason was terrified—not so much about finding Caranza, but rather for her mental health. He went to her and slipped down to one knee.

Looking directly into her eyes, Jason whispered, "You *will* be all right. You *will*. You have to be... for me... please?" As he intoned the words, he realized he had never quite spoken to a woman that way before. He did not plan his words as he usually did. He simply said them, totally unaware of what he was saying and what the impact might be on her. There was suddenly nothing frightening about it, nor was there anything macho in the words. They simply *were*. There was monumental liberation there, something he had never experienced before.

Her eyes, though, still stared. But there was something else. A single tear slipped over her lower lid, then a tear sliced a jagged line on her cheek, both cheeks. In a strange way, it was hopeful. In a few more seconds she started to shake, and then she pitched forward into Jason's arms, sobbing almost silently. He was holding her and stroking her hair when the police and the medical team arrived.

The rest of it was a fog of questions and police moving through the office taking pictures and examining things. Jason knew little of police procedures but was glad to see that as the session proceeded, Lupe was starting to return to at least a shell of the woman he had known. It was nearly ten o'clock when the police officials said they could leave, adding that they would have to come to the station to dictate statements in the next day or so.

Jason shepherded Lupe from the museum and into a cab. He managed to get her through the lobby of the hotel, where the clerk told him there was a huge amount of correspondence for him from "Los Estados Unidos." He simply pointed to a box of mail that was too large, by far, to be tortured into the tiny pidgeon hole. Jason waved the man aside, saying he would be back for the mail, and went to the elevator. He got Lupe to their floor and to her room door. For the first time since the discovery of the body, her eyes were clear. She looked up at him for a long moment.

"I am all right now."

"I'm glad. You're sure?"

"I'm sure."

Jason reached down, unlocked and opened her door. He took her by the shoulders and looked intensely at her. "You are certain? I can get someone to come up . . . to stay with you."

She shook her head, her eyes never leaving his.

"No. You stay with me, Jason. You . . . you . . . Please?"

He put his arm around her shoulders and took her inside.

It had all happened as if in a dream. Moments after they entered the room they shared the shower, bodies soapy and steamy. They dried one another, and without a word Jason scooped up the small but exquisitely proportioned body in his bronzed arms and moved her to the bed. He combed his fingers through her slick wet hair and she curled her arms around his neck. Her mouth was warm against his and her tongue gently probed his mouth. He slipped a hand down the damp small of her back and cupped a buttock. She shuddered slightly.

They fell asleep in one another's arms, her head, still damp, nestled against his chest.

12

Jorge and Manuel, his assistant, looked like masked and gowned ghosts at opposite ends of the table as they looked down at the corpse of Martin Caranza. This would be the third post mortem he had done in a short period of time. His other duties had taken him from the pure practice of forensic pathology for which he was trained. Teaching and supervising had eaten more and more into his available time in the last few years. But for the positions of two of the recently deceased, Rodgers and Caranza, he might not have seen three post mortems in three weeks for a long time. But Rodgers had to have the best medical examiner, and so did Caranza. As for the old woman, well, Jorge thought, that was curiosity. He could still see little reason for her death. The woman's heart had simply stopped. Whether old Xacha had stopped it herself or not was more a question for theologians than doctors. But Rodgers and the old woman seemed to share the same experience. The former had died, perhaps of fright at Tomb Seven, and the latter had warned of the horror of further exploration of the site when she mysteriously died.

And now there was Caranza, dead in his office with much the same look on his face as the American had. He pondered the thought that he'd had when he had done the post mortem on the American. Death by fear. But as he started to eviscerate the corpse of Caranza, he saw there was a good chance that this was another case entirely.

The abdominal organs were in poor condition. The spleen was enlarged, as were the liver and the pancreas. There were a number of kidney stones, though none that would have been in a postion to cause pain, let alone a seizure. Jorge was sure that a liver section would reveal an early cirrhotic pattern. While the chances were that Caranza was not yet an alcoholic, he had been headed in that direction. He moved on.

"Chest, Manuel."

Manuel nodded and opened the cavity.

The lungs were in as bad a shape as were some of the other internal organs. But the heart—there was something else odd about the heart. The organ was always of vital interest, not just to Jorge in his position as a medical examiner, but also because there was a time when he considered cardiology as a profession. This heart had been severely damaged. He eviscerated the heart and lungs and the arterial and venus system that connected them. He did not have to excavate far into the tissues to find what he sought.

Embolism! Air embolism. It had to be. There was no massive clot nor was there a single blowout that a clot might have caused. The path started to clarify itself. The air—or air mixed with something that could have caused the swift rotting—demolished the subclavian vein and ripped its way into the superior vena cava. The right atrium and ventricle fell to it and the blast ripped into the pulmonary artery and into the lungs. A blast of air... but there had to be something else. The microscopic tissue examination would find it, if it was there. But that would take time, and there were other things to be considered. He noted embolism and induced heart failure as the preliminary cause of death and left open the possibility of further examination.

Jorge went back to his office and checked his calendar, which looked like the entire population of Oaxaca had run across it barefoot. He dashed to attend two staff meetings—

TOMB SEVEN 149

the first related to the assignment of interns to various programs, the second and by far the more boring of the two related to funding for the construction of the new wing.

Through the second meeting, while Julitora droned about government regulations, Jorge mused over these three deaths. Finding the existence of an embolism in Caranza at least indicated the possiblity of an explanation. He could be an investigative scientist again rather than a superstitious fool. He had left instructions that the Caranza remains were to be gone over again, telling Manuel to search for skin punctures to account for the admission of air into the body. He moved his thoughts to the American. There might be a connection in the cause of death.

If there was a connection, there would have to be an exhumation order on the body of Rodgers. Well, he thought, all in good time.

"Dr. Lopez?"

"Hmm?"

The man at the end of the table, Senor Julitora, was the chairman of the board for not only this hospital but several others in the city. At least, Jorge thought, I can pretend to be interested. He looked up from his notes.

"Yes, Senor?"

"Doctor, what do you think of the incorporation of a new pathology lab into the additional wing?"

There was nothing to think about. "I see no need for it in the practical sense, Senor Julitora. There might be a need for the medical school side of things, though I confess that I cannot even see that. What we have will suffice. I suggest we give the space to beds and perhaps to an expansion of surgery. Unless, of course, there is an objection from any of my learned colleagues."

Jorge looked around the table. When it came to forensics and the allocation of space, all of them knew that Jorge could do an autopsy in the back of a Volkswagen and teach three interns while he was at it. There was no objection.

Jorge appeared to listen while his thoughts drifted back

to Caranza. There were the pieces of information that would have to be developed. It was still nagging him. There was—

There was a curt knock at the door. Julitora looked at the door as if he were the pope being interrupted by a curate.

"Yes?" Even his tone was pontifical.

The door opened slightly, and a dark skinned man in white peered hesitantly in through it. Jorge recognized the man instantly. It was José, one of his assistants.

"Pardon me, gentlemen, but you see... ah, Dr. Lopez requested findings immediately on an autopsy." He looked to Jorge as a man might look to God in a time of crisis.

Jorge smiled, first to Julitora and then to José. The latter smile was one of reassurance that the man would not lose his job for the interruption. José was one of the best in the pathology business and Jorge was proud that he had trained him. The man was the chief pathological assistant, one of the three who had worked with him on Caranza. Jorge made it a practice to have José on all of the tough and/or interesting cases. He had also worked on the Rodgers post mortem.

José approached the table and slipped a small routing paper to Jorge. He smiled meekly and dashed from the room, slamming the door behind him.

"Forgive the interruption, gentlemen. This is a vital case. There is police interest." He knew that was enough to stop any objection and to get José off the hook. Indeed, there *was* police interest.

He looked down at the sheet.

Doctor Caranza—needle puncture in interior of left
elbow. The puncture is fresh. The rupturing of part
of the vein above the entry mark indicates injection
of possibly air. This would support embolism.

José.

Jorge smiled to himself. The hunch had been right. But now there were many other things that had to be followed up. While appearing to make notes on the meeting, Jorge was starting to assemble his thoughts on the finding and the follow-up.

1. Reexamine the body and get photos of the puncture.
2. Send copies as addendum to the police.
Check police investigation for presence of a hypodermic at death scene.
3. If present ... suicide?
4. If absent ... murder!!!
5. Rodgers?

As Jorge looked up, thinking that all of the notes were complete, his mind wandered back to the Guelaguetza and the death of the old woman. There, the autopsy showed, a clear case of heart failure. There was no evidence of embolism. Wait. Again he had not done a coronary dissection. He made a mental note to ensure that in any suspicious case in the future, such a dissection would be common practice. What had her name been? Oh, yes. Xacha. And it had been the young girl, the tearful Marcos girl with the great sad eyes, who had claimed the body. All Jorge could tell the girl was that the old woman's heart had stopped. For the briefest second he was angry at himself for the possible oversights in the post mortems. Then he mollified himself. Xacha could not have been the victim of foul play. The old woman's heart stopped. That was it. There was nothing more. The stress of the strange speech that she had made that night, and perhaps the additional strain on the heart brought about by the climb up the mountain—these were the causes. He realized the chill he had felt at the old woman's words. He knew that the whole thing was native foolishness. But there had been a second of fear in him that night. He made half a mental note to contact the Marcos girl and reiterate his condolences.

Rodgers was something else. That was going to have to be looked into again.

The meeting ended and Jorge made grand rounds with the resident staff. It was late in the afternoon when he managed to get back to his office, which was meticulously ordered, thanks to the efforts of José.

He picked up the phone, deciding to call Sergio. The conversation was brief, as his nephew had spent the entire day on the bench and was about to go home. Jorge mentioned that the chances were that an injection of air killed Caranza, and Sergio was grateful to hear of it.

"The newspapers are pressing me and the police department. They are trying to find a way that they can smell the blood where there is none. But there might be blood, as you say now. I'll call the chief and have him check the report. In fact, I'll get them to go over the death scene again. Perhaps there is something there. A hypodermic, you say?"

"Yes, Sergio. It would have to have been found very close to the body. He would not have had time to hide it. But there is always the chance that it fell from his hand and rolled under the desk. There is one thing that bothers me about this new finding."

"Only one?"

"I am being serious. Do you know how hard it is to give oneself an injection?"

"Don't drug addicts do it all of the time?"

"Yes, but there is much practice there. This would have been one time only. There was only the one needle mark on the body. Caranza was not an addict—that I can tell with certainty. More than that, he did not, from his reputation, seem to be a suicidal personality."

"Uncle, pardon me, but I am more familiar with such things than you. One never knows about suicides. They happen suddenly, with notes and without. There is no sense in psychoanalyzing such things after the fact. I will have the police go after the report and check the office again. What if nothing is found?"

"If that is the case and the first search was also thorough, then there is a chance that you can release the jackals of the press."

"What would it be?"

"It would be murder, Sergio."

There was a pause at the other end of the phone. "That, uncle, would not be simple either. Caranza was a respected and powerful man. The pressure would be on to find the killer."

"Sergio, if this was a murder—and of course we are not sure of anything yet—the method used tells me that the chances are the murderer would never be found. He would have to be someone known to Caranza to get access to the office, and he... or she, would also have to be someone who knew medical practice well enough to know about embolism."

"Then that would allow the police to start looking in the right direction."

"No, nephew. Something tells me that if indeed there is a homicide here, it was done professionally. I can't tell you that there is any logic behind that statement. I just feel it."

"Well, I'll get on it. Meanwhile, I have to get home. There are three cases waiting on the tribunal for tomorrow, and all of them are complex. I will have to study."

They ended the conversation and Jorge turned to look at the setting sun. He had wished he could have been satisfied, but the satisfaction in his work would not come.

He turned back to the phone and called in José with a stab at the intercom. The small man entered the office with considerably more confidence than he had entered the conference room earlier in the day.

"José, get me the record of the remains disposition on George Rodgers. You remember... the American?"

José cocked his head to the side. "But Doctor, I thought—"

"So did I, José. I thought that it was wrapped in a neat package... but really I didn't. That one gave me a great deal of concern."

"Well, Doctor, remember that we had three of them in less than two weeks."

"Three?"

"Yes. The old woman... the one at the festival."

"Oh, yes. That reminds me. Find out about the disposition of remains there too. Check the name Marcos. I think I will want to send a note, or perhaps flowers for the grave. That young girl was so shaken by the death."

José nodded and left. Again Jorge turned to the sunset. It gave color to the office, something Maria had always said it needed. It was not more than a few minutes later when José returned quietly.

"Doctor?"

Jorge turned back from the sunset. "Yes?"

José stood in the center of the office, scrutinizing two files. Each had multicolored tabs that indicated circulation to various departments of the hospital. José frowned.

"What is it, José?"

"It is very strange, Doctor. About the American?" José stopped. He mused again over the files. "I just do not understand it."

"Understand *what*, José?"

"Well, Doctor, it seems that the American did not have a family, and that the American institute had claimed the body for shipment to the United States. I expect they were going to bury it there."

"*Were?* Get to the point."

"You see, the request came too late."

"Too late for *what*, José?" Jorge was impatient. This was the routine José went through every time there was some sort of anomaly in the order of things.

"It seems, Doctor, that the American request came too late because the body had already been claimed. They presented a paper and took the body. It seems there is no chance to exhume Rodgers, if that was the plan, Doctor. You see, this record indicates that the body was cremated."

"What?"

"Yes, cremated... on the day that it was claimed."

Jorge was furious, not only at the fact that there would now be no chance at exhumation, but at the fact that those who claimed the corpse were not family, nor did it appear that the cremation had been ordered by the American institute. Indeed, the man was ashes before they had a chance to finalize the shipping instructions.

"Who the hell claimed it, preempting the Americans?"

José flipped a few multicolored sheets. "It seems that it was an international organization, Doctor. Perhaps this Rodgers was a member of the organization and his wishes were to be cremated. That is, I believe, what the organization presented when they picked up the body."

"What was this organization?"

"InterHelp, Doctor."

"They are the ones in Mexico City?"

"Yes, Doctor."

"And they presented a paper that Rodgers had signed?"

"Yes, Doctor."

"Damn them."

"But, Doctor, if they had his permission, then—"

"Still damn them, because I wanted to get that body back." He looked at a nonplussed José. "I'm sorry, José. It is something both personal and professional. There is something that I might have missed in the Rodgers post mortem, and now... well, I will never know. You understand, I'm sure."

José smiled. "Yes, Doctor. You are a perfectionist, and if I might say so, I am, too, in my way. I do understand. When there is something that eludes me in your files or in your work, I will not rest until I get it right."

Jorge looked at the little man. He was indeed a friend. On more than one occasion they had gone to the bodegas together and gotten roaring drunk on mescal. Jorge's colleagues would have disapproved if they had the nerve to say anything at all, and Jorge was sure that they did disapprove among themselves. To hell with them, he thought. It was indeed a special friendship.

"Oh, José, what about the Marcos girl and the old woman, the one who died at the Guelaguetza?"

"Oh, yes." José started to flip through the second file, and gave the doctor a small slip with the address of Anna Marcos. José's look again became cloudy. He looked to one of the sheets and then to the doctor. Jorge watched him again look to the sheet and then slowly back up.

"There is something unusual . . . in this."

"What is it?"

"When the Marcos woman picked up the body and I was only looking for a gravesite here . . . you mentioned flowers."

"Yes?"

"Well, there is no gravesite."

"How do you mean?"

"It seems, too, that the old woman was cremated."

Jorge wondered if there was a rush of cremations starting in Oaxaca. Actually, there should have been very few indeed, as the Catholic Church despised cremation—it was a sin to cremate remains, something to do with history, the Council of Trent . . . ? the heresy of saying that a cremated corpse could not be pulled from the grave on the Judgment Day? He pulled his thoughts back to José.

"What is odd, José, besides the cremation?"

"It seems, Doctor, that the organization into whose hands Senorita Marcos gave the body for cremation . . . hmm."

"What?"

"It was InterHelp!"

13

The sunset spilled across the large bed, and shadows curled in small eddies as they moved against one another. Jason's eyes snapped open. He tried to peer down at Lupe without moving. He didn't want to disturb her increasingly restless sleep. How strange it was. Caranza, the madness of it all, and now this.

Her hair, splayed out in an ebony sunburst against his tawny chest, slipped a bit. Her head moved and the sleepy eyes opened. After a moment her eyes were on his like an awakening cat.

"Hello," she whispered.

"Hi."

He could feel her take a deep breath and slowly exhale. "I think we have to get up," she intoned. With her head perched on his chest, he could feel the words against his body far more than hear them.

"I know," he grunted, like a child with stolen candy.

He knew that a raft of work awaited in the lobby mail drop, and there was more at the dig. There was a need for supervision and...

Suddenly, he hated it—all of it. But with a look at her, he knew it had to be done. They were a hopelessly intertwined Gordian knot of arms and legs and he didn't want to try to unravel it. Like Alexander, she had cut through it with the sword of a few phrases. He resisted them for a moment but then she started to get up, leaving a cool hollow where she had rested. He was suddenly empty. That, too, he pushed away.

She crossed the room slowly and slipped into a robe she pulled from somewhere in the deep recesses of a dark closet. It was blue, and somehow—he was not sure how—it *had* to be blue. Had he known it before she'd reached?

"You know..." He tried to sound logical and rational, but suddenly started to laugh, a deep, hearty Welsh laugh.

She turned to him as she tied the robe and cocked her head to the side. "You know, don't you?"

"Know?" he asked through the laugh.

"About all of this... here today!"

He shook his head, the laugh subsiding. "All I know is ... is that I knew that robe would be blue... maybe should be blue. It's all very confusing."

"No, it's not. It's very simple... very. Don't analyze it to death. That laugh fitted you best."

He ran a thick, strong hand through his hair. "Well, it's been a strange day."

Suddenly there was something he remembered, something from the flight to Mexico City.

"*You* knew. You did. It was that small something that crossed your face on the flight down here. I mentioned it, asked about it, and you just smiled. Even when I pushed you about it, you just smiled. It was this... today."

She came to the side of the bed and sat gently on it, placing a hand on his chest. "Yes, Jason. It was. I didn't want to say it. I didn't want to look like, you know... promiscuous or unprofessional. But, yes, I knew. I didn't know when or how, I just knew that it was right and that if I mentioned it, it would color the relationship and everything else."

He could see the brightness of her eyes start to dim and grow sober. "I didn't *see*, as you call it, the death of that poor man." She started to fold her arms, pulling her hand from his chest.

He grabbed the hand rather than let her close like a turtle. "No one saw it. It just *was*. I don't know what to make of it and I'm sure you don't. Besides, what could either of us have done if we had known beforehand?"

"Nothing."

He pulled her down across the bed, allowing her head to fill the empty space that it had left on his chest. He sat up and she was across his lap. He took her head in his hands and gently lifted it. Her lips were amazingly cool in the warmth of the late afternoon.

Then she pulled away slightly, looking up at him. She was quiet for a long moment. "We'd better get to work, Jason—even though I'd rather be here."

"Me too."

Half an hour later he knocked at the door, one arm loaded with mail. She opened it, wearing shorts and a halter top.

"I don't want any today. You might come back another time."

He stood in the hall and pondered dropping the mail where he stood, charging into the room and making love to her on the floor. But he smiled to himself—there was time for that later.

"I'll have it burned," he said as he came into the room and deposited the mail on the bed. "But we have to read it first."

They started with the MRI reports Jerry Tanner, considering their complexity, had sent in two copies. It took them half an hour, Lupe reading slightly faster, to complete the abstract. At the very end she looked up and out of the shuttered doors to the portico and the garden. When Jason finished he also looked up, at her. He was looking for understanding. After all, she was the one who directed him to the chamber in the first place. It was insane. He kept telling himself that there was some mistake. There was no chance that a skeleton in such a fine stage of preservation could have been something like a quarter of a million years old. A root canal? A laser? The emeralds. The riddle became a powder keg. If the findings held up, there was a chance that the entire archeological community would descend on MRI like locusts... with torches, axes, and bombs. He would be called a fool, or worse, a charlatan. But the information was there in front of him.

"Lupe?"

"Hmmm?"

"The age? What about the age?" His tone was suddenly that of a small child asking why the sky was blue; or worse, why water was wet.

"I'm thinking," she said. "I know I was drawn to the chamber... I can't say why. I didn't know we would find what we did. I didn't know anything more than I told you at the time." She stopped for a second and looked into his eyes. They had gone totally professional. She knew what he was thinking. She was about to say what she hoped she would not have to say.

"I know I remained silent about... us on the plane. But that was something personal. I explained that. This is professional, and I can see that you're wondering about that."

A thought suddenly struck him. He grasped it like a man clinging to a canoe in the rapids. "What about the incident up in the plaza? The time that you knocked me down and said you had died there?"

She thought for a long moment before she tried to form an answer. She was forcing herself to move from the archeological professional to the role of the psychic and back again. It was an emotional Ping Pong match she was unsure whether she was up to just now. She tried, nevertheless.

"I think... that was something else. I can't say it was a Jungian gestalt... a feel that I had died there."

"But you hit me with the strength of a man."

"It was a *very* strong feeling. But I don't see the two as connected—the chamber and the moment of trance in the plaza. The chances are that I *did* die as a sacrifice in the plaza in a prior life. But—"

"I still have a lot of trouble with that notion."

"Please let me finish."

He nodded. He had not meant to interrupt her, not when he was looking to her to make sense of things.

"I say that I died there and in trance, even light trance, I might have had considerable strength. That might mean—and I ask that you accept the premise of reincarnation for only a moment, not that you believe it—I might have died there and because of the physical strength, I might have been a man."

"You don't remain a woman and I don't remain a man if there is, indeed, life following life?" he asked.

"There is no need. In fact, ideally, according to a number of theories, you should have equal numbers in each sex. There is a yin-yang thing about it. But still, I see no real connection between the event in the plaza and *anything* that went on vis-à-vis the chamber and the skeleton and the small gold artifact. That was psychic skill simply being used like a bloodhound."

"There's still the bloody age and the rest of it," Jason said. "I think that either we have the greatest archeological find in history here, and there is not a chance that I can explain it, or someone got there before us and, forgive me love, somehow led you there on a false trail."

"There is a chance of that, but it's a very small one." Her reaction showed that she had not been threatened by the comment at all. That eased the qualm Jason had about making the comment in the first place.

"Then, we have a whole new ball game. Remember Leakey? Each time he plowed a new depth of the Olduvai Gorge, mankind got older. At the last count it's something like three and a half million years old, I think. I'd have to look it up to be sure. But deeper means older. That has become an axiom in archeology."

She got to her feet, moved in the direction of the window, and turned back. Jason thought she wanted distance between them before she made her next point. He was right.

"That's not the only axiom, Jason," she said.

"Oh?"

"Yes. There is always the gradualist versus catastrophist thesis."

"If you mean all of that stuff about peaks and valleys in the evolutionary process, then—"

"Wait, Jason. If we deny the possibility of such a theory, which I think you are doing now, then we also deny any chance for an explanation. We are stuck in the rut of trying to reconstruct how they built the pyramid of Giza in a fixed amount of years with a fixed number of men and with tools and technology that we *assume* they had. That's the rub. Don't you see? We have to allow for a catastrophist approach. Besides, forgive me, but I don't think you know enough about the theory to reject it out of hand."

He simply nodded. He had been too awestruck to make sense of the data. If she had a framework, no matter how strange or occult, he would listen. Criticism would only come, he reasoned, at a time when he could find an honest intellectual, rather than prejudicial, approach.

"There has been more and more writing about the hypothesis," she said as she came back to the bed. She sat beside him and lowered her voice. He was, it seemed, going back to school in more than one way. "I'm not talking about the lunatic fringe, either. I don't contend that we were put here by space people or anything like that. By the same token, darling..."

He noted that it was the first time she had called him that, and it seemed to muddy his mental waters for a second. He tried to force them to clear as she spoke.

"...*that* is something we cannot deny, either."

"Yes, when I was at Swansea there was a professor who said there was a chance that we, homo sapiens, were actually someone's eighth-grade science project. So, you see, even conservative Wales had such glimmers on the hypothesis. I'm sorry to interrupt. Please go on."

"Well, the cyclical nature of just about everything we know about in our field and a number of others dictates that there is a periodic cycle to everything in the universe. Even the Big Bang, the Sandage Theory ... well, there is a chance that that *too* could happen again. More than that, there is evidence gathering year by year about every facet of this. Let's just use one example. Giza. The Great Pyramid, we believe, was built in about twenty years. Why? Because we think Khuphu or Cheops lived that long. So, two and a half million blocks of a weight of two plus tons each, plus the limestone facing are put in place in twenty years. That's piling one assumption on another.

"Assume the Gradualist theory for a second. Suppose this man Cheops, and we have no other information about him except his name, lived seventy years. If twenty years, they would have to have placed one stone every four minutes day and night, day in and day out for the entire time to finish it by the time he died. If seventy years, assume fifteen minutes. Then, there is the assumption that the tools and mathematics were as we think them to be. If that was so, there wasn't a chance that they even could have built it at all, given *any* time frame. So, the other possible option is that they didn't have the technology that we assumed from that period in history. They had something more advanced ... something left over from another civilization... a more advanced one, that somehow ended, with the survivors leaving a legacy that was used at Giza and then, in the intervening centuries, forgotten?"

Jason looked at her for a long moment. "But there is another point we are forgetting," he said. "All that you mentioned, if it were true, might have had something to do with Giza or the fashioning of the gold figuring—the dolphin and the other ones we saw in..." He paused. He thought of the visit to Caranza's office and the hasty departure. He remembered that was the last time they had seen him alive. "...Caranza's office."

He could see again the cloud that came over Lupe. She had been bouyant during their argument. Now there was a flicker of the look he'd seen in the office in the morning.

Still, he had to say it: "That would not account for the size and the dimensions of the skeleton. This Dr. Kumasaka says there is little or no chance that this skeleton is an anomaly. The damn thing was eight feet tall, and that's just the skeleton. What and how tall would the real thing have been? No, you can't refute a paleontological argument, especially with the thoroughness Kumasaka provided in the summary. That's why we charged in here today. We had to get Tanner and Kumasaka and the others up there to keep it longer. UFO types talk about little green men. Was this a big green man?"

She looked at him and he at her silently and intently.

"All of it baffles me." She reached across the table and took his hand. He could feel that hers was suddenly moist and cool. "Oh, Jason. Caranza, and poor Rodgers . . . something is screaming at us to stop looking into all of this and—" She stopped and shook her head. "*Something* wants to see all of this horror to go on." She ran her hand through her hair and again fixed him with her eyes. "We're caught in the middle of all of it. You might have been right."

"About what?" He held her hand tightly.

"I might have been fooled into going down there to . . . release something. I don't know."

He got to his feet and crossed to her, not letting go of her hand.

"Jason, I'm sorry. I just—"

"Shh." He slid an arm around her and picked her up, moving to the side of the bed and sitting her down on his lap, her head burrowed into his chest.

"Jason . . . ?" There was a slight hitch in her voice.

"Hmm?"

"I'm a good pro. I am. It's just that . . . we don't know all of the answers. Perhaps we should just leave the tomb . . . not push."

He paused for a moment to feel her pulse and her breathing. She was fighting the fear and hoping he could help.

"You sound like the big green men can kill us."

She reached back and pounded a fist against his chest. "I'm serious. I'm past my depth." She pulled her head away and stared wild-eyed at him. "If there are big green men, they're fighting each other and using us in the middle, and we're powerless against them. I've never felt like this before and..." Her voice trailed off into sobs and again she buried her head in his chest. After a moment she lifted her head and there was another look in her eyes. It was one he had seen only a few hours before.

"Make love to me, Jason. Make love to me...now."

He drew her to him across the bed and kissed her. She molded herself to him with incredible warmth and the pliant quality of a dancer. They slid backward onto the bed, neither of them wanting to end the kiss. He slipped a hand inside the top she wore and fondled the breast without the intervening confining cloth. Her nipple came suddenly erect in his hand. He could feel the stirrings of an erection through the thick cloth of his khaki slacks. He moved her into a position where he could slip off the snug shorts she wore.

There was a knock at the door.

They ignored it and he started to unbutton her shorts, his hands fumbling in anticipation.

Another knock.

He didn't stop, though she pulled her mouth from his.

"We have to—" she whispered.

"They'll come back. If it's important enough, they'll come back."

A third knock.

The moment died. Flushed, they pulled away. Angry, he straightened his shirt and slacks and headed soldier like to the door. He determined that if it were anything frivolous, he would slam the door.

He quickly swung open the door. A young woman and

a man stood in the hall. It was the woman who spoke first.
"Are you Doctor Farewey?"
 He nodded.
 "My name is Anna Marcos."

14

Jason stood at the door and blinked for a moment. He remained silent.

There was no question that the woman who stood at the door felt awkward. She fumbled before the silent and more than disturbed Jason. "Ah, Dr. Farewey, this is my fiancé, Carlos Ramirez." She gestured to the man who stood slightly behind her.

Jason, pulling himself from the strange montage of feelings that blanketed him, reached for the man's hand. He paused, mentally. He knew the man, or at least had seen him. He filed through a mental deck of cards. Yes. At the dig. Ramirez was one of Ugo's assistants.

"A pleasure, Mr. Ramirez. I believe we have already met."

Carlos smiled. He was broad-shouldered and strong, though shorter than Jason, as were many of the Mexicans he had encountered.

"Yes, Doctor. A pleasure," Carlos said in very heavily-accented English.

What were they doing here? Jason wondered. He had gotten the address of the woman from Caranza and had never gotten the chance to get in touch with her because of the find in the dig and the resulting furor.

"What might I do for you both?" Jason said. "Oh, please come in."

They sat at the table near the window that looked over the garden. Jason called the desk and asked that coffee be sent to the room. "Well, Miss Marcos," he said when he seated himself. "I was going to get in touch with you as soon as I could about the artifacts you found, but we made a huge breakthrough at the dig. I'm sure Carlos has told you all about it. We got very preoccupied with it and I didn't get the chance. How did you know to come here?"

"It was at the end of last week that Dr. Caranza contacted me and said you wished to see me. With Carlos already working at *Tombo Siete*, I felt that any information I might provide could help you. But there were some other things I wanted to tell you about *Tombo Siete* and what it means to the local population. Those are things that are perhaps more important than what you were going to ask me."

"Yes, Dr. Caranza was very helpful in getting in touch with you. It was a great shock."

"A shock?"

"Yes... you don't know, then?"

"Know what?"

Lupe gestured to Jason and interrupted. "You see, Senorita, we found Dr. Caranza dead in his office this morning. It seems that he died there in the middle of the night. There is no clue as to how he died. He simply died in his office chair."

Carlos rocked back in his chair and Anna stared at Lupe. Her expression mixed fear and disbelief, but as Jason peered into Anna's face, he began to think it was fear that was predominant, a deeper fear than he had seen at the news of death in the past. He tried to make sense of it as he looked at her. His glanced moved away and he could see Lupe studying her intently. He let the silence pass for a second before he spoke.

"I'm sorry we had to be the bearers of this news."

Anna was nodding ever so slightly, and Jason was trying to understand what it meant.

"Doctor, Miss? *Dios mio*," Anna intoned, as if unable

TOMB SEVEN

to momentarily form the words through the shock of the news she had just heard. "If the digging continues," Anna finally said, "there will only be doom, and it will not come only to the diggers and those connected to the excavation ... it will also come to the city and the entire state. This is not just something that I feel. It is a fact that was said by my grandmother. Her name was Xacha."

There was silence for a second, then all four of them seemed startled by a knock at the door.

Jason got to his feet and answered the knock. It was room service with the coffee. He did not allow the man to enter, but took the rolling table at the door and maneuvered it into position next to the table where they sat. He served the coffee, allowing Lupe maximum time to observe the two. As he served and poured, he could see Carlos looking back at Lupe, and could not miss the look in Carlos's eyes. He was devouring Lupe with them. A heated territoriality started to bubble up in him, but he forced it back. There was no sense in starting a confrontation over a look, no matter how lascivious it seemed. Besides, it was too important, at least to Lupe, that the rest of the story be heard. He had been looking at Carlos so hard that he didn't realize Anna Marcos had started to speak again.

"... she had expected it all of her life. She said that she was not sure of the time but that she would be when the time came. I feel t-terrible. Now she's d-dead and ... and I might have ... have caused ..." She suddenly burst into tears, and turned to Carlos. He reached out and held her, though Jason saw the gesture as one more of duty than anything else.

After a few moments Anna composed herself, drying her eyes with a small, tortured handkerchief that she gripped tightly in a fist. She took a few deep breaths. "I am so sorry, Doctor ... Senorita. Today ... all of it ... I don't know. I don't usually cry. But you see, my grandmother died just over a week ago and I can't help but think that it was my fault. Then, with what you said about Dr. Caranza, I thought that I might have caused yet another death. You see, it was to him that I sold the small pieces I found on the mountainside. I could not help but think I was responsible. My grandmother... she knew too much before it happened. She predicted things and she always said she would have to give ... g-give her life if... I never thought..."

Lupe reached across and placed a hand in Anna's. "I had a grandmother, too, who knew such things. I am the legacy that she left. Perhaps you are a legacy from Xacha?"

Anna nodded, her eyes not leaving Lupe's. "I always felt that way, though she did not teach me any of the secrets of the shaman. She told me things and then they happened. When I took her the pieces, she went white and said that the time had come. She told me to leave."

"Did you leave?"

"Yes. I always obeyed her. She had said that the dig at *Tombo Siete* would come to no good, and now there has been that cave-in that Carlos mentioned—"

"Did Carlos mention that we managed to get the men out alive... all of them?"

"Yes, he did. But that is only the first of many things my grandmother said would happen. The whole city will suffer...."

"How are we to know unless we dig?" Jason said. "I can ask that honestly. I am an archeologist and I wouldn't have given so many years of my life to a search for the past and the truth of it, if it didn't mean something."

"Well, I guess I understand the question. But the deaths and the rumblings of the earth... these are things that all say to stay away. My grandmother burned her hut and hiked to La Guelaguetza and she warned them. She warned the master of the festival and she warned all present. Then she died...."

Jason made a mental note to check on the death of the old woman... what was her name? Yes, Xacha.

"Since then there has been the death of Dr. Caranza. Don't you see? I disobeyed her. I found the things and I sold them to the museum. I didn't think at the time. It was sacrilege. I might have been directly responsible for the death of the doctor. And there might be more."

"Don't you think that Dr. Caranza knew the risk he might have been taking?" Lupe asked. "He was Oaxacan, wasn't he?"

"Yes, he was. There is a chance that he knew."

Jason pulled Anna's eyes to him. "We're professionals, in the same way that Dr. Caranza was, Anna. If there are risks to be taken to gain knowledge, we take them. That's just the way it is. I'm certain Dr. Caranza knew about the curse. There would have been no need to warn him." Jason stopped, having no further way of reassuring the woman. After all, he was going against everything his profession and the entire scientific community preached in terms of objectivity and methodology.

"What was it that your mother died of, Anna?" Lupe asked.

Anna shook her head for a second. "The doctor said it was heart failure. She had burned her shack and hiked all the way up the mountain on foot to the opening of the Guelaguetza. Heart failure, yes, that was what Dr. Lopez said."

Both Jason and Lupe reasoned that, in the final analysis, all death could be called heart failure. Jason, particularly, wanted to probe further, but decided to seek answers from the doctor in question rather than push Anna further on a delicate subject.

Jason got to his feet and moved to the window. The sunset was now marred by a line of scud clouds which raced across the northwest end of the valley. The chances were, he thought, that there would be rain during the night. He wondered if there were a chance to get back to the dig and Ugo, to ensure that there was additional shoring in place to support the massive weight of the red clay. Then he looked at Lupe. Perhaps Ugo could handle things by himself for a change, he mused, at least for the night. He marveled at how suddenly his priorities had changed. He turned back to the other three and his eyes again caught Carlos staring at Lupe. This time he caught a subtle flicker of a reaction from Anna. She, too, had seen it. Jason smiled inwardly. Perhaps there was a chance that he need never make anything of it. He hoped that was so. He could see the flash of anger in Anna's dark eyes after she had recognized the look on Carlos's face. No, there was nothing that had to be done or said. If he read Anna Marcos correctly, she would handle everything privately. He decided to make the point that caused him to stand in the first place. He was going to be gentle about it, but still it had to be made.

"Anna, you, and certainly Carlos, should know that scientists cannot be put off by fear, whether real or imagined. Understand me. I do not say there is nothing to fear. My work with Miss Muñoz, who is a psychic as well as an accomplished archeologist, has started to teach me about the powers of the mind. I also know about the deaths surrounding the opening of the Tutankhamen dig and the deaths surrounding the early excavation at both Giza and Luxor. There are no scientific explanations for these, and moreover, much of the scientific community simply shuns any consideration of them. There was a time when I, too, shunned consideration of such things. Honestly, I am still tempted to simply dismiss them. But let me tell you this—we will still go on with the dig. There is, especially in light of the discoveries made recently, simply too much to be learned. We really have no choice. Some men put out huge oil fires and take risks. We dig in the earth to find the truth of the past and perhaps run some risks. As I say, we have no choice. Do I make sense?"

"You do, Doctor. But I am talking about the danger to our city. It is said that the earth shakes to warn all interlopers, and we have had a number of tremors recently . . . since the dig has been in progress. The village . . . perhaps you have seen it? It is on the road to the airport. The village is alive with talk about the dig and the cave-in that happened. They are also saying that you took the bones of one of the guardians of the place."

"What exactly is the basis of all of this Anna? Perhaps I can get a better picture of the terror here if I know it."

"There is little to tell because there is little that we know," Anna replied. "The shamans—the holy woman and men—are the ones who know and knew all of the secrets. And they did not reveal all of it to the people, even in the ancient times. But I do know that the ancient ones or their descendants lived here. They came here too long ago to remember. They gave us technical things of which we had no prior knowledge. They taught us to grow maize... ah, corn. They brought law and many other things. But the things that they left they meant not to be touched, until mankind was ready."

"We've come back to that again. Who would determine when we were ready?"

"The story is—and this is only part of it... as I said, the shamans only know all of it—It is said that the guardians were left with powers, and they were to stop anyone from going to the sacred places."

"But if the skeleton that we found at the dig is one of these guardians, then, they, too, are dead. How does the power work?"

"I cannot say, Doctor. *Something* determines the readiness of the species to gain the secrets, and that is what moves the earth and causes the deaths and cave-ins at the dig. If we were ready, then there would be no impediment to the exploration. That is all that I know."

"Were these ancients the builders of Monte Alban?" Lupe asked with intensity. It seemed she was on the same trail as Jason.

"Oh, no. No, Senorita. They came much later. They built Monte Alban because the site was already sacred. They disturbed nothing that was there, or that is what Vieja told me...."

"Vieja?" Jason queried.

"My grandmother, Senor. That is what she told me. They

built there to somehow have the temples of their gods carry the power of the location. They had many priests and a very great power. They used the site but there was nothing disturbed, as I said. Otherwise, there would have been no Monte Alban. It would have tumbled to the ground. Still, there has been great turmoil there. Many conquerers have come and destroyed. It is said that this conquest, including the last one by the Spanish, was a subtle reflection of the power of *Tombe Siete* and the entire complex. But they did not gain the hidden knowledge, and that simply means that what happened was only the roar of a distant cougar, as Xacha would have said."

Instantly, Jason thought about the small figurine in Caranza's office. "Is there any clue as to where the ancients came from and went to?" he asked.

"Senor, there are many. Some say that they came from the sea, and others say that they came from the sky...."

Jason had to force himself from rolling his eyes to the ceiling and swearing in Welsh. Christ! Not *that* theory. "But there is another thing that I do not understand," he said. "We are nearly at the peak of our evolution in terms of technology, science, and knowledge. How is it we cannot elude this curse you speak of? What kind of evolution are *they* talking about in the legend?"

"Spiritual evolution, Senor."

It stopped him cold. Yes, well... that *was* something. He was far from a philosopher and there was little chance that he could manage to pursue that argument to any conclusion.

"Anna, thank you for coming with the warning, and I am sorry we had to break the news of the death of Dr. Caranza. But there is nothing else that you can do. Just say to yourself, as your grandmother might have, that we have been warned. So, in his way, was Dr. Caranza. There is nothing more to it. If there are any accidents, they came from our actions. There is an end to it. Does that make you feel better?"

She stared at him for a long minute before she spoke. "A little. I will have to think about it, Doctor. But, yes, it does make me feel better."

"Doctor?" Carlos chimed in.

"Yes," Jason responded.

"A number of workers left the dig today. I am sure from hearing them talk that they will not be back. Many of them are living in the village and they *do* believe the stories. We are running short. One of the reasons that I came in, aside from being with Anna, was to tell you that Ugo is getting so shorthanded he is crazy. He sent me to find as many men as possible. But you know getting experienced men is difficult. I was going to call to Yucatan and the capital to try to get more experienced men, *con su permiso* . . . ah, with your permission. I don't know how many I can find but I will do my best."

"Certainly. We will need all that we can get. Do the best you can. And Anna?"

"Yes, Senor?"

"Carlos is one of us. That is something you will have to find a way to accept. You two will have to discuss it. But Carlos is one of the best men we have."

The good-byes were brief. In the elevator Anna did not say anything to Carlos. He tried to put his arm around her but she pulled away. Carlos shook his head and said to himself that he would never understand the vagaries of women. In the lobby he excused himself and went to a phone booth. He said that he had a chance to get a few workers with a call.

He dialed through the switchboard to Mexico City. The call, as did all calls in the tourist season, took an eternity to complete. Finally the phone rang and there was an answer at the other end. Carlos was brief.

"We need fifty men. We are close. Is there a chance that we can get them tomorrow, or even tonight?"

The voice on the other end paused only for a second. "They will be there in the morning."

"We are close, I think."
"Evidence?"
"A feeling."
"Excellent."

Carlos hung up and moved from the booth to Anna, who waited in the lobby. "I was lucky. I think I got several workers with just one call."

"I don't care," she snapped. "I still don't want you to be working there."

15

Jason looked across the table at her in silence. With equal silence, she looked back. After a moment he smiled. "Where were we?"

She giggled. "You Capricorns don't ever lose your place, do you?"

"What? Oh . . . yes, I guess I am. I never followed that."

"Somehow, I didn't think you would. That's typical too. There might be too much earth in you for my fiery Aries nature."

He sat back in the chair and assumed a look of mock seriousness. "Madam, I'm afraid that you have the advantage of me in this area."

She giggled even more. "I know. I want to keep it that way."

He grew sober, but not from her remark. One part of his mind replayed the tapes of the conversation with Anna and Carlos, while an ever-enlarging part spoke of her. There were things he would have to think more about, but there were other things he was going to have to begin to accept, even now.

"She made quite a case, didn't she?"

"About what?"

"About your thesis for catastrophism. It wasn't totally lost on me—that sly smile of yours. Or perhaps the smile was meant to convey something else?"

She grinned. "Perhaps."

"Oh, that's right. Well, we didn't have to answer the door, did we?"

"Yes, we did, love. There was nothing else that we could do."

"I think there was."

"No. Both of us would have wondered, and there was always the chance that they might not have come back. Both of us would have felt guilty about that. No. We had to see them. I felt it . . . if only because she had to verify many of the things I have said, not only about catastrophism but also about mysticism. You *had* to hear that. And it was not for any 'I told you so' reason. It was simply something that had to be."

"I'm not going to ask how you know all of that. That much I've learned in the last weeks. But I think I start to see what you mean about this catastrophist thing. We automatically make assumptions and then we're stuck with justifying and making sense of them. If we look at things from the other point of view, there seems to be more sense in things. But all of this is so radical in terms of the accepted views . . . what evidence is there?"

Lupe looked to him with a smile still on her face. She shook her head silently. "There is a great deal of evidence, Jason, if we look in the right place. Plato tells of Atlantis in one of his tracts. He says that the Atlanteans were the greatest sea merchants in the ancient world. He says that Posedia, the chief island, was four hundred leagues west of the Pillars of Hercules. . . ."

"Gibraltar?"

"Yes. This is documented. In the late seventies the Soviets dove with a team there and found the ruins of a massive city at just over four hundred feet. A news release that came through Tass and Reuters quoted the head of the expedition as saying that they had found Atlantis."

"What happened then?"

"Nothing. There were no other news stories and there was no further exploring. The Soviets went home, satisfied with that much and nothing more. My grandmother, I remember, was furious. So was the late Dr. Moreland. There was nothing they could do at the time. There were no funds to be had. Since then, Jerry has been planning on the integration of archeologists and psychics. One of the places we are going to work together, as two groups of professionals, will be four hundred miles off the Spanish coast at Cadiz. That is one of the reasons I am here with you now. Since the late seventies there has been a great deal of government money poured into the Institute. All of what is going on here is prelude."

"I didn't know that Tanner was that interested in all of this, I mean I knew that parapsychology was his thing, but I didn't make that connection. I thought your coming with me was something of a side road to the things the Institute was after. I didn't know."

"I am ranked as the number one psychic, specifically psychometrist, at the Institute. When all of this is over, I am supposed to train the team of psychics that will work with the divers at the site the Soviets left. Four hundred feet is a treacherous scuba dive, and there are only a few minutes that each diver can have on the bottom before he or she has to be brought back up in stages. They would have to know *exactly* where to look to find things that could be brought back to the surface. Otherwise they would be in the same position as that Soviet team. They would see the ruins, say they were there, and go home."

Jason thought of Yuri and his KGB watchdog Valarin, and the way both of them had lingered at the site of the new chamber, and he wondered why such a group would spend such an amount of money on much explored Oaxaca when a similar team would find ruins of Atlantis and simply go home.

"Is there any reason why the Russians simply packed it in the Atlantic, I mean aside from the diving difficulties?"

"I can tell you if Jerry Tanner had made the find, we'd still be there combing the ocean floor, no matter what the cost. The site is in international waters, and whatever was raised would be salvage. There would be no claim to them."

"Are you saying it would be financially worthwhile?"

"Jason, darling, is everything conventional archeology for you? The chances are that the find would be monumental. That's another reason Jerry wanted me here. He thinks, and so do I, that the gold artifacts we found were originally made somewhere other than in Oaxaca. The emeralds are an indication of that, wouldn't you agree?"

"I'd have to. But you think that the 'somewhere else' is Atlantis?"

"How would the Zapotecs know about the exterior biology of the bottle-nosed dolphin? It would take a nation of seafarers to know that. According to esoteric sources—"

"What esoteric sources?"

"You know, the ones you would not believe in no matter what they said—according to them, the dolphin was the national symbol of Atlantis, that and the Eye of Oris—the symbol the United States placed on the back of the dollar bill."

"But that's Masonic, isn't it?"

"Yes, but where did the Masons come from? We know there were Masons in ancient Egypt and that they claim to an even more ancient heritage. The gold of Troy was supposedly smelted in Atlantis. If there's something in the Atlantic, then there's a fortune there."

"Jerry wants to prove catastrophism with all of this. Atlantis is not the only site. There are others and there is a long term plan."

"Stop. I have to take things a step at a time. All of this and the things you have done here are too much to gulp down. You know that if any part of this pans out, the chances are that the wrath of the archeological establishment will land on the Institute?"

"Jerry knows that. That was why he had you look at a demonstration of psychometry before you agreed to take on this assignment. He wanted you to see that it worked. Look what we have found. The next step is to put all of that into a framework that works toward building a case for catastrophism. So, you see, there is indeed a long term plan, and the things that I mentioned were just probes, designed to see if you were ready to accept further assignments in this area, employing psychics."

Again he smiled. "With you? Anytime."

Though there was a warm, almost liquid look in her eyes, she shook off the comment. "Jason, I'm serious. We . . . we are another thing entirely. Neither of us could have predicted what was starting to happen. Well . . . perhaps I could a bit on the plane, but I've been wrong more than once, and I didn't want to push things. But why we're here . . . that's something else. Us . . . well, it's a magnificent bonus."

"But what about all of the rest of it, Lupe? The things Anna spoke of. Fear and legends and the deaths and some enormous power, earthquakes . . . and the rest, about a species not ready to understand power. I know there is something frightening you about Caranza and some of the other things at the tomb. We're talking about two breeds of cat. What if Atlantis, or whatever it was, displeased something and earthquakes blew it up? If you, a psychic—and a hell of a psychic—are frightened about this dig and the things surrounding it, where the hell do we go from here? I'm sorry. Perhaps I'm just confused."

She stared at him for a long moment with her hands folded beneath her chin. She breathed deeply, exhaling with a sigh.

"Yes, I'm frightened, more than you know, and you're not the only one who's confused. When I said that we were caught in between two things, I wasn't sure what I meant. I start to see it now. There's something in that tomb that is stupendous, vast . . . what can I say? Ominous? And terribly powerful... more than we can even imagine. It could be strong enough to create earthquakes and more...."

She stopped and seemed to think for a long second before she went on. Her voice was quiet and tiny as she spoke again. "Jason, I'm more frightened than I have ever been in my life. I just want you to hold me forever and for us to never go back into a dig again."

He got up and pulled her to her feet gently. He circled her with his arms and nuzzled her hair for a moment. "I'll go back alone. I don't want to put you in any more danger."

She pulled away from him. "Oh, male ego, Jesus, Jason. You don't see it. We're pawns in a game and there is a chance that all of us have been since the first of the figurines was discovered there. They *had* to be found. We *have* to be here. And I beg the spirit of my grandmother to help me. *We* have to go back in there and play out the roles set for us."

He cocked his head to the side, staring at her. "I'm sorry. I meant what I said. I would go back. The rest of what you're saying just baffles me."

"Jason, it baffles me too. Maybe we're tools in a larger game. I know that sounds... corny. But there will come a time when there is no choice for us. The script is written. I just hate to hell the way it's been written and the roles we've been given."

"What... cast are we?"

She came back to his arms. "I don't know, Jason. I don't know, darling. I don't know." She looked into his down-turned face and took it in her hands. "But I know that us coming together the way we just had is something that is a part of the script."

"I wish I had the chance to talk to the old woman before she died. I wonder if there is anyone that I can talk to about it?"

"I wish I could have talked to her too. But all that we could do, and I maintain that there is no value in finding how she died, was learn a few fragments more than Anna told us. Remember that she said her secrets were not divulged by the shamans. Occult means hidden, Jason. To spread such knowledge, more than was needed, would be to diffuse the energy and allow the negative energy of the unbelievers to blunt the purpose. That is simply the way it is. There is nothing that could have been learned."

"I could have learned what killed George Rodgers, who had a coronary in his twenties, being a runner and physical fitness buff. It might have told me that."

"I'm almost certain that the diagnosis of heart failure would have been accurate. I begin to think that sheer terror killed Rodgers. I really think so. That is something I could not have said to you a few weeks ago. I think that something frightened George Rodgers to death, and I also think that old Xacha died because there was nothing left to live for. Her mission was complete and it was something that she spent her life waiting for. Aren't there old couples to whom this happens? One dies and the other follows within a year because there is nothing there anymore. They want to join one another. There is a rightness to it. There was an American general, a man named Patton in World War Two. He died a few weeks after the war was over... as a career soldier, there was nothing for him to live for in peacetime."

"But Patton was killed in an accident, wasn't he?"

"Yes. But he was also a reincarnationist. He believed that he had been many generals in the past. There are no accidents. There are only things we plan for ourselves. There is always the chance that we fool our egos into calling them accidents, while all the time our reincarnational subconscious has planned them. There is always a reason."

"God, I've been saying that all my life as a scientist. I never thought of it in that context." He stopped for a second and looked at the great sad eyes that had started to grow fiery. "Was what happened this afternoon... us... was that something reincarnational? Was it something we planned?"

She shrugged and started to smile at the same time. "Jason darling... it was fun. It was more—it was fantastic. There is something very special about us. Very. I'm not sure about anything more than that. There *is* a deep reason for all of this that we have hidden from ourselves. I know *you* think that I might know about it. But aside from that slight premonition that I had on the flight, I knew nothing. Honestly. All I know now is that I am very happy. I don't think that I have ever felt this way in my life."

She reached a hand across the table to him and he covered it with his. Her eyes were liquid again and there was nothing of the scholar in them. There was nothing of the psychic. There was only the loving look of a sensuous and exciting woman, one who had moved Jason in a way he had never been moved before. He had always been cautious, careful, suspicious. He had never jumped headlong into an unknown place, not until today. There was no guilt, no suspicion, and no hesitation. It had simply happened. He squeezed her hand.

"I think I'm starting to get a premonition right now. I think I see..." He got to his feet, came around the table, and lifted her to her feet. "...us making love in the freshly made bed." He slipped an arm around her slender back. She could feel the strength and the warmth of his hands. They excited her. "Yes, I think I see that right now." He turned her and started to walk her in the direction of the bed.

Suddenly she pulled away from him. He looked startled and then there was a look of disappointment in his eyes. She started to realize more than ever how sensitive and delicately balanced he was. That excited her more and totally endeared her to him.

"Wait."

"What's wrong?"

"Even Pharaoh fed the slaves. We haven't eaten all day. I'm starving for you, darling." She came forward and caressed the stubble on his face. "But I'm also starving. Is there a chance that we could get dinner? There seem to be tables down there in the courtyard. Can we? You wouldn't want to make love to an unconscious woman, would you?"

The hurt look evaporated. "There have been times in the past when I thought that some of them were unconscious. Well, let's not discuss that."

"No. Let's not."

He looked to the dinner tables in the courtyard, then to the sky. The clouds were still moving through the mountains, but he thought the chances were good for them getting through supper before the rains came. They did not have to get back to the dig until morning. He was sure Ugo would be able to take care of things until they returned. Besides, this woman was fast becoming a top priority in his life, and he had to reorder things.

"Dinner it is. Let me go over and change. I actually brought one suit with me. Is there a chance I could meet you in the lobby? I have to get a cable off to Tanner about the death of Caranza. We're going to have to find another method of dealing with the Mexican government and this group called InterHelp. I have to get that off as soon as possible. I would have sent it as soon as we found the body, but there were other things that . . . ah, intervened."

"The lobby then." She smiled. She knew it would give her the chance to primp, get into her best dress, and make something of a grand entrance. "Half an hour?"

He nodded and reached down again, slipping a strong, warm arm around her waist. He kissed her gently and then left.

In his own room Jason scattered his clothes as he headed for the shower. He took the single wash suit from the closet with him, like a strange companion, to the shower.

Clean and shaved, he dressed in the now wrinkle-free suit and the one white shirt that hung in the closet next to the single blue-striped tie. Then he sat at the small desk in the corner of the room and started to compose the cable. It didn't take him long. There was little good news in it.

Tanner from Farewey:

Caranza dead mysteriously. Contact with
government and InterHelp gone. You will have to
do something on your end. Perhaps State Dept.?
Otherwise, dig progresses. Will advise if anything
startling happens. Lupe Muñoz is brilliant!

J.F.

He smiled at the last comment. It was not something he had to do. It was more of a pun than anything else. Tanner would never realize that he was speaking about something other than archeology. And, Jason mused, at the same time Tanner would be excited about the comment in light of the ambitions Lupe had conveyed to him.

He glanced at his watch, and left from the room. He took the stairs rather than the elevator and crossed the lobby. He saw there were no messages for either of them. There was, blessedly, no further communiqué from MRI. He had the desk clerk take down the message and was assured it would be sent before ten in the evening, when the telegraph office closed. It reminded him that this was a land of siestas and therefore longer days, often stretching store and office hours to after eleven in the evening. Strange, he thought, since this was not a hot part of Mexico. Indeed, much of the day was like early, cool summer in Wales. Still, there was siesta and the closing of everything between one and four in the afternoon. Tradition, he thought, nothing more or less.

He waited another ten minutes... fifteen. He looked at his watch and smiled. Why was it that women took so much longer than men to get ready for anything? He used to get impatient and even angry at such things. But they did not bother him with Lupe. Instead, there was only the excitement, the anticipation of seeing her. He wondered for a second if that was the reason she took her time. He conjured up a mental picture of the look in her eyes and realized that that *was* the reason. It made him smile. How little he actually knew about women!

The elevator opened and Lupe strode out. She did not see him for a moment and he was glad for that. She was magnificent. He was not sure that he wanted her to see the considerable impact she had on him in that moment. Then, there seemed to be nothing wrong with it.

"Lupe. Over here."

She smiled and started toward him, wearing a pink cocktail dress that was deeply cut to reveal the cleavage between her dark-skinned breasts. Her hair had been brushed out and shimmered down across her shoulders. Her smile was breathtaking. There would have been no question that she was a woman in love, even if Jason were a stranger seeing her for the first time. He knew if he were that stranger, he would have instantly envied the man with whom she was in love. Now, he thought, he could allow other men to envy. It didn't matter. As she moved, there were a few male heads that turned her way. Two of the men he noticed were with older women. They managed to sneak a surreptitious peek at her before their mates noticed that they were noticing. Jason smiled at that.

She grinned. "Good evening, Senor Doctor."

Jason remembered her, grime-covered and exhausted at the dig. He also remembered her up in her room, her fingers kneading his back as her hips undulated beneath him. She had said nothing. There had not even been a moan from her at the moment of climax. Yet, he felt he knew how good they had been together without being tactless enough to ask. He took her arm and they started toward the patio dining room without a word. It seemed to Jason that it was something they had done all of their lives.

El Presidente had a superior kitchen, and they feasted on five courses of Oaxacan cuisine. At least one of the courses—a sort of beef roulade with a pungent green sauce—

made Jason's eyes water, and he managed to down the better part of a bottle of mineral water following it. Lupe, it seemed, didn't mind the hot main course. She giggled quietly as he mumbled to himself about it, and gulped down the mineral water.

Following the main course, while they were lingering over fresh fruit and cheese along with steaming black coffee and two tiny glasses of fine mescal, they chatted.

"I was an only child too," she said. "My grandmother, rest her soul, had nine children. Only seven of them lived, but she managed to raise a strange brood. They are my aunts and uncles. Some of them you will have to meet, professionally. Two of my aunts work for MRI. Both of them are psychics, though their talents tend to be slightly different than mine."

"How is that?" he asked as he held her hand across the table. She might have been saying that bananas were yellow as far as he was concerned. He would have been happy to hear that voice say anything.

"Well, Flora is something of a telepath, but she has no skill with artifacts. She has no ability as a psychometrist. Inez is a retrogressive sensitive. That is something like what I do, but much more specialized. She can provide the period and the life, in the case of a skeleton, that the artifact or the deceased went through. Of course, there is a great more conjecture there, especially in a life. There is no way to easily verify what she says. It is much easier for me and her with artifacts. It makes things easier for Rosemary McGee to feed information into DANIEL, where she can make sense of things."

"Daniel?"

"Oh, yes. Didn't Jerry mention DANIEL to you?"

"No. But I'm sure that Tan . . . ah, Jerry had a great deal to do at the time. Remember, we got down here in a considerable hurry, without the usual leisurely tour through the Institute, as I might have expected. Obviously that news about Rodgers—"

"I'm sure we will find what caused the death before we leave everything here. I am certain of it."

"Is that something...?" He gestured to his head with his hand. "You know..."

"I think it is, Jason. I think it is. But, you know, I can make guesses that are not psychic and still be right. I know that you know I can make archeological judgments and decisions. You have seen me do that and so I am sure that ... how do I say it? I am sure that you are sure. About a psychic premonition... well, they are there and I recognize them. But they do not always come in the same way or with the same strength.

"You see, many of these things are body feelings. They are not quite the same as empiric information. It's sort of like a radio picking up a distant station that is drifting in and out. One has to catch what is there when the station is in range, and one has to be able to hear and... I guess amplify that signal. Everyone is psychic, Jason. I am sure of that. For example—"

"Even me?" he asked as he sipped at the firelike mescal.

"Even you." She squeezed his hand. "See? I say everyone and I mean everyone, even close-minded Welsh diggers and scholars."

"I stand... ah, sit humbled before you, madam. Seriously, why everyone?"

"All of us have had a psychic experience or two in our lives. Many of us push them from the conscious because we are afraid of them. We say that they were a coincidence, or something like that. We are afraid of them. The Western tradition does not prepare us for such things. It tells us that everything can be measured, analyzed, placed in a clear Aristotelian category. Not everything can. Thus we have cut ourselves off from a wellspring of mind power."

"But there must be phonies among psychics. The whole field must be rife with them."

"Oh, Jason, you have hit the core of things. When you mention that to Jerry Tanner, he starts to grimace and roll his eyes. He says that when he first studied under Channing Moreland in graduate school, he investigated literally hundreds of cases and some three quarters of them were either not psychic at all or were willful fakes. Jerry found that, like UFO investigations, the reports must be culled. By the time he and Channing got professionally under way and the Institute was formed, they could smell a phony at a great distance. Most sincere psychics are interested in *how* the talent works. They want to understand the things that might have frightened them through their lives. They, for the most part, do not charge for their readings and cannot read things on cue. If they can, they tend to be suspect. It is the stage mentalist who *must* be right to impress his audience. So he uses props and becomes an illusionist. All of the data Jerry could put together about phonies has been assembled and fed into DANIEL, an immense computer complex that Channing, God rest him, Jerry, and the Institute staff have been stuffing full of programs in the area for years. They screen everyone who comes to the Institute and they have a good system. At least at MRI there are no phonies. There *are* questions that have not been answered. But that is the reason we are here, isn't it?"

He smiled slyly. There was a brief flash of lightning in the north, over her shoulder. Jason considered that he—they—were fortunate that the rain had held off through dinner. They would make love in a thunderstorm: What a wild thought.

"Is it?"

"Well, partially. There is us. Is that grammatical?"

"I don't care. It's true. That's all that matters. Why don't we—" There was yet another flash to the north and with it came a low, deep-throated rumble. That, Jason reasoned, would be the sound of the first flash. Some rapid calculation told him that the storm, if it was going to get to them, would arrive in less than an hour, considering that he could feel little wind.

Jason glanced around the terraced dining area. A number

of the tourists were also looking at the sky, wondering if their dinners might be drowned. At the far end of the dining area, half obscured by a huge potted plant, there was a small table, close to the door. As the man at the table leaned forward to speak to the waiter, Jason caught a glimpse of his face. Valarin.

He wondered why the KGB man was not off hounding the steps of Yuri Kurtzov. He shrugged. Even KGB men had to have some time off, and there was little chance that Yuri would be pounding at the doors of the American consular office in Oaxaca, not with a wife, four children, and a number of inlaws still in Leningrad. Again he thought of the way the man had looked at the figurine in the dig. What had that look meant? Could it have been recognition? Was there a chance that he had seen the dolphin-shaped object before? Could it have been in the ocean exploration of Atlantis? He pushed the wild speculation aside.

Valarin's head turned in his direction and for a second the two men's eyes met. Valarin smiled, as if surprised. He raised a glass as if in toast and drank it down. Then he got up from the table and left. Had he just finished a meal? Or had he left because his presence had been discovered? Jason pushed the thoughts away.

Then there was something else. It was strange at first. Nothing in the courtyard seemed to stir, as if the wind— actually the gentle zyphr—had stopped. Then there was a slight sway—not of the wind, but of everything. He looked at the bottle of mineral water on the table. Inside the glass the water was doing a slow dance. The trees around the courtyard seemed to emulate the movement of the water. For the first few seconds the waiters and the other patrons did not seem to notice the same things Jason did. He looked to Lupe. It was clear she was feeling the same thing.

"What—" she asked.

"The same thing as in the park—last week, I think. A tremor. This one seems stronger."

"Yes." Indeed, it was. The trees shook and there was a

creak in the structure of the hotel. Still, there was little notice taken by the restaurant staff other than a quick look to the sky or a slight hesitation in the serving of wine at a table. Jason could hear questions being asked—some in Spanish, but most in English—by the tourists. The one-word answer he could understand was *"tremora."* It was the same term he had heard in the plaza the week before.

In a matter of a few more seconds it was over, and except for a few exclamations from tourists who were obviously American, business went on as usual.

"They must really be used to this kind of thing." Jason said. "The only thing like it in Wales would have been..." His look grew distant and Lupe could see that there was something wrong.

"What is it, Jason?"

He shrugged. There was no way he was going to spoil the evening he saw ahead, the one he also hoped she saw ahead.

"Jason?"

"Nothing, not really."

"You were worried about the dig?"

"Well, a bit of concern. I think it will be all right. We've done a great deal of additional shoring, especially after the cave-in. There has not been the rain that there was before the last one. I think everything will be fine."

Lupe did not believe him, not completely. She knew he had a depth of concern greater than he was admitting. She pressed. "There is no sense in us staying here for a romantic, passionate evening if you are going to be worried about the dig. Perhaps you should get in touch with Ugo. Did you get one of my... feelings, Jason? Was that it?"

He shrugged. "I don't know. I can't say if it was the experience of the last cave-in or just paranoia. I was just worried for a second. Simple as that. If I were more concerned, I'd call Ugo. But he knows where we are and how to reach us."

She reached her other hand across the table and took his

TOMB SEVEN 193

in hers. "Just remember, all of us are psychic. It is all right for even *you* to be psychic. The voice is a small one and we can dismiss it or ignore it."

He was disturbed and both of them knew it. He tried for a few minutes to listen to the music of the guitarists and singers who drifted quietly from table to table. There was something odd about the words and the way that they were pronouncing them. He tried to focus on them. They were soothing, though alien.

"What is that language? It's not Spanish, is it? It doesn't sound like it."

She also tried to listen to the words through the four perfectly harmonized guitars. After a moment she turned to him with a quizzical look on her face. "A native language. I heard a tiny bit of it last week. I think it is Zapoteco."

"Do a lot of the natives still speak it?"

"I'm not sure. But I distantly remember that it is a dying language. I think less than one percent, or at most two percent, of the Oaxacans still speak or understand it."

"Like listening to ancient Egyptian, isn't it?"

She nodded. "Yes. I can't understand a bit of it. It does not resemble Spanish even slightly. None of the native languages did."

It was ten minutes later, when he had paid the bill and they were about to get to their feet, that he saw the assistant manager of the hotel come into the courtyard and peer around. He was followed at a distance by a bedraggled grime-smeared man who looked about urgently. The assistant manager spotted Jason and Lupe at their table near a bed of hibiscus.

"Senor Doctor," he called, not too loudly.

Jason got to his feet and the grime-smeared man who had followed at a distance saw him. He bolted through the tables to Jason, almost upsetting several tables and trays as he ran. The manager was more than upset by this, and followed the interloper almost at a run. It was unthinkable to interrupt the dinner of the guests with such a person's presence. The man was only a few feet away when Jason recognized him as one of the faces at the dig, a man who had had a lot of conversations with Ugo in the last weeks. He was not of the status of Carlos but he was a valued digger.

The man's eyes were wild as he ran for the table. "Senor. Senor!"

"Yes? What is it?"

He spoke in bursts of rapid Spanish and Jason looked in panic to Lupe. "What is it? What is he saying?"

"It's too quick, even for me. Wait."

She spoke to the man and tried to calm him. When the speech had slowed, she listened for a long moment and Jason could watch her eyes turn to him as she listened. After a few moments she placed a hand on the man's arm and stopped him. The grimy man stood there in a strange blend of exhaustion, panic, and bewilderment.

"Jason," she said. Her dark eyes penetrated his for a long moment. It was as if there were something she was dredging up, a memory from the distant past.

"He says there has been another cave-in at the site. He says it was again in the main tunnel and that there are men trapped again. He says only one or two this time."

Jason thought of the feeling he had over dinner during the tremor. She had made such a point of it, such a strong point. Was it that she also . . . he didn't even know how he could think of it . . . frame it with logic. It was not logical at all. Had she caught a premonition he'd had and used it to teach him that he, too, was psychic?

"At least that means the shoring has been better this time. Tell him to— Oh, how many men and are they sure that the men are still alive?"

All thought of a night together vanished from both of their minds. Jason tried for a moment to put those thoughts on hold, but couldn't do it. It was like a doctor and a nurse trying to be romantic in an emergency room. At that point there was nothing to be done except care for the patient. They were professionals.

"He says that there are three and they can hear sounds from the other side of the cave-in. He says he needs to know what to do."

"Tell him to get back out there right now. Say that we . . ." He looked at her and she knew what he was going to say before he said it. ". . . will join him as soon as we can change. Tell him to tell Ugo we might need the core drilling equipment again, and that the rescue diggers should avoid disturbing any dirt even within a few feet of a vertical support. Say that—"

"Jason?"

"What?"

"You don't seem to understand. The man needs us out there to start things right now."

"Please, Lupe, tell him to have Ugo start. That way things can be under way before we get there. Time is crucial. It—"

She interrupted. "Jason," she said firmly.

"What?"

"We *have* to be the ones who start things. It seems that Ugo is one of the three men trapped."

16

Mexico City.

Don Diego had stayed late at his office in the headquarters of InterHelp, which occupied three floors of prime location on the Paseo de la Revolucion. Although it was his custom to leave near four and get back to the hacienda, there were several things that had to be cared for tonight. One of them meant money, and one of them could prove to be a threat to the money. Such things always delayed Don Diego, because he was so meticulous with them.

He was holding the phone and listening. Occasionally he would nod, as if the speaker could see him. This was a way of confirming to himself that whatever was being discussed was going well. Tonight Diego smiled as he nodded. Things were indeed excellent.

"Yes. You will have to get them there tonight." He listened for a second. "I don't care. I know that we said tomorrow. I understand you have made the arrangements, but the situation has changed quickly. You will have to get them there tonight."

Again, he paused. "Yes?" There was something being straightened out on the other end. He started to smile as Senor Tres, the man on the other end, spoke. Diego listened.

"Excellent. Late in the evening, then?"

After a few more minutes he hung up the phone and glanced at his watch. The second task of the evening was about to begin, and with the first solved, Diego felt confident about the second. The man who had made the appointment had made it hurriedly. Normally Diego was a man whom it took months to see. Diego smiled. The visitor who would arrive in a few minutes was one who did not know how lucky he was.

Then there was something else. The visitor could well endanger the operation which was so near fruition.

He waited, considering the tactics he might use in dealing with him. Etiquette was, of course, mandatory. There was a chance the man would come into the office with guns blazing, ready to accuse Diego of everything from grave robbery to child molesting. But any man had his price. Diego knew that from long experience and he also knew something else, which was less reassuring. He had to find the right currency. That was not always easy. Many times it was not something as simple as money. But, he said to himself with assurance, the right currency was something he had always been able to find. It was necessary in his position.

The phone rang—not the office line, the personal one. He picked it up before the second ring, pausing just long enough to consider who it might be.

"Yes?" He did not identify himself. Anyone calling on the special line would know the voice of the man answering. Before there was an answer, Diego reached down and snapped on the scrambler, which he had snapped off after the previous caller. Despite the fact that there was no extension and absolutely no bugs on the line, there was always the chance that a task force working for some agency or other would have a way of intercepting the call. So the scrambler was insurance. Everyone who might have called on the line also had a scrambler on their end. Everything was covered.

"This is Dos."

"Is there something new?"

"Yes. In fact, it happened less than a half hour ago."

"Well?"

"Monte Alban has suffered another cave-in. It will set the dig back."

"Do we know how long?"

"Not precisely. We think at this time that the delay might be a few days to a week."

"Is there something we can do to expedite things? I don't want that freighter on station at Plato y Oro too long. The Coast Guard and others might get too curious. She cannot afford to have herself boarded."

"That has been taken care of, sir. She has a load of explosives in her keel and is anchored in deep water. If there is a hint of anything amiss, she will scuttle and there will be little trace of what she carries. The captain will, if the event occurs, be held for smuggling. But as there is no evidence, he will be released. However, I remind you that the ship has altered her position each day, and she does carry a small cargo that is legitimate. If there is to be a considerable lead time between now and her utilization, I will have her deliver the cargo to Tampico and return. That would remove any suspicion."

"Since you mentioned a delay of only a few days to a week, I don't see that that will be needed. I think she should remain on station, pending information from the dig. Things will be moving too quickly when the find happens. We also have more men—"

"I know. Tres told me. I'm adjusting."

There was a pause in Diego's side of the conversation. Tres knew that Diego disliked being interrupted. But he also knew that under these circumstances, the less said on the phone the better.

"Very well. Let's speak again at the staff meeting. If anything happens at the dig before that, call me immediately. We will have to move with speed. I'm sure you know that."

Diego hung up without allowing Dos to answer on the other end. There was no slight intended. It was simply a question of efficiency.

He opened the file on his visitor and perused it for a final time. He wanted to be sure there was nothing he had missed. He always believed in knowing the enemy. It told you more about the possible currency of purchase, as well as giving you a tactical feel for the confrontation. He would counterpunch. It was what he had been considering earlier. Yes. There was no way he could admit to the knowledge he really had. He would look at the opening gambit and play things from there. Most importantly—

The intercom buzzed and he answered it, glancing at his watch. Yes, the man was on time, exactly. That would mean his mind was orderly and that would make him, to an extent, predictable.

The huge door opened and Dr. Jorge Lopez strode into the office.

"Dr. Lopez, welcome to InterHelp." Diego got to his feet. There was no question about the initial advantage Diego had. He stood nearly half a foot taller than the diminutive doctor. "Please, sit down. Might I offer you some coffee?"

The doctor smiled winningly. "Certainly. Thank you very much for seeing me."

Jorge sat across the desk from Diego. The latter buzzed an unseen personage and ordered coffee. While they waited, they chatted.

"I've noticed that the summer has come early to the capital."

Diego glanced perfunctorily over his shoulder to the afternoon sun streaming across the Paseo de la Revolucion. "Yes. It has been here for a few weeks now. But I am fortunate to live out of town, past Chapultepec. It's cooler there. I imagine it is considerably cooler in Oaxaca. I remember cool summers there when I used to vacation there, many years ago...."

He thought about the other arrangements he was going to have to make as a result of the delay at the dig. His lone contact across town was not going to be happy at the delay.

The trawler that was to intercept the freighter on her northbound journey was known only to him and his associate at the other end of the city. After the transfer, the freighter would be given another set of course coordinates, and after traveling on them for sixteen hours, she would fall prey to a monumental explosion, one that would kill all hands. The submarine that lay in wait would have to be advised of the delay, but he assumed that would be no problem. Both the sub and the trawler were in international waters, as the freighter would be. If his newly acquired business colleagues were miffed by the delay, they could mollify themselves with the thought of their reward.

"A lovely city, as I remember," Jorge Lopez was saying. "I'm sure there has been a considerable amount of growth in the last few years?"

"Yes, a considerable amount." The eye contact between the men did not waver. Neither blinked.

The coffee arrived on a glistening silver service, wheeled in by a shapely, dark-eyed secretary. Diego waved her out and served the steaming coffee in delicate china cups. Both men took it black. It was as they sipped that things started to move in the direction Diego had anticipated.

"What can I do for you, Doctor?" he asked.

"I am concerned, Senor, about the fact that your organization has been involved in the cremation of several deceased upon whom I had performed post mortems."

"I wasn't aware that among your other duties you were also a medical examiner," he lied. "You seem quite a diverse man."

"Thank you, but diversity in a small city's medical community is a necessity."

"You are too modest, Doctor. Now, specifically, who are the people you were concerned about?"

"They are an old Indian woman, essentially an indigent, known only as Xacha. The other deceased is an American archeologist named Rodgers, George Rodgers. Can you give me any information about any post mortem procedures that might have taken place prior to the cremation and subsequent to my investigation?"

Diego thought the doctor either naive or playing naive. "Just a moment. Please enjoy your coffee. I'll get the files myself."

He left the room and returned quickly with two files under his arm. Jorge was impressed. "That was quite efficient, Senor."

Diego smiled as he placed the files on the desk and sat down to sip the coffee. "Well, we pride ourselves on our retrieval system. It took a good many years to develop." He looked through the first file, then through the second. After a few minutes perusal, he closed both of them and looked across the wide desk to Jorge.

"It seems that there was no additional work done. I was fairly certain there had not been. We never engage in post mortems. It is far outside the scope of our organization. I had no way of anticipating a need for exhumation."

Jorge shrugged. "There was not actually a need, nor was there a court order... though I could have gotten one if it would have done any good. There is no sense in trying to do a post mortem on ashes, Senor... and that brings me to the second question. How does an organization that purports to be philanthropic and archeological/historical involve itself in cremation of bodies that die in Oaxaca? This is not an investigation." It was his turn to lie. "I am merely curious."

Diego did not believe the lie for a second. "Actually, the reasons you state are the very reasons for the cremations. It is because we support the indigent that we offer a cremation service and, I might add, we have sixteen branch offices, one of them in Oaxaca. It was not the original purpose of the organization, not in the least. It was one of the things that we, you might say, drifted into over the years. It came to our attention that burial facilities and costs were out of the range of some of the poorer of our countrymen and women, particularly after the number of outbreaks of disease that occurred off and on in the poorer rural areas. But I am sure that you, as a man of medicine, are more than aware of that?"

Jorge nodded slightly with a smile.

"At any rate, we started a service for the poor, though we could not arrange for the burial disposition of the body. I'm sure you understand the logistics of that kind of operation?"

Another nod.

"We decided that cremation would be dignified and sanitary. So there are offices in the sixteen cities I mentioned to you, and one of the functions they carry out is the cremation of the indigent. I remind you that this is done by a release of the deceased while they are still alive, or by releases signed and witnessed by the next of kin. Of course, it is necessary to prove that the deceased was indigent, but we do not stress this too hard, as the bereaved family would only be placed under more unpleasantness if the requirements were too stringent. To sum up, the service is indeed one of philanthropy, with a side purpose of sanitation."

"How did the cremation of Dr. Rodgers come under that heading?"

Diego did not pause. The question was easily anticipated and answered. "It didn't. It came under the arm of our operation that deals with the preservation of archeological sites and the watchdog service that we provide against illegal smuggling or export of national treasures. A part of that operation, since a number of our offices happen to be near archeological digs, has connected itself to the watchdog service. This brought us into contact with a number of diggers and professionals. After canvassing them, we saw that many of the workers were almost archeological migrants. They had no real place of residence. But once they had acquired the skill of digging at such sites, they moved constantly from one to the other, as foundations funded more digs. Many of these diggers were men with no families, and though they did not fall under the category we have called indigent, there were no family members to make the arrangements, should there be an accident at the dig and a fatality occur. While these don't occur every day, they do happen... and with considerable consistency. The trip you made to see me today was, in part, about such a death, was it not?"

"That's correct, as I mentioned," Jorge replied mildly, though Jorge's mind flashed to the post mortem on Rodgers and he had to push his anger back. Damn! He still wanted to get his hands on a no-longer-existent corpse.

"Well, you see then. We offer the service to everyone at the site. To exclude the professionals, while the chances are that they *have* families and means to pay for interment, would be harder than to offer the service to all. From the professionals we ask a small donation, whatever they choose to give. When we approached the staff at the new dig at Monte Alban—it is at Tomb Seven, is it not? At any rate, we offered it to all of the staff and one of the professionals, Dr. Rodgers, indicated he would like to avail himself of it. We have here..."

He opened the file and passed several official-looking papers across to Jorge.

"You will notice that the first of the papers is a release by the doctor himself for the service. It has been signed in the presence of a local Oaxaca notary. The other papers are also, you will see, totally in order. I cannot say why the doctor wanted our service. But there is a mention in the forms that he had no family, and he seemed to indicate to the representative to whom he spoke that it seemed simpler to avail himself of the service rather than burden the... I believe it is the Moreland Research Institute... with the disposition of his remains, should something unforeseen happen.

"I understand that the Moreland Research people subsequently requested the body for interment in the United

States. This was unfortunate. But we did cable them and send the information about the doctor's choice in the matter. It is unfortunate that at the same time we had been—and indeed still are—in some dispute about the return of some of the artifacts that were found at Monte Alban and shipped to the United States."

"Why is that, Senor?" Jorge found himself suddenly curious.

Diego looked intense. "It is a matter of track record, Doctor. This has little to do with the record of the Moreland people. In fact, truthfully, we have never had any dealings with them. We found in this case that through pressure brought to bear on our government by the United States State Department, pressure clearly initiated by Moreland, the remains or whatever the artifacts from the dig were, had been shipped from the country as soon as they had been crated—less than twenty-four hours after their discovery. This alarmed us. Common practice is to have the Minister of the Interior and the Department of Antiquities examine the artifacts before shipping. I, again, do not criticize Moreland. Rather, to violate such a practice and set such an alarming precedent with the shipment of native Mexican artifacts, opens the door for other breaches in the practice. In a few years we would be back in the nineteenth century, when our heritage was robbed wholesale. You see then, it was common practice for us to register a complaint."

"Were you affiliated with Dr. Caranza, of the museum? It was mentioned, and I did the post mortem, that there were a number of InterHelp documents among his papers."

Diego paused. It was a question the doctor should not have asked. He did not know what had been found in Caranza's office. But he was sure that he was going to find out.

"We still are aff— Did you say post mortem?"

"Yes."

"I didn't know. When did he die? Why did my staff not know of this?"

"It only happened yesterday morning. He was found in his office early in the morning by some people from the dig."

"How did he die?"

"That's curious. I believe he was murdered."

"Murdered? Not Caranza. He was such a warm, vital man. I only met him personally once, but I spoke many times to him on the phone. He seemed like the kind of man who would have few enemies. I hope that robbery was not involved."

"The police don't think so. But I am certain he was murdered. He died of a coronary embolism and there was a needle mark on the body. There is no chance that the death could have been suicide, as he would have little chance to rid himself of the needle and the syringe. None was found in the office. That is the reason I wanted to exhume the body of Rodgers. I also diagnosed heart failure in his case. But I neglected to have my staff check for needle holes, and I did not do a coronary dissection. The latter was where the possible . . . I might say *probable*, murder of Dr. Caranza came to light. You can see that I might have wondered about InterHelp—with the connection that Dr. Caranza had to your foundation, the cremations of Dr. Rodgers and the old woman, Xacha."

"What did she die of, Doctor?"

"Heart failure also. On the surface you might see how the connection could have been made. Of course, her case was considerably different. She was rather old and not in good health to start with. I witnessed her death at the first night of the Guelaguetza Festival. She simply fell over. She was a local shaman and was involved in curses and other folklore. She was, I was told, also concerned about the opening of the tomb at Monte Alban. But I can see no connection there. In fact, Senor, aside from the bit of frustration that I experienced when I found that there was no Rodgers corpse to exhume, I can see no connection between InterHelp and all of this. As far as I am concerned, you are performing a valuable service to the health of the nation."

He got to his feet, carefully placing the delicate china cup and saucer on the desk.

"So, Senor, I think I might have wasted a trip here and a bit of your valuable time. I thank you for seeing me."

Diego was also on his feet. "Not at all, Doctor. I was only glad we could have settled things the way that we did. I was happy to be of help in the matter. I'm glad I found out about the death of poor Dr. Caranza. I will make immediate arrangements for flowers and an appropriate message to be sent to the family."

"I am sorry to have been the one—"

"Not at all." He extended his hand to the smaller man. "No. It was something I would have learned eventually, and this allows me, on behalf of the foundation, to do the right thing, if you know what I mean. I wish you a safe trip back to Oaxaca."

As Jorge moved through the well appointed outer office, he replayed the mental tape he had made of the conversation. He hailed a cab to the airport. He would just make the return flight. As he rode through traffic, he also made another decision, based on his pondering the conversation. He was going to contact Sergio as soon as he returned. He did not believe Senor Herrerra. He didn't know why. He just didn't believe the man. He didn't know why. He just didn't believe him. Besides, he knew of the offices of InterHelp in the sixteen cities. There was something sinister in that too. Yes. He would call Sergio, and have his nephew put someone on the computer and run a thorough check on InterHelp.

In the office, Diego sat for a long time and thought. The sun was setting below the Paseo when he picked up the phone and dialed a number. There was an answer on the first ring.

"This is Diego. I have a job for you." He paused while the party on the other end spoke.

"It seems that there has been some question of the death

of Caranza in Oaxaca. It is not that things were handled poorly, though I think they might have been better handled. The death could have been made to look like a suicide. The coroner is the one who suspects something, and there is no way I will endanger this operation with his snooping." Diego *knew* he hadn't convinced the doctor, though the little man acted as if he were.

"So, I want you to arrange something for the Dr. Lopez when he returns to Oaxaca. Have him checked through Dos. Examine his patterns. Arrange an accident. A *convincing* accident. No more needles. Is that clear?"

Again he waited while the party confirmed the instructions.

"Very well, then." He hung up, pleased that all of that was finished. He was sure the operative he had chosen would carry out the orders effectively. The man knew that if he did not, after creating a furor with the death of Caranza, then Diego might arrange an accident for *him*.

But there was something else—something that had puzzled Diego since the doctor had left. Who was this Rodgers? How did he die? And how did the old woman die? What did they have to do with anything connected to InterHelp?

He pushed away the thought. People died in the archeology business all the time.

17

Oaxaca.

Jorge came down the gangway of the Mexicana flight to the tarmac of the Oaxaca airport. He was still reviewing his conversation with Diego Herrerra. There was no way the documents he had seen could have been forged. Or if there was a way, perhaps Diego might have found it, but it would have required a great deal of trouble. There was only one possible reason Jorge could think of to connect Diego with the death of Rodgers: InterHelp did not want to have the Monte Alban dig continue. On consideration that evaporated too. There was every reason for them to foster the dig, as the stated purpose of InterHelp was to gather and keep in the country all of the records and artifacts of the past that it could. They were the watchdogs of Mexican cultural heritage.

Jorge stopped in the small second-floor glass-walled cafeteria and sipped a cup of coffee. *What* exactly was it in the conversation that bothered him?

He thought for a long moment, took a sip of coffee, and realized there was nothing suspicious that he could directly point to. It was a hunch, the same way that the coronary dissection on Caranza had been. He had always followed his hunches. There was *something* that connected the death of Caranza to InterHelp, and another *something* that connected InterHelp to another facet he could not pinpoint. But he could not let it alone either. He finished the coffee and headed to the parking lot.

Less than half an hour later he managed to find a parking space three blocks from the state government offices that housed Sergio's office. As he walked to the building he silently cursed the tourists who crowded the streets and the storefronts, who slowed him and forced him to walk the extra blocks. He pushed the thought aside. There were more important things now. He got to Sergio's office and saw, as he pushed his way through the barrier of secretaries, that Sergio was just starting to don his legal robes.

"Jorge! This is a surprise."

The diminutive doctor crossed the room and shook his nephew's hand.

"Oh, I see that look, Jorge. It means you need something and you want it yesterday, right?"

Jorge smiled, then started to laugh. For a second all of the seriousness of the moment—the trip to Mexico City and the meeting with Herrerra—was lost.

"Well, whatever it is, I will do what I can. But I have to be in court in a half hour and the case is rather important. I can get you started looking for what you want, but there is no chance that I can follow up on it, not today. Will that do?"

"That will more than do, Sergio. I have just come from Mexico City. It was there I met with a Senor Herrerra...."

He explained as quickly as possible the possible connection between InterHelp and the death of Caranza.

"But, Jorge, as you explain it, I can see no real link between the two. I don't see that gathering information will do us a bit of good in finding the killer. I *do* believe that there was a killer, though. The police went over every inch of the office and the grounds below the window and they found nothing. Not only was there no needle or syringe, but there was nothing that could have been used to tie off the vein. You will remember that you asked us to look for elastic or some such? We found none."

"There was a tie-off mark on the upper arm above the puncture, Sergio, and that would indicate he would have had no chance to remove it. An embolism acts that fast. But as for one other thing, I know that I cannot *prove* there is a connection, I just want to see if there is the thread of one. What can I say, nephew? You know how I work. You have seen me get too many results from autopsies—things another pathologist would not have found. That was not skill, not some sort of genius—it was simply playing a hunch. More have been right than wrong over the years."

"I know, and there is no harm in gathering evidence or sifting through information if that information can prepare an indictment. That is well within the jurisdiction of this office. Let me take you to the man who can do all that rather quickly, then I will have to get to court. If something, anything tangible comes of it, let me know as soon as possible and we will put more people on it. That will have to do for now. Come." He started for the door. "You see, if I introduce you to him personally, he will know that the power of this office supports the endeavor. You will not have to wait for computer time. They will start digging today. You can stay there and play with our new expensive toy. Pedro plays it like a piano. Come."

They moved from the office and down the hall, crossing into the new wing of the building. As soon as they did, the surroundings changed dramatically. Indirect flourescent lighting and modern paneled walls replaced the marble and brass that marked the nineteenth-century part of the building. It was, Jorge thought, like passing through some sort of time gate in science fiction.

At the far end of the annex, they entered the computer complex. Jorge saw that there were banks of machines in an almost chilly, air-conditioned room.

"Pedro?" Sergio called to the tall, slender man in the business suit who stood hunched over a console that contained a flashing screen.

Introductions followed and Sergio made it clear that the doctor was to get all the cooperation he needed, and that the work was of a high priority to the Ministry of Justice. Sergio left after a few moments, and Pedro himself—not one of the half dozen or so computer operators—sat at a console and snapped it on. He turned to Jorge and politely asked what he needed. Jorge had to consider which information he wanted to evaluate first. He decided to go back to the conversation he had had in Mexico City.

"Can I get a history of an organization called InterHelp? They are based in the capital."

Pedro nodded. He turned to the machine and started to hit the keys. As Jorge watched, characters and lines of data began to appear on the screen. He was fascinated by the speed of it all.

"Is there a chance that a record can be made of this?"

"Certainly, Doctor. When we are finished, we can print out all or part of what we have accessed, so if there is something you are certain you want to keep, tell me and I will earmark it for printout. The printing will come out over there." He gestured to the far side of the room.

"That's our new high-speed printer. We were pleased to get it. It can print something just under sixteen hundred words a minute."

Jorge whistled through the gap in his front teeth. "The chatter must be amazing."

"At that speed, Doctor, there is no chatter. There is only a quiet whine. You will see. InterHelp, you say. Well, let's see what we can do."

He turned to the machine and again his hands flew across the keys. "Pull your chair close and you can see as it comes up on the screen."

Jorge did, and watched the cathode-ray tube flash with InterHelp data.

The organization, Jorge learned, was just over fifty years old. But it had grown immensely in the last fifteen, under the directorship of Herrerra. It had multiplied itself more than five times since then, as it moved into different areas—among them, free or nearly free cremation. From the data, it appeared to have been Herrerra's idea.

"If Herrerra is president of the foundation, who is their board chairman?"

Pedro punched in the query.

HERRERRA Y QUINTOS, DIEGO.

"Well. Both jobs. Where exactly are the offices?"
More punching of the keys by Pedro.

MEXICO CITY
CHICHEN ITZA
LA VENTA
UXMAL
DZIBILCHALTUN
MAYAPAN

The list went on to name eight other offices. It seemed that with the exception of the capital, all of the other fifteen were in archeological areas, where digs had been just opened or were being reopened.

"Pedro, is there a chance that this machine of yours can give us financial statements about the assets of the organization?"

Pedro paused for a second, pulling his hands from the keyboard. He turned to Jorge. "What we can get is the printout of the statements they file with the Ministry of

Taxation. That we can get by accessing the Mexico City system, as His Honor has ordered it."

"Isn't there a chance that that information would not be accurate?"

Pedro laughed in spite of himself. "Senor Doctor, doesn't everyone cheat on his taxes? I am sure it is not accurate. Any organization that large probably has some place they hide funds."

"Is there a chance we can find that place? I ask unofficially, of course."

"Ah, there are ways. None of them..." He leaned close to the doctor. "... none of them is quite legal, if you know what I mean. None of them could be used for evidence in a court of law."

"I am certain that His Honor knew that. What we are after here is information that will lead us to other information. If there is a lead to be found, then I think we should find it. By the way, how do you do it?"

Pedro thought for a long time before he answered. When he did, he leaned conspiratorially close to the doctor. "You see, what we do is search for the access code of their computer. The chances are that the *real* books, assuming that they are cheating, would be kept in a closed portion of the computer record. What we do is access the open portion of the record and request entrance to the closed portion."

"Does the machine simply give it to you?"

"Rarely. No, Doctor, there is an access code that must be fed into the computer, then their computer opens the door, so to speak."

"How do you get this?"

"You guess. But there are times that the computer you are searching through can give you hints, not voluntarily, of course. You start to look for repeated phrases in the answers you get. Actually, in the end it boils down to playing a hunch."

Jorge started to laugh, and for a second Pedro was not

sure but that he was laughing at *him*.

"I'm sorry, Doctor, but that tends to be the way that it is when you are attempting what we are attempting now. Is there something wrong? You asked about it."

The doctor stopped himself and placed a hand on Pedro's shoulder. "No, my friend. I was not laughing at you. It was at something that Sergio . . . ah, His Honor and I said earlier. Please, let's try."

As the computer was already inside the InterHelp system, Pedro simply requested further financial data. The first thing that flashed on the screen was a history of the public statements for the last twenty years of the organization.

"This is something of a smokescreen in the system, used while the larger system evaluates the nature of the request. In a moment we will see, I think, that there must be an access code submitted. If there is not, the computer programmer should be fired." He reached to wipe the information and ask for more.

"Wait," Jorge said with a slight tone of disbelief and urgency in his voice. "Is there a chance that we can now get what is on the screen in a printout?"

"Of course." Pedro pressed a few keys, and across the room the printer started to whine at sixteen hundred words a minute. The print took some fifteen seconds.

As it printed, Pedro asked the Mexico City computer for yet more information. After a few more details flashed on his screen, he saw what he expected:

ENTER ACCESS CODE FOR FURTHER DATA

"See. There it is. The chances are that the access code, whatever it is for InterHelp, is one that has been there for a considerable amount of time. It would be changed if they were in a business where penetration would mean considerable business loss. As that is not the case, the chances are that this little devil has been there for a time."

"What kind of business would change fast? I don't fully understand."

"Stock houses and banks transfer funds by computer. If their systems are penetrated, there is a chance that someone could alter a transaction or transfer funds to his or her own account, then tell the computer to forget the transaction. It would be, in effect, untraceable."

"I see. Can you wait for a moment?"

Pedro nodded and looked back to the screen while the doctor headed across the room and took the sheet of printout information from the tray. He looked down the list of numbers. The statements had made quantum leaps in the years of Herrerra's control. He estimated that the net worth of the foundation must have risen more than a thousand percent in fifteen years. He took the sheet back to Pedro.

"There seems to be a great deal of money involved here, and the numbers have risen sharply in the last fifteen years, under the present president. Is there a chance that we can find where they get the funds? They are a foundation. There must be someone or another organization that, in turn, funds them."

Pedro nodded. "Good idea."

His hands again flew across the keys. On the screen the lights flashed, and line by line, the information was displayed.

PAN AMERICAN ASSISTANCE GROUP
FEDERAL REPUBLIC OF MEXICO
EDUARDO FERNANDEZ MEMORIAL FUND
AMERICAN FOUNDATION FOR ARCHITECTURE
INTERNATIONAL ARCHEOLOGICAL SOCIETY
TOMAS ARRONTOS MEMORIAL FOUNDATION

There were perhaps a dozen in all.

"Have you ever heard of any of these, Pedro?"

Pedro stared at the board for a long minute. "With the exception of the government itself, I have not. But this is not my field."

The hunch that Jorge hoped for was starting to form in the back of his mind. "Is there a chance that we can get the officers' names from these organizations?"

"Of course, Doctor. That, too, is public information. Do you still want to get into the InterHelp closed system?"

"Yes. I'm trying to think of that access code. How many letters would it be?"

"That is hard to say. The chances are that it would be an eight-character word... a maximum of eight characters, that is. Then there would be a period, and as many as three characters following. However, if could be as small as a single digit, a period, and a single digit number after it."

"That sounds like it would be too easy to find."

"The computer is a large haystack, Doctor. The access code is a very small pin."

"Very well. Let's look at the officers."

Diego Quintos y Herrerra turned out to be an officer on six of the organizations that funded InterHelp.

"Why would he do that?" Pedro asked as he looked at the glowing screen.

"I begin to think why, Pedro. Why, indeed, would a man sit and move money from one pocket to another? The money from the funding organizations that feed InterHelp would be made from investments. I wonder what they might invest in?"

Pedro started to laugh. "Well, with the peso where it is, Doctor, the chances are that they would not invest domestically. There is not too much return on investment. I would think that reasonably stable portfolio structures would be something they would be after. If I were them, I would not use the domestic banks or investment houses. I would invest abroad, and the best thing that I can think of vis-à-vis investment, is either foreign currency or gold, silver, and precious metals. Of course, you understand that that is simply a personal opinion. I am not in the field. But my personal holdings, modest as they are, are in those things."

"What concerns me is the fact that Herrerra is an officer of those other foundations. He sits in board meetings and makes sure that funds are moved to InterHelp. All of this makes me wonder if Herrerra is feeding his own money to the other groups so that it will reappear in InterHelp. Then he would have free access to it as chief executive officer."

"It is, Doctor, what the Americans call laundering money, if that is actually what is going on."

"I know. And you think that the chances are good that this is in the master computer?"

"Yes, I do. But there is always the chance, if there is something illegal—really illegal going on—that he has it all in another machine... perhaps a personal one."

"Is there a way we can determine that?"

"It is longer and somewhat slower, but there is, indeed, a way."

"I would like to try it."

"Certainly."

As Pedro worked on the problem with the machine, Jorge again took information from the printout tray across the room. All of the other funding agencies squeezing their money into one. Why? He considered what Pedro had said about the American term *laundering*. It meant that nefariously gained funds were turned into legitimate assets as they were shifted from one company or organization to another, he thought. If party A stole money from wherever, and spent the money through company B, then assuming company B was owned by the same person and the money was spent for something like services, it would come back into the same pocket. The arrangement Herrerra had, if indeed there was an arrangement, *could* work something like that. He knew he was reaching, but he still looked at the memberships the man held and the enormous growth of InterHelp.

"Doctor?"

Jorge turned back to the console. "Yes?"

"I have managed to find Herrerra's computer. It seems, though, that this one will also have the same kind of access code."

"I see."

Jorge headed back to the terminal in measured steps. What would the man invest all of it in? he wondered. How would he get the money in the first place? There were almost too many questions to deal with, but Jorge stopped after the question of *where*. He thought of the offices of InterHelp. They were all at archeological digs, or near them. Was it possible InterHelp was feeding the money to the other corporations and getting it back? Where did it come from, then? He was back to the same questions.

"What have we got, Pedro?"

Pedro pointed to the screen. On it were a series of numbers denoting the fact that they had been knocking at the door of Herrerra's personal system.

"It is the same thing, as I mentioned. There would be a key word or phrase."

What would get them in? What would the investments be? What was the common—

Jorge stopped almost in midstride. The sites. Perhaps they had been siphoning off artifacts from the sites. All of that silver and gold invested in another country against the value of the peso, as Pedro had suggested. All of that silver and gold... silver and gold.

"Silver and gold..."

"Pardon, Doctor?"

"Oh, silver and gold. I was thinking to myself."

"*Plata y oro. Plata...oro.* Eight characters," Pedro mused.

"Try it. What have we go to lose?"

"We have nothing to lose." Pedro coded the eight characters and pushed the Enter button. In a flash they were inside of Herrerra's system—his private one.

Both men laughed and patted each other on the back. Another hunch. Pedro started to fly across the keys, looking for the possible ledger sheet. Jorge was amazed at the way the man seemed to ask just the right questions of the computer. In a few minutes the statement of net worth was flashed on the screen. Diego Quintos y Herrerra was a billionaire, and it seemed that all of his money had been placed in both holdings abroad and securities in immense chunks, as if he had made killings in stocks or something. The irregularity of the additions to his assets intrigued Jorge. He thought about it as Pedro had the information printed out.

"Remember, Doctor, if anyone other than us or the judge even knows about this, there is the chance we could go to prison."

"Don't worry about that, Pedro. I would know how to use the information." Again he tried to put elusive pieces together in his mind. Chunks of money... possible laundering through several foundations. And all of this tied to archeology. Something flashed through his mind, but initially it seemed too preposterous. Then, as he thought further, he realized there was always the chance that the very fact that it *seemed* preposterous might be what made it above suspicion. He paused, thinking of a way he might frame it for Pedro to feed into the computer.

"Pedro, can we shift to another realm when we get the information printed out?"

"Yes, Doctor. We do not even need to wait. All of that is already waiting to be printed in another location of the computer. We can go on right now."

"You might think that this is strange but... can this machine find a record of losses of artifacts from archeological digs?"

"Ah... yes, it can. That would come under the criminal records, and we have just finished programming them in the last few months. It was no easy feat, reducing all of that old paper to computer data. It took more than a year...."

Jorge knew that Pedro was proud of his operation, and he let him explain the problems of transcription he had overcome. After all, Jorge was sure Pedro was doing something that few others could have done for him. It was a few minutes later when Pedro realized he was rambling in language the doctor might not understand. Somewhere in the monologue, he had almost stopped speaking Spanish and started speaking fluent computerese.

"I am sorry, Doctor. I have forgotten myself. I guess you can see that I love my computers and what they can do."

"I see that you can make them do extraordinary things, Pedro. The more I see, the more amazed I become. What about those loss records, the ones from the sites?"

"Oh, yes." Pedro shifted the frame of reference to another set of files. Jorge noted that the man did not have to refer to a single number from a manual or other source. He seemed to have all of the access codes for the files in his head.

"There, we are in the file. Now, how far back did you want to go, Doctor?"

"Fifteen years."

Pedro looked up and his eyes met Jorge's. They sparkled for a second. "Exciting, Doctor. But we are stretching a long way. Let's see."

>UXMAL
>LA VENTA
>CHICHEN ITZA
>DZIBILCHALTUN
>MAYAPAN

Five of them, Jorge thought. Five of the sixteen locations

near where InterHelp had branch offices. All of the losses were in silver and gold—the access code to Herrerra's computer. All of them were considerable and unsolved.

"Can we get the dates?"

"In a second."

As the dates printed out, Jorge shuffled the papers in his hand from the printer until he came up with the one that indicated the entries into Herrerra's personal finances. *He had it.* All of the entry dates were within a month after the thefts. He cross-checked and found that all of the major contributions from the other funding sources to InterHelp were within sixty days *after* the thefts.

"Do you start to see a pattern here, Pedro?"

"Yes, I do. But if any of this that we gained even legally is to be used—let's even include the surreptitious information, for the purposes of argument—if all of it were put together, it would still be circumstantial. There does seem to be more to investigate, but this alone would not be enough, I think, for an indictment. If there were a *direct* connection to a specific case, then we would have something indeed, Doctor."

Jorge remembered that the initial purpose of his visit was to get information about the connection of Caranza to InterHelp.

"Can we get a list of the employees of InterHelp?"

"First I will record all that we have collated. Then I'll see what I can do. It would help if you knew for whom you were searching. Do you have someone specific in mind, Doctor?"

"Yes. I am looking for a Dr. Martin Caranza."

"Is he the poor man who was found dead in his office a few days ago?"

"The very same."

"Is there a connection there? I mean, was the man murdered or something? If..." He stopped and looked to the doctor sheepishly. He remembered who had brought the doctor to the computer center and ordered him to have full run of the place.

"I'm sorry, Doctor. I don't know. Are you permitted to divulge that information?"

"Let's just say, Pedro, there might be a connection. When there is more, I will be able to tell you."

Pedro accessed InterHelp again and specifically asked their machine for their personal files, querying the name of CARANZA, MARTIN, Ph.D.

The answer came in a microsecond. Yes, Caranza had been an employee for something less than a year. This in itself meant nothing. Diego Herrerra had himself admitted that. But there was something else Jorge could not push to the surface. It was something Herrerra had said, or intimated. He forced his mind back to their conversation of the afternoon.

Yes! Herrerra had said he had known the man longer than that, intimating that the man had been on the staff earlier. He thought for a moment, and realized he was on a false lead. All Herrerra had said was that Caranza had been known to him for some time, and that he had only met him once. That was nothing damning. Jorge was frustrated. If there was a hook that could connect Herrerra and InterHelp to the death, then there was something more than circumstantial evidence. Jorge paced the room and tried to find another mental thread. There was none there, he realized after a few minutes. He returned to the console where Pedro patiently waited.

"Pedro, I don't think there is much more we can cull from the machine. I will give it some thought and get back to you in the morning. Is there a chance I can get a printout that collates all of the data we have here? If there is, I can take it home with me and study it tonight."

"That would be no problem, Doctor. It will only take a few minutes. I'll—"

The lights started to flicker in the building. Jorge could

feel a slight sway beneath his feet. Both men paused to feel it. Suddenly, Pedro looked to the screen. The blinking words chilled him. It was something a computer operator in an earthquake area always feared.

SYSTEM GOING DOWN...SYSTEM GOIN—

The screen went black, and all of the tapes that had been spinning in the room stopped. The screen flashed to life again in a matter of seconds and the tapes started spinning, though this did not seem to make Pedro any happier. He sat and stared at the machines. The doctor was confused.

"It felt like a tremor, but it seems as if your machines were only interrupted for a few seconds. Does that mean everything will be all right?"

The question was sincere and so was the concern. Jorge was starting to admire this man who could get him all of the information he needed. Indeed, he liked him. But the consolation clear in his voice was not enough to pull Pedro from deep concentration and more apparent depression.

"Hmm? Oh, I'm sorry, Doctor. Yes...ah, we have a device that fixes most of the data in the memory when there is a power outage. The Japanese developed it for their computers, as they are in a heavy earthquake area. But there is always the problem of data in transit between the terminal and the memory banks. That is something that has to be checked out item by item. I'm afraid our system will be down for at least a few hours while we do that. When I think of all of the users we serve and the demands they will put on the system in that time, I cringe. Well, it will take longer to get you that collation you wanted, Doctor. There is nothing I can do about it. Even the great machine sometimes fails us." He managed a smile.

"You have been more than helpful, Pedro. I will make a point of telling Sergio that. I will work with what I have for a few days, and if there is a chance to come back for the collation, I will do that. I will, of course, call first."

Pedro got to his feet, and after his eyes scanned all of the machines, they came to rest on Jorge's.

"You have been easy to work with, Doctor. I cannot say that about all the users who come in here. Besides, I was starting to get the feeling that we were involved in a true mystery, and such things intrigue me. You are always welcome here, sir. You might consider integrating more computer facilities into the wing of the central hospital. Medical computers have grown enormously in the last few years. I *do* consult in that area, when I am not trying to keep all of this from coming down around Oaxaca's bureaucratic ears."

The doctor shook hands with Pedro, and after a bit of small talk on the way to the door, Jorge found himself again moving from figurative century to century as he walked into the older portion of the building, which was all but empty. He looked at his watch, saw that it was well past seven, and realized that Maria would be frantic. He had not called her from the airport as he had intended. The whole InterHelp intrigue had overwhelmed him. He made his way to Sergio's office and found that there was no one there. The chances were that Sergio was long gone. Even contacting him at home was doubtful, as Jorge knew that Sergio many times simply did not answer his phone after a busy day. In one respect, Jorge could understand that. He had often felt that way himself. But he could not simply not answer. He did not have the luxury of that. He was a doctor. He went down the marble stairs and headed for the main entrance of the building.

The guard waved him through with a smile, and he strode out into the street. The warm moist air told Jorge there might be a shower, or that there had been one while he'd been in the windowless computer center. He stood and sniffed at it for a moment. In another setting now, he tried to piece all of the parts of the puzzle together.

No, there was not enough to get an indictment on the death of Caranza, though it was absolutely certain the case was one of murder. He had to think of Herrerra and the entire organization. What were they after in Oaxaca? He remembered the old woman and the speech she had made on the ill-fated night at the festival—the words she spoke just before she fell to the quagmire the dancing circle had become. It was a curse, though the doctor could not understand Zapoteco. It was about Tomb Seven. Tomb Seven! Yes! Herrerra was planning it carefully. There was going to be more missing art. That connected to the old woman, and possibly to the death of Caranza. By God, Herrerra was planning to steal gold and silver—probably anything he could get his hands on—from the newly opened dig. He prodded the thought from every critical angle he could. There was no other answer. When would it happen?

That was another easy question if he followed the hypothesis he had just devised. The robbery would take place as soon after the discovery of the artifacts as possible. That way, there would be no real index or annotated list that could be traced abroad, where the artifacts might have been sold. If that were so—Jorge realized he was piling assumption dangerously high on assumption—there was a good chance that there were operatives, subversives from InterHelp, on the site now. He wondered if they might be traceable through the computer, but decided Herrerra would be too clever for that.

Then there was Caranza again. Was he connected? Was he blackmailing Herrerra? He pushed the thought from his mind. Where, he wondered, were the archeologists staying? Only a few feet from a pay phone, he went into the booth and dialed Sergio's number, only to get no answer. It was as he anticipated. As he hung up, he decided he would not be too much of an alarmist if he did call the archeologists. Their place of residence popped up in his mind: The Presidente. It was where Rodgers had stayed.

He dialed the number of the hotel and the desk phone was picked up on the second ring.

"This is Dr. Jorge Lopez. I am trying to get in touch

with the archeologists from the Tomb Seven excavation. I assume some of them are staying there?"

There was a pause at the other end, and Jorge began to worry that he might have the wrong hotel. If they were staying somewhere else, the chances were that he would need the help of the police to find them, which would take time.

"Dr. Lopez?"

"Yes?"

"We have two of the people you are seeking. We have a Dr. Jason Farewey and a Senorita Lupe Muñoz. They have been here for some time now, and spend a lot of time out at the dig. We pile up a great deal of mail for them."

"Are they at the hotel now?"

Again there was a pause. Jorge assumed the clerk was checking the key slots.

"I'm sorry, Doctor. They are not here. Is there a message you wish to leave?"

Jorge thought for a minute. There was no sense in trying to explain the scenario in a message. But it was important that he get in touch with them.

"Yes. Ask Dr. Farewey to get in touch with Dr. Jorge Lopez as soon as possible."

He gave the clerk every conceivable number at which he could be reached. After he was sure that the clerk had them right, he hung up and left the booth. He tried to remember where he had parked the car and realized with a frustrated grunt that he had an almost four-block walk. He shrugged and started across the street.

He only heard the roar of the engine at the last minute. The small car roared from the curb and was only feet from him as he turned to it. He could see there were two men inside and that there was no time to get out of the way.

There was a scream from a woman on the curb as the car slammed into the small doctor. Jorge was hurled ten feet through the air before slamming sideways into another car. Unconscious, he slipped to the concrete.

The car sped off as the woman, though still screaming, managed to get three digits of the license number.

The man in the right seat of the fleeing car turned to the driver. "Is he dead?"

"I'm sure of it."

18

The dig.

Halogen lights, torches, and flares cast eerie dancing shadows across the plaza as Jason roared in a cab up the winding road. He could see the lights at a considerable distance. Lupe also peered through the windshield over the driver's shoulder.

Jason's eyes snapped to her and then back to the lights. "Anything?"

"No. Nothing." She shook her head. "I think I have to get closer before I can feel anything. I also have to relax a bit. I'm too keyed up. There's too much static."

"My doing?"

She turned to him and smiled. "Yes, part of it. Don't worry. It will not impede me. I just have to adjust a bit."

Jason was both sad and happy. He was flattered that what they felt for one another might have an impact on her psychic operation. On the other hand, he had come to rely on her accuracy and would miss it, especially in a crisis situation. He focused himself to think that he had contended with crises before and he could again. But he was more than glad she was at his side.

The cab roared to a stop near the site, and Jason paid the driver. He helped Lupe from the car and they trotted in the direction of the undulating pool of light and the voices yelling frantically in Spanish.

Jason turned to Lupe as they ran. "Make sure you stay very close, love. Aside from you and Carlos, there isn't a person on the site who can make themselves understood to me, and vice versa."

Again, still running, she turned to him and managed a smile. "Darling, they won't be able to pry me away from you."

She had to begin translating as soon as the diggers saw them. Three of them came to him, spewing out a stream of rapid-fire Spanish. Lupe gestured the group in the direction of the canopied command post.

Once there, she spoke at length to the diggers. Among them Jason recognized the man who had come to the hotel. After the conversation was over, the men backed off a few steps. Lupe, looking slightly frazzled, turned to Jason. Her eyes were dark and her expression all business.

"Let's look at the map. By the way, their Spanish is even a bit fast for me."

They looked at a cross-section map of the entire dig that had been amended to include the new shaft and the chamber discovered in the previous rescue effort.

"It doesn't seem," Lupe said, "that there is as dangerous a situation here as the first cave-in. They say Ugo was down at the very bottom of the shaft with two other men when the tremor started. Apparently they knew they could not make it back to the surface. As the tremor hit its peak, there were two simultaneous landfalls. The first was about forty feet down the incline. It was small, and almost totally cleared by the time we got here. They are in the last stages of that right now. They have added shoring to the spot. The second, more serious one was here."

She pointed to the very bottom of the shaft on the map. "There was a man a few feet on the near side of the slide, and he said Ugo and the other two disappeared. They didn't appear to have been hit by any of the falling debris. The witness, standing over there"—Lupe pointed to one of the men who had spoken to her—"says they simply seemed cut off in a pocket. Of course, this happened so fast that he could not be sure. As they have been in there for almost two hours now, and as we're not sure of the volume or quantity of air, we cannot count on anything. I suggest we use the core drill we used the last time, and punch a compressor hose through to them as soon as we can."

Jason looked to the map and the overlay. Ironically, it still contained the dotted-line plans for the first evacuation. "Where was that, exactly?"

Lupe took a grease pencil and inscribed a small circle at the bottom of a shaft, indicating in dotted lines the place where the smaller upper slide had occurred.

Jason took care to examine all aspects of the possible rescue. He knew the deeper the dig got, the more treacherous the possibilities of dropping the entire mountain into the excavation tunnel. It was a red clay house of cards. He remembered as a child in Wales the sudden and totally unexpected slides of slag heaps into towns. They had killed hundreds on occasion, simply because the heaps had been there for almost half a century and the people who lived beneath them had thought they would never move. Jason knew all too well that this mountain could move at any second. Being in an earthquake area was living in front of a gun. He glanced at the map and could see that the chamber wall and the existing shaft at the point of the slide were close to each other.

It took him a few minutes to make a series of calculations before he pointed Lupe in the direction of the map. "You're going to have to give them these instructions and warn them that this is going to be delicate. We'll need a team of the most experienced hand diggers to move into the existing shaft at the point of the slide. Remind them that everything has to be moved by hand and with great care. There are two shafts running quite close, which means the existing shoring will not support too much mucking about. If there is another slide because of something we've done wrong,

TOMB SEVEN

there is a chance the entire mountain will fall into it and no one down there will get out."

Lupe turned to the men and was about to speak when Jason added, "Oh, and I'm afraid you'll have to be on the hand-dig side with me on this, otherwise I won't be able to say anything to the workmen."

"I wouldn't be anywhere else, Jason."

In the midst of a flurry of frantic planning, he suddenly wanted to reach over and touch her hair. He dared not. It would have dissolved all of the professional composure he had mustered from the moment the assistant manager of the hotel saw them at dinner.

"I just thought for a moment of what we might have been doing tonight," he said.

"So did I. But I think there will be other nights, Jason. I want there to be."

"Well, about the other part of the plan—I want a crew to go to this point of the chamber and dig, again carefully and by hand, through the side between the buttresses. That way, there are two avenues that we can use. It's risky, but there is a good chance that if one group gets through first, we can stop the other one from pushing through. That would eliminate a lot of engineering problems. The main shaft will be designed for the air supply. I think the second one will be the actual rescue shaft. I'm afraid you will have to be running from one to the other. But I know you can do it."

"Well, I was planning another sort of exercise for tonight, but I think I can manage," she said, and went off to give instructions.

A few minutes later she came back with a curious expression on her face. "Do you remember when Carlos said he was searching for new workers?"

"Yes?"

"Well, he seems to have gotten them rather fast. There is a crew that arrived just before we did."

"That *was* fast."

"They seem to be professionals from a company or something. They all wear black coveralls and the local workmen said Ugo was very pleased with them as he started down into the tunnel before the cave-in."

"We can be happy for small favors. When this is all over, I'll talk to the head of their operation. It will be good to have experienced men on the scene. You'll have to remind me to tell Jerry Tanner that we have them. I'm sure they're costing more than the locals we already have here."

Lupe nodded and turned to the men, issuing orders as she went.

Jason donned a hard hat with a fresh battery in his head lamp and headed for the opening of the inclined tunnel. One of the black-uniformed new men handed him a small hand shovel, exactly the kind needed for the digging in the main tunnel. He looked at the man for a long moment. "Thank you . . . ah, gracias."

"De nada, Senor," the man said with a slight incline of his head.

They certainly were professionals, Jason thought.

At the bottom of the incline Jason could see Lupe directing the work of several of the new black-uniformed men in the shimmering dusty light. "Where are we with things?" he asked.

"They started a few minutes ago. I have two taking soil to the surface. They will be sifting it just in case. Three will be digging, and when we think that we are close, I'll have a hose and an air spike sent down from the compressor on the surface."

"Good." He headed in the direction of the men and prepared to help them. "Oh." He turned back as she was starting up the tunnel. "How do I tell them to stop . . . in case we have to suddenly?"

She turned back and smiled. "Sign language is the quickest way, but the Spanish word is *alto*. You can pronounce it?"

"Alto."

"Fine."

He turned back to work. It was a slow, agonizing hour later when Lupe came down the shaft again. She was dust-covered and it was obvious she had been digging on the other side.

Jason moved from hands-and-knees digging and turned to her, wiping jagged lines of sweat from his forehead and brushing damp hair from his face. "How are we doing?"

"Good, so far. We've gotten some four feet from the buttresses and the other supports. We used small lengths of shoring and the new shaft seems quite stable. Perhaps that's because it's only two and a half feet tall. What about this side?"

Jason momentarily looked back at the diggers, whose coveralls had turned from black to a ruddy shade from the mud and the dust. "They work well. I don't know where the hell they came from, but they work well. I think we're only a few feet away. Another foot or two and we can push that air hose through. In fact, there's a chance we might get through to them before the other team does, though I hope your team can get the tunnel through first."

"Are you rooting for us, Jason?"

"I like to say that, but the reasons are more practical than that. That's why I've got the other team there in the first place. They're coming from a more supported area. This is where the slide occurred in the first place. It's the most unstable area. The more we dig here, the more dangerous it is. That's why I don't want both teams to get there at once. It's sort of like sawing a limb out from under you, or it could be. See if you can get a local weather forecast from the radio. Or better yet, have someone up there listen for one and feed the information down."

She nodded exhaustedly and headed back up the ramp.

"Lupe?"

She turned at his call.

"I love you."

"I love you, too, my darling."

They said nothing more. She simply turned and headed back up through the murky dust and light. He watched her go for a long moment before he turned back to the men who had not ceased moving earth.

It was half an hour later when Jason got back to his feet and started measuring the distance they had covered. Yes. The chances were that if the witnesses' information was correct, they could punch the air line through from this point. He started up the shaft to get Lupe.

"Dr. Tanner?" He could see the figure partway down the incline. He had spoken English. It was Carlos.

"Carlos?"

"Yes, sir. I came as soon as I heard the news. I brought Anna with me . . . she wouldn't let me come alone, actually."

"Good to see you. We need more people who speak English. Lupe is being run ragged."

"What do you want me to do, Doctor?"

"Get them to run a hose from the compressor with an air spike down to us here. I think we're about ready to punch through. Have you got that?"

"Right." He waved and headed off, yelling to the workers in Spanish.

It was only a matter of moments before the spike was rigged and in Jason's hands. It was something like a large hypodermic needle with a mesh filter on the front. With its three-foot length, it could penetrate the barrier of earth that separated them from the trapped men, and when attached to an air compressor hose, would supply them with air until one of the two tunnels was completed. Jason took the end of it and waved the men away from the small end of the narrow tunnel. He was going to have to do all of it by feel. But he had done it before in cave-ins in Wales. He was glad the Royal Navy had invented it for the rescue of submariners.

He gently pressed the point into the soft earth. He moved it an inch at a time until it was more than a foot in. Then something seemed to block his way. This was the tricky part. He had hit something, perhaps a rock. He tried to jockey the point to the left, but after shifting the angle more than a few degrees, he realized there was still an obstruction. He backtracked and moved to the right, moving the point expertly. He knew that there was only one spike at the site and they might have to send to Mexico City for another. By that time, Ugo and the others would be very dead.

About six degrees to the right of center he again found soft earth. He breathed deeply and started to nudge the point forward. He was another foot deep in the clay when the tip broke through. He was sure this was the place the men were trapped. He turned back to Carlos, who stood halfway up the incline.

"Start feeding... slowly. We don't want to give them the bends."

Carlos called out in Spanish and Jason could feel the slack hose suddenly stiffen in his hands. Yes, the air was going somewhere, or the point would have burrowed itself back out the way it had gone in. He got to his feet and gently handed the hose to one of the new workmen. The man handled it as if it was an infant, and Jason was satisfied. He started to head up the incline but was met near the top by Lupe.

"Jason! You are going to have to go in this way. We hit a solid wall."

"There's no way around it? You're sure?"

"I'm sure. You will have to see this wall to believe it. But I assure you there is no way around it. It angles past the dig at something more than forty-five degrees, but I have no way of knowing just how far it reaches. You can understand that I don't want to push the overhead support too much. I know," she said as she came down the incline to meet him, "that this is the more dangerous of the two options, but you will have to take it."

Jason did not question her judgment. He knew it would be flawless. He looked down to the end of the incline and then back to her. "We'll keep going on this end. We've gotten air through to the pocket. I hope there's someone there to breathe it."

She looked quickly at her watch. "Three hours and thirty-five minutes, as best as I can judge. From what that digger said, I think they have enough air."

He moved close to her. "Can you feel anything about them, or was that a professional judgment?"

"Both, I think. I'm not sure. But I do know that you are going to have to go in this way. But I am more than glad that we dug on the other side."

"Why?"

"The wall, coming as it does at a forty-five degree angle to both digs, seems to be what is supporting both of them. Jason, I think that this wall is the entrance to another chamber. There is a chance there was an ancient earthfall that covered it. I'm having the diggers brush away the loose dirt now. I told them they should stop after there was a good clear spot we could examine. They are to move no more dirt than is necessary. We can get a good look at it when we get the men out."

Jason stretched his tired arms and took her by the shoulders. "Have I told you you're fantastic?"

"You don't have to, darling. You are the one who makes me feel that way."

He smiled and reached down, kissing the top of her dusty nose. They shared a small moment before he returned to the bottom of the shaft and she headed to the top to get fresh diggers to take the place of the men with Jason. She had asked Jason to come up but he insisted on staying until they had broken through to Ugo and the others.

Jason did a great deal of the digging himself. He knew exactly how much to take and where to place the tiny three-sided frames that served as supports. It took the better part of an hour, and then he could feel his hand push through to an opening.

He dropped the shovel and started to claw at the loose earth with his hands. In a matter of a minute or two he had the opening wide enough to get his head and shoulders through. He took off his hard hat and pushed it in the hole ahead of him. He played the light through the dusty, fetid air.

"Ugo? Ugo?"

"Senor?" The voice was a tiny whisper. *"Madre de Dios . . . Dr. Farewey!"*

Jason followed the sound and saw Ugo only a few feet away, cradling a man in his arms.

"Get him first, Doctor. I think he has broken some ribs—José, there." He pointed to another man, curled a few feet to the left. "He's unconscious off and on. He took a blow to the head. I think there is a concussion. He was vomiting."

"How are you, Ugo?"

"Alive, *gracias à Dios*. Alive, Doctor."

"Are you hurt?"

"Bruised. My back got hit with some rocks. But there is nothing broken as far as I can tell, and that fresh air is helping me."

"Let me get some help down here."

Jason yelled to the top of the incline, and Carlos and the new diggers came running down with a first-aid kit and a stretcher. Within half an hour all of them were on the surface. The two men who had been with Ugo went to the hospital in an ambulance that had been standing by. Ugo refused treatment after he had been looked at by the on-call doctor. He wanted to see the new wall that had been discovered. Jason grudgingly agreed and the two moved around the side of the mountain in the direction of what had come to be called the chamber dig.

"Where did you get these new men? They're quite good."

"Carlos got them, Doctor. I think he got them from Mexico City. They talk like they came from the north. I don't know what they will cost yet, but with so many of the old crew deserting, they will be needed."

"They were needed tonight. They were the ones who dug you out, Ugo. I'm just glad you're well. You're too damn good to lose. We'll let Tanner worry about the new men and payrolls. We just dig in the earth, right?"

"Right, Doctor."

They turned down the steep incline and headed to meet Lupe at the bottom of the narrow, newly carved shaft. She came to meet them with a shocked expression.

"What is it, Lupe?"

She shook her head.

He waited. He could see she was trying to form words, and the formation was not going well.

"Is it something psychic?" he asked.

She nodded. "But something else too. I've never seen anything like it."

"Where?"

"The wall... there." She gestured. "You'd better look at it before I say anything else. Just go look at it. See if you think what I think about it."

He took her hand and led her to the wall as Ugo trailed behind them.

The headlamps of workmen played across the surface of the diagonally placed wall. They were brushing off a five-foot rough square of it with damp cloth. Jason was about to warn them about weakening adobe with water as he looked at the wall. It was onyx white and appeared perfectly smooth. He pushed past one of the diggers and placed a hand on the wall. It was cool to the touch and felt as smooth as it had looked from a distance. He took off the hard hat and placed the light close to the wall as he ran his fingertips across the coolness. He stayed there for a long minute before he got to his feet. He looked around, only to find that Lupe had moved off quietly to the far end of the chamber.

"Lupe. It's marble. Marble! There was no marble of this kind in Mexico."

"I know." Her voice seemed tiny and distant. Jason could feel something in it that he recognized.

He started in her direction. "Do you understand the implications of that? I think it's Italian marble. Perhaps Carrara

TOMB SEVEN

marble. This had to have been brought thousands of miles to get here."

"I know." Despite the fact that he was only a few feet from her now, her voice was even more distant and frail. Instead of turning her to him, he moved to her side and looked into her eyes. They were distant and glazed.

"What is it, Lupe?" he said gently.

"Something evil... something bad is going to happen, Jason." She folded her arms across her breasts as if she were cold in the warm, close chamber. "The woman... Anna and her grandmother—they were right. We are not..." she shook her head as if she were pushing away a dream. "We are greedy and childish and not ready...." She again shook her head, more strongly this time. "Not for what they have to give us. No. And yet, we will... we must go on. I know we will, to prove that they were right. And then it will all be gone... and we will have to wait centuries again ... again until we are ready. It will be so long...." Her voice had become a strange monotone droning a litany.

She stopped and looked at Jason. She pointed to a spot on the chamber wall. "The entrance through the wall will be right there Jason. They will only have to move a foot of earth to find it. We can enter through it. It will be the only entrance to be found."

As she stopped, she did not look at him. She stood stone silent. He was afraid to touch her. She might shatter, he thought, or there was the chance that he might find she had turned to stone. He had to hold her, but he dared not. His emotions curled together in his stomach, becoming a rock-hard presence.

"Lupe?" he whispered.

Nothing.

After a moment, she turned to him. Her face was somber. "We will have to dig here, Jason."

"But what you said... perhaps we should not?"

"If we don't, then someone else will. We are the ones here now, and we have to dig."

"But the things you said. . . ."

"I know what I said and what I saw, Jason. Still, I know that no matter what I said, we have to dig."

"Will you be all right?"

"No one can say who will be all right, my darling. But we are here to dig. We must."

Jason took a deep breath and turned to the confused Ugo, who stood only a few feet away.

"Ugo, bring the crew and the lights over here. Have them start to dig right here."

"Immediately, Doctor." He trotted off, yelling commands in Spanish.

It took them less than half an hour to clear what appeared to be a Roman arch entrance of some three feet. The height of the arch told Jason that perhaps the floor they stood on would have to be excavated further to reveal the original height. But it was Lupe's enigmatic words that haunted him.

As the last of the loose debris was cleared, Ugo approached Jason with a large searchlight. "It is open, Doctor. Would you like to be the first to enter?"

Jason's eyes moved quickly to Lupe's, trying to probe, to read something there. She smiled distantly and nodded to him. Jason took the searchlight and started to the entrance, with diggers scrambling out of his way. He pushed through the low arch on his hands and knees. As he got to his feet, he played the flashlight around what looked to be a smaller chamber than the first.

My God!

He moved the light more slowly. He was numb, and suddenly knew the feeling of Schleimann at Troy . . . of Carter at the Valley of the Kings . . . of innumerable others. His jaw hung slack for a long moment as he stood there in excitement and shock, happiness and awe. Then there were Lupe's words—why they had to dig, why he had to be the first to enter. It all jumbled itself together.

"Ugo?" he blurted. *"Ugo!"*

"Yes, Doctor?"

"Get a complete crew in here and have them touch nothing until I can get pictures. As soon as we do that, I want to start collecting and tagging. Hurry."

"Very well, Doc—" Ugo came through the opening and got to his feet. As he looked at the room, he stopped in midword, transfixed.

"Dios mio. Dios mio."

Jason nodded to him. They needed to say nothing. The room was filled with waist-high piles of gold and silver implements and ceremonial knives. There had to be a billion dollars there.

Jason turned and moved through the small opening. Lupe stood a few feet away. He went to her. "You knew what it would be. You knew what we would find."

She nodded. "And now there will be those who will want to take all of it, destroy its value and replace it with money. They will want to kill us and take all of it for themselves."

"Will they succeed?"

She smiled an enigmatic smile. "No. *They* won't . . . nor will we."

"I don't understand."

"I don't know if I do, either. But we won't succeed. Remember what Anna said about the curse and the gods? Well, perhaps we aren't meant to succeed, and those who come after us are. I just don't know, Jason."

19

Jason looked down at her, knowing she was right. Still, they stood at the door to a knowledge of the past no one else had even approached. He owed it to the Schleimanns, Carters, Lucheses, and the others who sifted through hundreds of ancient digs in search of the truth. He looked down at her with a dour expression of resignation.

"I've heard everything you've said... I mean everything, Lupe. But—"

"But you're going in, and you want me to help. Right?"

All he could do was nod. He knew she hadn't read his mind, as she had in the past. Any fool could have read the look on his face. He was addicted and beyond all redemption. He was an archeologist.

"Jason," she intoned, the slightest hint of sadness and resignation in her voice. "I love you. I think you know that. But that's not the reason I would consider helping you. I'm also a professional, but even that would not make me go in there, not with the feelings I'm getting from the entire dig."

He shook his head. "I really don't understand. Of course, I need you in there. There is no one else who can do what you can, short of flying Jerry Tanner in or yelling for help from Kurtzov and his people. I *have* to go in. I have no choice in the matter. But I understand the way you feel and all that it means to you. I couldn't ask you to go against that. You can run a catalogue check here or up at the top of the tunnel as I send the stuff up."

She shook her head. "You didn't let me finish. There's more to it. I *have* to go in too. The same way you do. Not for the reasons I mentioned. You see, I'm part of this scenario now. I'm linked to it in the same way I'm linked to the whole expedition down here. The very words I'm saying to you at this moment are like a massive, confusing déjà vu, something programmed for me to do a long time ago. What I said before, about love and professionalism... they are things I firmly believe, but they have no part in my decision. Something dreadful is coming and there is nothing we can do to stop it. My role is to be there with you. There is no way on earth I can begin to change that. I'm sorry, Jason. I would like to be going in out of love. You had to know that."

There was nothing Jason could think to say. In the last days, his profession, his philosophy, and his life had been turned upside down and shaken. He knew if he started to think about things, he would come apart. He simply reached down and held her for a long moment. As they separated, he drew a deep breath, and exhaling audibly into the dank air, led her in the direction of the entrance.

Ugo stood alone in the room and stared at the mass of gold, jewels, and platinum ten feet across and over five feet high. The digger, whom Jason should have packed off to a hospital after the ordeal of the cave-in, stood stupefied for a long moment before turning to Jason and Lupe.

"I'm sorry, Doctor. I should be getting a crew down here, but I never... I mean—"

"I know. Neither have I. Start getting the room dimensions, and get that photographer down here—what's his name?... Pablo? I want shots of the array as it was found, before we start to move anything. Then I'll want shots of each piece as we start to remove it from the site. Then I'll want a second shot of the piece after it's been tagged and assigned a number. But you know that routine, I'm sure."

"Of course, Doctor." Ugo sped out of the chamber and started to organize the forces that were going to be needed.

"Jason?"

He turned to see Lupe at the far side of the treasure heap. She was holding a small goblet that had come from the top of the pile. She held the small piece out to him as he approached.

"What do you make of it?"

The piece was heavy for something so small, and he speculated on the purity of the gold. Still, it was solid, and he was sure they would find an alloy—something like the titanium that had bound the earliest pieces found by Anna Marcos. He turned the small wine cup in his hands and looked at the brilliantly molded decorations. A naked youth with roped hair and wide eyes wrestled with the horns of a huge bull. On the opposite side, tiny, naked human figures worshipped an oversized figure. The legs were human but the upper torso and head were that of a raging bull.

After a long moment he looked to Lupe. "The Minotaur? It's classically Minoan, but—"

"There's more! Look." She handed him what looked like a decorative breastplate. It was crescent shaped, small and delicate, something that might have been worn by a woman. The small bas-relief carvings were exquisite in detail. The profile of a man reached up to the image of the sun while tiny rays, each ending in a stylized Ankh, showered on him.

"Amenhotep worshipping Aton in the Amarna period. Fifteenth Dynasty... just before the Hyksos." He was mumbling. There was no way that a piece from Minoan Crete and another from the Egyptian feudal period could be found in a Mexican dig that antedated the discovered pieces.

"Lupe, this is like Alice in Wonderland! The skeleton outside was infinitely older than these pieces. How...? I mean, it's an anachronism."

"No. It's simpler than that. Whoever placed these things here invented the imagery. The Egyptians and the Minoans and God only knows who else—they were the inheritors of the design. They were the descendants of the original jewelers and craftsmen. That's not Amenhotep on the breastplate. There's no elongated headdress to cover the fact that he was a hydrocephalic. The Ankhs are elliptical at the top and not circular, as the Egyptian ones were. Don't you see? The Egyptians inherited these designs and everything that they copied originated here, or perhaps it was moved here so it could be kept in a safe place."

"Moved here from where?"

They stood silently for a moment. Jason realized there was no need for an answer. It was some place far more ancient than any that archeologists had ever found.

"Atlantis, Lupe?"

"Or something before that we don't even have a name for . . . something so old that every ancient culture that we know of emanated from. Look!"

She pointed to a long scroll made of gold beaten almost paper thin. Part of it rested beneath the pile and part was exposed. They knelt and studied the visible portion, not wanting to disturb the rest of the pile until a record was made of exactly how it was stacked.

It was perhaps eight inches long and three wide. The gold was as thin as onionskin paper, and the marks on it were tiny engravings with interspersed pictographs. Jason shined his light on the scroll. There was a stylized writing that looked vaguely Cyrillic, but it was the pictographs that made Jason's stomach tighten. Men with large headdresses rode atop birds in flight. An inch away, men in gowns labored in what could only be a lab—the machines behind them could be nothing but computers. Stylized high technology, perhaps made at a time when the artisans could still remember what *had* been. Perhaps the original models had been done centuries before, Jason thought, and the style was simply additive, something common to the later culture. At the very edge of the scroll, before it was shrouded by the artifacts above, there were lines of symbols.

"Can you make out anything of these?"

Lupe crouched close to him and stared at the symbols for a long moment. "That one symbol there?" She pointed to a tiny engraving almost obscured by dust.

Jason peered closely. "It looks familiar somehow, but I don't know why."

She looked up at him and her eyes met his. "It's an integrate sign. It's calculus, Jason. And Newton didn't reinvent it until less than three hundred years ago. Jerry Tanner is going to be beside himself."

"*Aqui*, Senor?"

Jason and Lupe turned to the entrance. Two men stood with cameras and photographer's shoulder bags. Jason nodded to them as Ugo slipped in behind them. He issued orders in rapid-fire Spanish and the men started to take pictures.

Ugo barked orders to other men who entered the treasure room. Each one of them stopped for a long moment and silently stared at a quantity of gold that might make all of them rich beyond their wildest dreams. Ugo directed them to the far wall of the dust-shrouded chamber, where they laid out tape and Ugo started noting the measurements of the room. He had paced half the distance across the far wall when he suddenly stopped. On the wall, underneath layers of dust, was a design. He pulled a rag from his back pocket and started to wipe away the grit. A sudden surge of excitement gripped him, but he had to be sure before he said anything. After all, he was a professional and not an alarmist.

"Ugo!" the digger on the other end of the line called, impatient to get the measurement. Ugo silenced him with a growled curse. Yes... it was, it was. "Doctor!" he shouted. "Here. Look at this."

It took only a minute to confirm what Ugo had discovered. It was the thinly blocked entrance to yet another chamber. After less than an hour of digging, they broke through into an inner chamber. Lupe and Jason, flashlights in hand,

TOMB SEVEN

were the first to clamber through the opening.

"Madre de Dios," Lupe whispered as she played her light across the new room, which seemed to be many times longer and wider than the first.

It was filled to eye level with gold!

"We have to get in touch with the Mexican government as soon as possible," Jason said. "There's more here than the treasuries of some small countries."

"And there *will* be other rooms."

"A feeling, Lupe?"

"A feeling."

In the hour that followed, diggers poured down into the room, taking measurements. Ugo set up a complete cataloging system and had the photographic crew take photos from every conceivable angle in both of the rooms.

"Doctor?" he called as he stopped to enter the inner chamber for what seemed the fiftieth time.

Jason moved slowly toward him, trying not to raise any more dust than was necessary. He was already thinking that respirators were going to be needed if there was going to be any more traffic in the room.

"Yes, Ugo?"

"I have called Mexico City." He looked around and consciously lowered his tone. "It's Sunday."

"I'd forgotten. Could you get anyone?"

"All I could do was to leave a message at the Bureau of Antiquities, one of those phone tapes."

"Well, it's been here for eons. I guess it will have to wait until tomorrow."

Pablo Ruiz shook his head dourly as he looked at the light-meter reading. He paced across to Ugo and offered him the meter. Ugo shrugged. "Pablo, you know I know nothing about all of that photography gear. I stick to digging. What's the problem?"

"Film speed. What I have is too slow. We could bring in more light, but with the dust, there's a good chance that we'd light fog the prints. This is too important to take that chance. Let me get back up and call into town for some fifteen hundred ASA stuff. With that we can watch a firefly blink at a mile."

"How long? The doctor wants to get things rolling as soon as possible."

Pablo spread his hands in a gesture of uncertainty.

"Sunday. Hmm. There is a shopowner I can call. He has the fast film I need and he's greedy. Say forty-five minutes to an hour. It will take you that long to get the other measurements you need."

"Get to it." Ugo moved in the direction of Lupe and Jason to inform there would be a slight delay in the procedure.

Pablo negotiated the steep incline and shielded his eyes against the midday sun. He wondered how long the gringo doctor and the Hispanic woman were going to hold up without a break. Both of them had been in the dig for more than eighteen hours and showed no sign of stopping. For that matter, he wondered how long Ugo was going to keep going, as he insisted on supervising the diggers personally. He grunted as he started to cross the open plaza. Any fatigue on their part was going to be a distinct advantage to him.

Yuri Kurtzov had been aware of the furor at Tomb Seven for some time. He hoped that Jason and the stunning Hispanic woman had not encountered trouble. Just now it was the relative sizes of the arches over the entry ports of the Seven Deers tumuli that concerned him. The uprights and lintels were straight across, forming a functional equivalent of a normal doorway. But it was only five feet high, and the ruin was clearly much newer than the classical temples less than half a kilometer away. Those doors were seven or eight feet high and used a Gothic arch at the top, a much more sophisticated engineering form. Had these ancients regressed? He wished he knew more about the period, but Central America was not his speciality. He used a small hand brush to remove the grime from the top of the door lintel. On it were carved the characteristic seven stylized deer that gave their name to the site.

And why am I here at all? he wondered while tapping on the lintel with the brush. Why not Galiashin or one of the others who knew South and Central America like they knew the back streets of Moscow? Galiashin would have been the perfect choice. He was a young man with a large family and a seemingly constantly pregnant wife. He was one that the KGB and their sinister Third Department would feel perfectly safe letting out of Mother Russia for long stretches at a time under little supervision, as long as the wife and household full of children remained in Moscow.

Yuri, a childless widower with no personal ties at home, shrugged. When they sent him abroad, Valarin and a whole entourage went along. In fact, he had never seen such an entourage before on any dig anywhere in the world. More than half of the force were KGB and the rest were unfamiliar enough with the most rudimentary archeological technique to assume they might also have connections to the Third Department.

Could they be? He brushed the beginnings of a thought aside and stepped out of the ditch. He barked an order to one of the diggers to retake the measurements of the lintel and the height of the door. He started to feel the sun on the bald spot at the back of his head. He had forgotten his hat. He hated hats and made a practice of forgetting them on digs everywhere in the world. But here in the northern outposts of the tropics, a hat was necessary. He could forget it in the cool of the evening but not in the heat of the day.

As he approached the trailer, he saw that Valarin was speaking to a digger, one he had not seen before. Frustrated with the slowness of communications, Valarin gestured to one of his KGB underlings who spoke both Spanish and Russian. Yuri watched as the trio moved off some distance and carried on an animated conversation. As Yuri was rummaging through the bedroom of the trailer for the elusive hat, a slight breeze from the valley brought a few words of the distant, animated conversation through the trailer window.

"Another room? How large?"

There was chatter in Spanish and then the translation.

"Huge...tons...more than a fortune...a treasury...."

"Have they informed Mexico City?"

Again there was the translation and the chatter in rapid-fire Spanish. Then, as the wind started to ebb, there was the translation back into Russian that drifted to him in fragments.

"Cannot...bureaucracy...shut down...Sunday...."

There was more to the conversation, but it did not reach Yuri, because the breeze had shifted to another direction. He thrashed through the room and found the hat under a blanket. He slipped out the back door and headed back in the direction of the dig. He could putter around there while he did a great deal of thinking.

They couldn't be planning something that insane! It was impossible to even consider. And yet there had been the sudden assignment here, and the extreme security precautions. And the only thing I know about this area of the world is the gold! he suddenly realized.

He walked like a man in a dream. Around him he could hear shouted orders. Diggers and supervisors, all of them somehow connected to the KGB, started to scurry in all directions. Yuri noted with the clarity of a man in a dream that their movements were not at all random. Rather, they were the movements of men trained for a specific operation, a specific task. The impossible is true! he thought, stopping to ponder the enormity of it. They were going to attempt to seize the gold.

With gold running at almost a thousand dollars for an impure ounce on international markets, there would be perhaps trillions of rubles, billions of dollars, uncounted pesos. And what they were about to do violated the most sacred laws of archeology. It was a desecration that would prevent Soviet archeologists from ever getting a permit to dig again, anywhere in the world. It was total insanity.

Yuri took off the hat and let the heat of the sun beat down on him for a long moment. He had to do something about it. But the price, oh, God, the price.

Jason paced slowly across to Ugo, who was conferring quietly with Lupe. As he approached, her eyes moved from the clipboard and met his. He could see worry and concern merge in her expression, and along with it something else—something he could not define.

"I think as soon as we get the rest of the photos and the sketches, we should get some security down here and close things down until we can formally inform the Mexico City people. Ugo, isn't there another local representative, someone who might have the authority to supervise the removal of the artifacts in Oaxaca?"

"I am sure that there is, Doctor. But I would have to get them at home. I will start to try to find someone, if you want."

"Do that, and get the diggers to stay here after we finish the shift. If they spread the word into the city about the amount of gold we've found here, there is a chance that everyone and his cousin will be charging up the mountain. We don't want a riot on our hands."

Ugo nodded and headed toward the entrance of the second treasure room. As he approached the arch, he stopped, and Jason and Lupe turned. In the outer treasure room there was the sound of a woman shouting, and the angry voices of men.

Ugo backed away from the low arch as Anna Marcos stumbled into the room. Behind her came Carlos, wielding a pistol. Behind him, one of the new diggers carried a menacing automatic rifle, which he immediately leveled at Anna and the three others.

"Why couldn't you listen? I told you not to come here!" Carlos hissed.

"So I couldn't see that you'd become a thief, a dog who steals the sacred things from our heritage!" Anna shrieked.

Incensed and confused, Ugo stepped toward Carlos. "Carlos, what is the meaning—"

"Stay where you are!" The order came from the man with the automatic rifle, which Ugo saw was leveled at his stomach.

The half-dozen diggers who labored at the pile of treasure had stopped working and stood for a second, frozen in a grotesque tapestry. Carlos's head snapped in their direction. "It begins. Get to the outer room and start loading."

They dropped what they were doing and started to move to the arch with the speed and discipline of a military unit.

Carlos's glance moved back to Jason, Ugo, and Lupe. "Go to the far wall and sit—you, too, Anna! I'm going to have to figure out what to do with you."

"How much of it do you think you can take, Carlos? And how far can you get with it?"

"Heroic statements are not in order, Doctor. This operation has been planned since long before you arrived here, and it will be carried out perfectly. The fact that it is a Sunday is that much more to our advantage. The workers above who know nothing about this have been dismissed and told to return tomorrow. Already they are on the two buses heading back down the mountain. We will have plenty of time to do what needs to be done. . . ." Carlos paused as he heard a moan and a slight, distant rumble. A tiny vibration moved through the chamber and dust sifted from the ceiling down on those below.

Lupe's eyes narrowed. "Your own ancients won't allow all of this, Carlos. Old Xacha was right. They will collapse the mountain on top of you before they let you take what is rightfully theirs."

"Talk all of the superstition that you want, Senorita. Every man on this team will be a millionaire for life. There is nothing the ghosts of the past can do to alter that. Now, move. Get to the corner and sit—the four of you."

They did as they were told. Jason curled an arm around Lupe's shoulder. He could feel her muscles tensed like steel springs. "I don't know what to say," he whispered. "I never even considered all of this . . . not until I saw the amount of gold here in the second room."

"I think I saw it, Jason. Evil piled on evil. It was what old Xacha was saying with her death up at the Guelaguetza."

"They're going to kill us, aren't they?" Jason said.

"Yes, Jason, they are . . . or they're going to try. They have to play out their roles in the drama too."

He pulled her close as they moved at gunpoint in the direction of the far wall. "You've mentioned this before. Is there no way out of this?"

"There's always a way. We have free will. Old Xacha could have chosen another way to die or she could have let nature take its course and die of old age. She chose to make her death a warning about just this sort of thing. Man is not ready for the secrets of Tomb Seven and that is the way it will end. There is always the chance that we will end with it, and there is little that we can do about that."

"The hell we can't. If we could get a few of those weapons, there's a good chance we can hold at least the inner room for a long time. They can't use explosives and risk a cave-in. If they start to truck gold out of here, someone *has* to notice."

She turned to him. Suddenly there were tears in her eyes, slipping over the rims and making jagged tracks in the dust on her cheek. She grabbed him by the shoulders and he could feel her fingers digging into his flesh.

"Please, Jason," she whispered with an agonizing urgency that tore his anger away from him. "If you love me at all, do nothing. Just wait. What has to be will be obvious when the time comes."

His arm circled her waist. Against all he believed, against all of his rage, against the desecration of what he held sacred, he would listen... for now.

Yuri jammed the hat back onto his head. There were only three diggers left at the arch where he stood. There had been seven before. The other four had left obediently when a shouted order from Valarin called them to the trailer. He was uncertain as to what to do. He was not a spy, nor a hero; not even much of a survivor. He boggled at the possibility that his own government could so obviously violate the sovereignty of another nation. This was not the Afghan fiasco, nor adventurism in Africa or Central America. It was surely not a time of détente, but it was also not the nineteenth century. Still, what he had feared *was* happening! And it seemed there was nothing he could do about it.

"Comrade Academician."

Yuri turned to see Valarin standing over him. The man looked imperious, military. His scowl was far deeper than usual.

"Yes?"

"You will come with me. There is important work that has to be done immediately."

"Why is it that you order me about, Valarin?" Yuri got to his feet. After all, he was a much honored fellow of the Soviet Academy and Valarin had to be reminded of it.

Valarin held out a small gold figurine. "I want the currency amount of the gold contained in this. I want the per ounce price relative to the purity, immediately."

"You have no right to make such a request. I am an archeologist not a gold broker."

"You will do what you are told. I represent the government here and I need that information, now."

"Do you really work for the government, Georgi Ivanovich, or are you working for yourself, for profit?"

"Do as I ask or I will not be responsible for the outcome!"

"Is it the Third Department? Are they behind this? Do you understand the international consequences?"

Valarin said nothing, but rather, gestured in the direction of the trailer. Yuri held his glance for a few seconds. In the small gray eyes he could see the standard, noncommittal look of the KGB operative. It was something practiced, designed to express nothing but confidence and cool resolve. But there was the hint of something else in the look. It was a vague hint of anxiety—a look of fear. Valarin was *not* working from patriotic fervor for Mother Russia, nor the Central Committee. It was a different kind of adventurism. But Valarin had always seemed the epitome of loyalty. It came down to the Third Department. It was the ultimate coup of the lords of Dzerzhinsky Square—the KGB itself. There was no other entity that could have been so daring. The theft, if indeed that was what was planned, would topple the power foundation of the Central Committee and renew the worst days of the Cold War. In the wake of the upheaval, the new power structure would contain a great many KGB faces. And why not? Yuri thought. They had a two-million-man army and were the consummate watchdogs of Leninist policy. With literally billions in gold, the KGB could easily change the course of the government. After all, Yuri Andropov's ascent to the leadership of the Soviet Union proved the power of the KGB. And now there were those within the KGB who would ensure that the billions would be effectively spent... perhaps on exotic new weaponry. The thought chilled Yuri.

"I will answer no further questions of you, academician," Valarin spat.

Yuri suddenly felt ten years older. He inhaled and breathed out a deep sigh before he started for the trailer.

Valarin waited quietly as Yuri sat at his small lab table and looked at the trinket. It was an exquisitely formed bottle-nosed dolphin with tiny emerald eyes. He subtracted the estimated weight of the emeralds from the gross weight he had established with his scales. The gold purity and acid tests were simple enough with the field kit Valarin brought on the expedition. He was astonished at the findings.

"It is incredibly pure. I would say close to twenty-three carats . . . ninety-five percent or thereabouts."

"And the estimated value per ounce?"

"The gold market fluctuates daily, Georgi Ivanovich. I'm sure you know that."

"Your best estimate?"

"Eighteen carat is the standard for trading purposes. This would be something on the order of twenty-five percent more. In American dollars, I believe the round figure is now close to a thousand dollars an ounce. This would come out to be something on the order of one thousand five hundred dollars an ounce."

Valarin nodded with the barest hint of a smile. "Come with me, academician. There is one more task for you."

The sun was hovering near the western mountain when Yuri entered the tomb. The gallery that had been discovered in the rescue attempt yielded to the first treasure room and then the second. Yuri was speechless, as much at the sight of the immense wealth as the sad picture of his friend and colleague Jason and the others huddled in the corner by armed guards.

"Over here, academician." Valarin moved Yuri to the other end of the treasure trove and out of sight of the quartet of prisoners. "Look." He pointed in the direction of markings on the red clay wall. There seemed to be the vague hint of an arch similar to the one through which he had just passed. "Is there a chance that there is another room in this direction?"

Yuri looked at the arch and allowed his glance to move upward. There seemed to be enough overhead support for another room. But the architecture was unfamiliar. He looked at the inset design of the arch. He had seen some like it in the orient but none in the West. Still, there was little chance that such an arch was decorative in such a setting.

"Well?"

"I am unfamiliar with this design. I will have to have some time to study it."

"There is no time for that."

"Then I cannot help you."

"What do you estimate the value of these two rooms to be?"

Yuri squared his shoulders and faced Valarin. "I will say nothing more about this dig, Georgi, until you have made me certain assurances."

Valarin eyed him for a moment, apparently assessing the possibility of bluff. "What assurances?"

"I demand that you assure the safety of Dr. Farewey and his party. What you are doing is outrageous enough without getting into the area of kidnapping and..." he paused, not wanting to say what he thought. "...other crimes."

Valarin stared at him. The academician did not blink. After a moment Valarin nodded. "As soon as the operation is completed, they will be released. You have my word on it."

The archeologist pursed his lips. "So... the value is perhaps five hundred billion."

"Rubles?"

"Dollars!"

Seemingly satisfied, Valarin led Yuri back in the direction of the entry arch. Yuri stopped short and turned to Jason and the others. "I have the guarantee of your safety from my... colleague here, Jason. Please understand I had no part in... this."

"I understand, Yuri. Thank you," Jason said as he got to his feet and stretched. A guard motioned him back to a sitting position.

"Do you think he means it?" asked Ugo in hushed tones.

"I'm sure Yuri is honest, but I don't think there's a chance in the world that any assurances will be carried out."

Yuri and Valarin moved slowly back to the plaza, where the shadows were lengthening. Valarin gazed at the sky and seemed pleased with what he saw.

"What is going to happen now?"

"That, academician, is none of your concern."

"And what is to become of me?"

"For now, you will go back to your trailer and wait. When everything is finished here, you will be transported back to the Soviet Union through the embassy in Mexico City. Most immediately, as soon as we finish, you will be taken to the consular office down in Oaxaca, where you will be held until transport to the capital is obtained."

"You will honor your word about the team down there?"

"Of course, academician. They will simply be kept until they can no longer endanger the operation by giving an alarm. No harm will come to them in any way. We are not barbarians."

Yuri said nothing as he moved in the direction of the plaza. Valarin had a digger in a black coverall head back with the archeologist in the direction of the trailer. The man was unarmed and smiling, in deference to the tourists who might happen by. Yuri tried to engage the man in polite conversation as they walked toward the Seven Deers area and the Soviet enclave, but he found that the man spoke neither Russian nor English, only an apparently Cuban dialect of Spanish. Still, the man was no fool. He stayed a few steps behind Yuri and watched him carefully.

They were on the narrow path that linked the narrow saddle of the Seven Deers to the broad plateau of the Monte Alban plaza when Yuri made his decision. He slowed his pace and then stopped. Behind him, the guard paused for a second, unsure about what to do. It was obvious that, while he had been told to guard Dr. Kurtzov, he had also been told the academician was a very important man and one to be given deference and respect.

"*Senor? Qué es esto?*"

Yuri turned to the smaller man and placed a hand over his chest, trying to remember the Spanish he needed. *"Ah . . . assisteme, por favor."* He tapped his chest. *"Corazon. Ohh."*

Yuri dropped to his knees and then to his back, feigning unconsciousness. It was only a minute before the guard ran in the direction of the Russian camp, calling for help.

Yuri waited until he was sure the guard was out of sight before scrambling to his feet and dashing back over the narrow rock-strewn path to the plaza. A few knots of camera-toting tourists dotted the leveled mountaintop. Yuri moved with speed across the grassy plain ringed by temples and pyramids. He slipped in behind a tour group as they made their way back down to the parking lot and visitor center a few hundred feet below the mountaintop, then managed to find a battered cab with a sleepy-eyed driver.

"Ah . . . Oaxaca, por favor."

The cabbie nodded, adding, *"Dónde en Oaxaca, Senor?"*

Yuri got into the cab and paused for a second. His career, his interntional status, and his ability to return to his homeland stood like shattered ruins behind him.

"Policía, por favor. Rapidamente! Ese es una emergencia!"

The cab sped off wildly down the twisting road, in the direction of the city.

20

Sergio looked down at his unconscious uncle. The emergency squad had gotten to him with blessed speed. Mentally, he went through the checklist of injuries the head of surgery had detailed for him. The right leg, broken in two places, was in a cast and held in place by traction wires above the bed. The skull fracture to the left occipid had caused no brain damage, or so they thought. Likewise, the three broken ribs were serious but would not be fatal. A great deal of the diagnosis would wait until the doctor returned to consciousness. Oddly, a doctor had said, the accident would clearly have been fatal if the doctor had hit the street as a result of the impact rather than the side of the car. It was the latter impact that absorbed much of the energy of the collision and prevented total disaster.

Sergio had always thought of Jorge as a surrogate father. He remembered the rage that he'd felt when the news of the hit and run had arrived. When the chief's car was roaring to the hospital, Sergio recalled growling to the chief that the criminal *had better* be found immediately, and that all of the resources of the Oaxaca Police Department should be brought to bear instantly in that pursuit. The chief had nodded and started to bark commands into the mike. Sergio regretted his tone but refused to mitigate the order. Not his own uncle, not in his own city. It simply could not happen.

TOMB SEVEN

He *was* comforted by the fact that Jorge was getting the best care the city could give, in his own hospital, under the care of his own staff. Sergio reached for a cigarette, then looked at the oxygen warning sign. He moved slowly from the room and headed into the hall.

He was lighting the cigarette as he turned into the lounge where he saw the chief of police waiting for him.

He had ordered the chief to start an investigation immediately. It was obvious the crime was a hit and run, and Sergio wanted the driver almost more than he ached for the recovery of his uncle. The chief knew Sergio when he was in such a mood, and the night shift at headquarters worked diligently through the night on the investigation.

"Yes, Chief?" Sergio said. "Is there anything new?"

"Yes, sir."

They moved to seats at the far end of the room and the chief took out a small notebook. They spoke in hushed tones.

"We spoke at length to the woman who saw the accident and she has been very helpful. She says she was sure the car was aiming for the doctor. It roared from the curb as soon as he was in the middle of the street and it did not brake or swerve to avoid him. Nor does she say that there was any effort made to stop after the impact. She said the car speeded up and turned from the plaza, heading out of town. Another thing. She says there were two men in the car."

"So you think it was deliberate, not just panic or intoxication on the part of the driver."

"I am certain of it. There are no tire marks on the street except from the acceleration point to the curb. From the distance that the doctor was thrown and the depth of the impact mark on the side of the car he struck, the chances are that the car that hit him was moving at something over fifty at the point of impact. Then, there was further acceleration as it moved from the scene.

"Also, the woman said that she had gone shopping and

remembered seeing the car as she headed the other way more than two hours earlier."

"How did she remember that? It's rather odd, isn't it?"

"Yes, but it is plausible. She says there were two men in the car when she first saw it. She thought they were waiting for someone in the government building. But mainly she noticed that the driver was rather good-looking. She says she got a very good look at him. Then, on the way back, she again noticed that the car was still in the same spot, with the same men in it. She was watching them unseen as she approached the car from behind. As the doctor started to cross the street, the man in the right seat pointed to him and the car roared from the curb. After it hit him, she managed to get the first three numbers of the license number before she ran to help the doctor. We are fortunate to have her statement, sir. We have gotten a lot of information."

"What about the car?"

"Rented." He turned the page of the battered notebook. "It was rented under the name Jesus Garcia."

"Have you got a line on the man?"

"Yes and no."

Sergio stared intently at the chief.

"What I mean, sir, is that the man does not exist. His address is a vacant lot. All of the other identification he presented was false and well-forged. We found the car at the airport and we can assume that he and the man in the right seat were headed back on a flight to the capital. There was no physical description of the men that the woman could give us except, as I said, that the driver was rather good-looking."

"Fingerprints on the car?"

"It looks like the prints have been wiped clean, but I have a team out there now going over the car again. If we get anything, they have orders to call me here as soon as there is a make."

"Why, Chief? Why? What is the motive. Especially Jorge!"

"As far as I can see, this was the work of very good professionals. They knew the time and the place and the location. There is nothing the doctor could have done to get out of the way of that car. All I can think is that he was getting too close to something, and someone with power and a considerable amount of money set up the hit. Do you know what he was investigating, Your Honor?"

Sergio paused, then nodded. "Yes. Let me think about it, though. He spoke to me during the day and he used the computer facilities. Let me think about that."

InterHelp!

A white-coated doctor rounded the corner to the lounge. "Your Honor?"

Sergio jumped to his feet and strode quickly to the man. "Yes?"

"Your uncle has regained consciousness. He is very weak. After all, he is not twenty. But it is starting to look like he will have little or no permanent damage. He was more than fortunate. I might say that God was with him."

"Can I speak to him?"

"For a few minutes. He asked if you were here."

"I sent Maria home—my aunt, his wife. My wife is with her and the doctor's children are flying in. I didn't know how bad things were. They will all be happy to hear of this. I'd like to see him now, if that is possible."

"Let's wait just a moment or two. They are still taking his vital signs now. Not too long, mind you. He has been sedated. But he did ask for you with some urgency."

The doctor nodded to Sergio and gestured to the other end of the hall. "You will excuse me, Your Honor. I have a critical case up here and I have to go."

"Certainly," Sergio intoned. "And thank you and the rest of the staff for all that they have done for him."

"Thank God, Sergio, if I may call you that. He was the one who did it. There was little we could do but wait."

With that the doctor moved down the hall, and Sergio noticed that the chief had approached, notebook still in hand.

"Yes, Chief? Did you hear?"

"I did, sir. I will tell the members of my staff who know the doctor. They will be happy. He was always a man who helped us and really made our jobs easier."

"Not *was*, chief, *is*. He is going to live. I want that driver and the other man. We'll speak later. Wait until I see my uncle."

"Of course, sir." He closed the notebook and slipped it back into a uniform pocket.

Sergio headed back down the hall to Jorge's room. "Uncle? How are you feeling?"

Jorge opened his eyes and managed a smile. "It *was* the car, wasn't it?"

"Yes. It was. We are looking into it now. We have many leads and there is a chance we can get the driver."

"A hit and run? They seemed to aim for me."

"They did aim. That was what a witness said."

"I knew he would try to kill me...he thought I knew something. Then there was the computer, and all the things that Pedro got. He has all the information. He can give it to you."

Jorge tried to adjust his position in the bed and was stabbed by the pain in his ribs.

"Oooh. That hurts."

"Don't try to move too much, uncle. There are some ribs there that have been rearranged. There is also the head and the right leg. You look like you are more plaster than person."

Jorge laughed and again was stabbed with pain. "God, Sergio, what is it the Americans say? It only hurts when I laugh?"

"In your case it's right for the time being, uncle. Rest and stay still. I sent Maria home and my wife is at your house. Your son and daughter are on the way here."

"All of this concern over me?"

Sergio knew there was no false modesty in the statement. "Yes, for you, uncle. They say you are going to be fine but that you are going to take time to heal." Sergio thought for a second. "You said someone tried to kill you?"

"It was Herrerra from InterHelp. I am sure of it. He thought I was getting too close, and the fact that he made the attempt so quickly means he is ready to strike. The things that I got from the computer... some of them we cannot use—Pedro got them illegally. But the information indicated that Herrerra is laundering money through foundations. It is money he has made through the theft of artifacts—gold and silver missing from digs across the country. His operatives get in soon after a find, before the gold and silver can be catalogued and before there is any security in the area. I had thought he was going to steal things from Tomb Seven if anything there proved profitable."

"Sir?" The voice came from the door. It was barely a whisper. Sergio turned to see the chief of police with a quixotic look on his face.

"What is it, Chief?"

"Ah, I am sorry to interrupt, sir, but there has been a communication from headquarters. Something urgent that you should know about. You will be the one to make the decision, and—"

"What is it?"

"A man came into the police headquarters about two hours ago. I just found this out, as I was involved in the doctor's accident. It seems the man claims he is a Russian archeologist. He says he wishes political asylum and that there has been a mammoth find of gold at *Tombo Siete*. He also says something about a KGB plot to steal all of the gold. He says armed men are currently in command of the site and that they hold hostages—other foreign archeologists and local diggers. The story sounds insane, I know, but as there was an international dimension with him asking for asylum, I thought you should be informed as soon as possible. It will take an order from you to prevent his embassy from freeing him and taking them back."

Sergio snapped his head in the direction of Jorge. "InterHelp, Jorge? You might have been right."

"You will have to get police there as soon as possible."

"I am afraid I will have to do more than that. Chief, has anyone come to ask for the archeologist?"

"Yes, another member of the expedition is waiting at headquarters right now, demanding the release. The on-duty staff is quite upset. The man is screaming and making demands and speaking of an international incident. I am afraid I need your help for this one, sir."

"Put the archeologist in protective custody immediately. I will take full responsibility. Why would a man go to the headquarters rather than calling the governor or my office about this? We have always had a good reputation with the mission here. Arrest this man who screams for release. Hold him too. I will get in touch with the embassy. The procedure is too far out of channels. The Russians would not act in that way."

"The man was insistent about the gold, sir. He said he thought the amount was in tons, that they are planning on moving it and killing the witnesses."

"How could they move tons? Did he say?"

"He said he had no idea, sir. His chief concern was that there be no loss of life and that this insane adventure be stopped. The captain at the station who has been speaking to the man says he seems to be speaking the truth."

"Get down to the lobby and phone in my orders. Then get me a line to the president in Mexico City. If there is any trouble getting him, use my name and tell him that it is a matter of national security."

"Si." The chief dashed through the door and headed down the hall.

Sergio turned back to his uncle. "I have to go, uncle."

"I know, the curse of the gods," he murmured.

"What?"

"The curse of the gods. The old woman at the Guelaguetza died without any real cause. So did the American,

TOMB SEVEN

Rodgers. No cause really, just the curse of the Old Ones. Perhaps it all had to do with this?"

"More like the curse of the gold, not the gods, uncle. I must go. Rest now. I will be back as soon as I can."

Sergio headed off in the direction of the elevator, wondering about the size of the find and the means that could be used to move it. They would need cargo planes, or trucks, or something big for that much weight. The scope of the operation must be vast if the defector was to be believed. He pushed the button for the elevator and tried to compose his thoughts for what he was going to have to say to the president on the phone. The matter was going to be delicate. As he watched the flashing lights head to his floor, he heard the deep-throated roar of an aircraft engine coming from the west. As the roar grew louder, other people in the hall also stopped and listened. The aircraft was large and flying low. Sergio began to think that it sounded more like a huge helicopter than an airplane. As it passed overhead and faded, he could hear a distant roar of a second machine coming from the same direction. By the time the elevator had arrived, he had heard the fifth and last set of engines. West to east—to Monte Alban—to *Tombo Siete*.

As the elevator door slid open, Sergio was already gone, dashing for the stairs. He was going to have to move with great speed.

21

Jason sat against the cool red clay wall with his knees drawn up and his arms folded. Lupe, near exhaustion, sat next to him with her head resting on his shoulder. He had no idea how long it had been since they had dined and laughed at the small hotel restaurant. The nightmare that began with the cave-in trapping Ugo and the others had now turned into something unspeakable. They were staring at men carrying automatic rifles, men who were fully able to use them and surely would, when given the order. To his left, less than a foot away, Ugo sat stiffly, seething.

"Ugo?"

"Hmm? Yes, Doctor?"

"What do you think the chances are?"

Ugo's eyes moved about the chamber and back to Jason. "From this position, and with these armed men, I don't see that we have much more chance than the bull does in the ring. They seem to be content with one man to guard us. They've rotated that man four times in four hours. There is no way a man will become tired at his post. They are professionals, Doctor. Their accents are Cuban. They are from the group that slipped in from Mexico City. It would seem someone had all of this well planned in advance.

"Notice that one?" His eyes moved in the direction of the guard in the distance. "He never gets closer than three or four yards...plenty of room to bring the rifle to bear and kill all of us with a single burst. With us against the wall, there is no chance that his firing could wound any of the others. What about that Russian, the one you know? And the other one. Were you doing some kind of bargaining?"

"No. Yuri abhors violence. His parents died in the Stalinist Gulag. He was doing the bargaining. I'm sure Valarin is in charge of the operation if he was making promises to Yuri."

"Do you think he will keep the promises?"

"No."

"Neither do I."

"When do you think, Doctor?"

"I suspect as soon as Valarin comes back. I don't think Carlos will be willing to give the order to kill Anna, nor will he want to be here when it happens. I think they will wait until the treasure is cleared and then kill us down here. The thing that puzzles me is the treasure. What do you estimate the weight to be?"

Ugo shrugged. "Dozens of tons, at least."

"How are they going to take it out?"

"I have no idea, Doctor, and there is a good chance that unless we do something to prevent it we will not live long enough to see how they move it."

"Good point." Jason assumed the thieves would move all of the gold from the outer room to a loading area on the surface before they started on the inner room. There was a considerable amount of noise from the outer chamber, and he surmised that the artifacts were being loaded onto something before being taken to the surface en masse, where they would be loaded. It chilled him to think that all the information that could have been gained would be melted into bullion and then bargained or sold somewhere on the world market. But he pushed the thought away and went to the more pressing matter—survival.

The single guard was not a large man, but the ease with which he cradled the AK-47 made it clear he was a professional killer who could kill the four of them in a matter of seconds if they showed the slightest interest in disarming him. He leaned against the wall adjacent to them with one of a series of unfiltered cigarettes dangling from his lips. Jason noted that when he removed the cigarette, he used the hand that supported the barrel of the rifle rather than the hand that gripped the pistol stock and the trigger. When he moved, he paced in a small arc near the treasure pile, his eyes occasionally glancing toward the gold then back to the four of them seated against the wall. They were going to need a diversion, something that would allow them to disarm the guard and hold the single entrance to the chamber against the others loading treasure in the outer room. If they could do that, there was a chance they could manage to maintain a stalemate. Jason was sure, given the fragile nature of the superstrata of land above them, the hijackers would not dare use explosives for fear of tumbling the mountain in on the treasure and themselves. He was also certain they were not prepared for siege and had designed the entire operation around speed and stealth.

"Ugo, do you think he understands English?"

"No."

"Do you think you could get very sick, have a fit or something in a few minutes?"

"If it would help us get to the gun, I could be very convincing."

"I'll tell Lupe and she can pass the word on to Anna. Make it a coronary, when I nudge you."

Ugo nodded, his eyes never leaving the guard.

Jason squeezed Lupe's shoulder and he saw her eyes open instantly. For a split second there was fear in them. As she looked up at him, the fear seemed to ebb.

"We are going to arrange for Ugo to be very sick, very suddenly. If that can divert the guard, I'll go for the gun. I might need some help."

"But you can't fight all of them out there, you—"

"We don't have to. There is only one small arch to enter

this room. We can control it with a single gun. They know that if they use anything heavier than small arms, they could collapse the dig. I don't see that we have anything to lose."

"I'll pass it on to Anna," Lupe said.

A few minutes later Jason caught Anna's eye. The pretty young woman nodded slowly. Jason turned to Ugo and he started to say something but stopped suddenly. In the distance there was a low roar, and in a matter of seconds it grew louder. For a second Jason thought it might be the beginning of another earthquake. But there was no ground tremor. The roar became a din and Jason suddenly knew how they were going to get the treasure out of the dig. It was a helicopter—a squadron of them from the sound. As they landed in the plaza above, the ceiling of the vault moaned and a few pieces of red clay detached themselves from the structure. Jason took a deep breath.

"Now."

Ugo screamed and pitched forward, gripping his left shoulder. Lupe started to her feet and hovered over him, screaming.

"Get him some help for God's sake," Jason shrieked. Most of the sound of the shouting was absorbed by the roar of the helicopters above.

The guard was confused. He looked down at the writhing form of Ugo, and at Lupe, who was trying to look as if she were giving first aid. He looked back in the direction of the arch and Jason dove at his feet.

The guard fell forward and rolled, aiming a kick at Jason at the same time he tried to bring the rifle to bear. Suddenly on her feet, Anna grabbed the rifle and yanked it from his grasp. She swung it wildly down and smashed the man across the face with it. The impact jerked her finger, which had been on the trigger, and a short burst of fire peppered the far wall.

She pulled away from the limp, bloody form of the guard. But before she could give the rifle to Jason, someone darted through the arch—Carlos. Jason watched like a man in a dream. Carlos, gun in hand, screamed at her to put the rifle down. She shook her head, and shrieking herself, pointed the weapon at him. They fired at the same instant.

The short burst caught Carlos in the neck and the face. It seemed that the last round removed the back of his head, splattering skull and blood across the wall. The single round Carlos had fired from his .45 caught Anna full in the chest and slammed her back into the opposite wall of the chamber.

Lupe and Ugo dashed to her as Jason grabbed the rifle and took a position against the treasure pile, guarding the low arch, now partially blocked by Carlos's body.

Lupe gently slipped her arms under Anna and turned her over. She was red with blood from her chest to her groin. Blood oozed from her lips, which quivered. Lupe pulled her up and cradled her. Anna's glazed eyes opened slightly.

"H-hurts," she whispered. She shuddered violently for a second, there was a spurt of blood from between her lips as she tried to form another word, and she went limp.

Ugo dashed across Jason's line of fire and scooped up the .45 from where it lay near Carlos's body. As he did, he came eye to eye with a man in black who was starting to come in through the arch. As the man bent low, Ugo had the advantage and fired once, the man toppling backward. Ugo fished for a second clip of ammunition but could find none. He scrambled back in Jason's direction and Jason fired a short burst from the AK-47 at yet another man in black coming toward the arch.

Lupe dragged the bloody form of Anna from the wall and propped her against the treasure pile behind which Jason and Ugo crouched.

"How long, Doctor, before they get the idea that they cannot get in?"

"Not long, I hope."

In the plaza above, the five helicopters stood in stark contrast to the ancient ruins. Their blades turned slowly against the lights that had been rigged to aid their landing. The front bay doors of the first, open like a clamshell, awaited the small forklift that eased its way up the cargo ramp. The treasure had been professionally loaded and tied down with tarp so that none of the precious pieces would fall. The driver gunned the motor and started up the ramp. In a moment he had off-loaded the skid and backed the lift off the ramp, deftly turning it to wait for the tying down of the next skid. He estimated that with the speed of the operation, all five of the machines and the men would be off the ground and heading to the east coast in about an hour. As the lift swung into position he saw them—three trucks of uniformed men screeching around the last of the hairpin curves on the access road to the plaza. He got up and screamed a warning to the men who had been posted as perimeter guards.

What followed was chaotic. The trucks screeched to a halt, and the heavily armed force of riot police fanned out in a skirmish line, grabbing cover where they could. The perimeter guards immediately unleashed a withering barrage of fire. Four of the police fell in the first burst and the rest scurried for cover. The forklift driver, who was about to start back the incline to the outer chamber where the pallets were being prepared, jumped from his machine and headed to the helicopter. One member of the crew had slipped from a hatch and was slamming the doors shut. He helped the crewman pull down the hatch and dove back inside with him. At the outer gallery the substitute diggers who were loading the skids dashed up the incline to join in the firefight. In a matter of seconds the diggers in the outer treasure room who were shuttling armloads of gold to the loading skid joined them.

After a few minutes Jason moved cautiously in the direction of the arch. He pushed away Carlos's body and peered through the opening. He could see little past the body of the man who had been shot on the other side, but there seemed to be no movement. He propelled himself with his legs holding the automatic rifle at the ready. The outer chamber was empty.

"Ugo, Lupe, Anna, get out here," he screamed as he dashed in the direction of the arch through which they had first entered the first treasure room. They could hold the first room as well as the second. With Anna and Lupe sheltered behind the wall, Jason and Ugo peered through the arch. The gallery was empty save for piles of gold scattered about and a pile of skids that could be used by a forklift.

"Should we go up?" Ugo asked.

Jason shook his head. "I don't know. Sounds like there's a full-scale war going on up there. There's a good chance we're safer here."

"Jason, we have to go—we have to go now." It was Lupe, crouched beside Anna's body, which Ugo had carefully carried with them.

"We can't. There's too much shooting going on up there."

"Jason . . . now . . . we must. The old gods *will* have their way."

Above, the situation seemed a stalemate. The police had taken good positions, and so had the hijackers. It was Chief Alvarez who sensed the possibility of a bloody tie and changed tactics. One of his ordnance men fired a shoulder-mounted rocket propelled grenade in the direction of the helicopters. The flash of the explosion shattered the night vision of the police and the thieves alike. The nearest helicopter to the police blossomed into flame, and the blast set fire to the second. The third helicopter gunned its engines, but before it could get airborne the chief ordered another rocket fired and the blast destroyed the skid of treasure, the helicopter, and the fleeing forklift driver.

Below, the blast and the falling debris had started an ominous rumble which chilled Jason's blood.

"The mountain, Lupe, the whole mountain . . . is that what you meant?"

TOMB SEVEN

"The gods of the ancients, Jason. They *will* have their way. I told you we would have nothing to say about it."

"Come on!" Jason shouted as he started a few feet up the incline. "We have no chance if we stay here!"

As he spoke there was another rumble of collapsing earth, and the chamber started to crumble. Ugo began to heft the body of Anna across his shoulder but could not manage to balance the weight. He staggered.

"Let's go! We have to leave her!" Jason shouted, barely able to see Ugo in the swirling dust. Suddenly there was a flicker of light and they were in darkness. The generators on the surface had been wrecked in the last blast. Leaving Anna's body, they began to creep up the incline as the chamber finally collapsed behind them in an explosion of smoke and dust. As they got to the mouth of the incline, Jason heard a voice bellow at him in Spanish. He couldn't understand what was being said. Two flashlights played across him, Lupe, and Ugo as they shielded their eyes from the light.

"Drop the gun, Jason," Lupe told him. "He said to drop it or he'll shoot all of us."

Jason held the gun for a long second until he heard the clash of metal on metal from only a few, invisible feet away. He dropped the gun and expected a burst of AK-47 fire to slam into him.

"Senor Farewey?" The voice came from the darkness.

Jason nodded.

The light in the darkness turned back on itself, revealing instead a badge and the brown uniform shirt of a Oaxaca policeman in a tattered flak vest.

"I am Chief Alvarez," the man said in broken English. "The fighting is over."

"Madre de Dios," Lupe whispered to Jason. "The gods were on our side."

22

Sergio looked down at Jorge's smiling face.

"Uncle, there is going to be a small award for you from the government when we get you out of here. After all, you are the one responsible for all of this. There was the chance that they could have gotten away with billions in what the Bureau of Antiquities likes to call, 'Our Cultural Heritage.' But you and I simply know it is gold."

"I don't want awards. I want that bastard in Mexico City behind bars for a long time. He was the one who set me up to die. Did they arrest him?"

Sergio shuffled. "Let's say they tried to. He jumped from the window of his inner office as the police were coming in. It's too bad. He had a lot of information they could have used in the formal complaint they are lodging against the Russians."

"What about the find at *Tombo Siete?*"

"It's all gone . . . under millions of tons of rock and earth. And the Bureau of Antiquities swears that it will be a long time before they allow *any* foreign archeology team to come close to digging there again. But there is a lot more to sort out, especially with the Mexico City officials. I—"

"Senor Chief Justice?"

Sergio turned in time to see a smiling nurse at the door of the room. "Si?"

"Phone, sir. They say it is important."

TOMB SEVEN

Sergio excused himself and moved to the phone at the nurses station in the hall. After a brief conversation he slammed down the receiver and strode back into the doctor's room.

"It does not look like the conversation was a happy one, nephew."

Sergio shook his head and ran a hand through his hair. "The Russian is dead."

"The man who defected?"

"No. The one who we put into custody. Alvarez says that despite a thorough body search he apparently had a pin embedded in a collar stay. He pricked himself with it and was dead before he hit the cell floor. This will damage the complaint the government is planning. The Russians will deny everything in any event and . . ." He paused and looked at the doctor, whose eyes had wandered to the window. In the distance he could see the looming presence of Monte Alban.

"Uncle? Are you all right?"

"Yes. I was just thinking . . . remember the Guelaguetza?"

"How could I forget it? It was the night the old woman died."

"Everything she said came true. Those who sought to defile Monte Alban died and the Old Ones now have their treasure forever, or until we are ready for what information and revelations are there. She was right. I was obsessed with the post mortem on the American, Rodgers. I shouldn't have been. There is a chance he frightened himself to death. But, we will never know. . . ."

"Perhaps some day, uncle." He pointed in the direction of the mountain. "Perhaps when the Old Ones think we are ready."

Lupe snuggled her head against Jason's chest and twirled his chest hairs between her fingers.

"A peso for your thoughts."

"Oh... I thought you might still be asleep."

"How could I be with you yanking my hair?"

"Good point." She patted his chest. "You offered a peso. I might almost take that against a dollar these days."

"Two pesos."

"Do you scuba, darling?"

"Do I what?"

"Scuba—you know, dive, mask, tank, all of that?"

"No... why?"

"Would you like to learn?"

"Why... are you going to tell me it's something like a vacation?"

"It could be, mixed with a little work."

"In all the time that I've known you, you've never mentioned diving as a hobby. I guess, therefore, this is about something else?"

She went back to twirling his chest hairs. "It would be a working vacation."

"Where?"

"We could have a few weeks in the Canary Islands and then have a few more in Spain. After that we could go on a cruise."

He sat up and put his arms around her. "Let me guess. The cruise would leave from Cadiz and head west—four hundred leagues west of the Pillars of Hercules... I remember that's where Plato put it. Is that where you place it?"

"Place what, darling?" She tried to keep a straight face but broke into a grin and then into laughter. "Jerry said I should approach you. You see, I told him I had some influence. Now that the Russians have purged the officials of the KGB who were behind the fiasco at Tomb Seven, there's almost no chance at all that they'll let an archeologist anywhere out of the country for some time. We would have clear sailing. Jerry is prepared to sink a great deal of money into the expedition if you'll lead it."

"Can we have Yuri Kurtzov for the gold analysis?"

"Jerry says we can have him as soon as the State Department finishes processing him. That will be in a month or so. Jerry already offered him a research position at the Institute. It was the least he could have done. The man saved our lives. What do you think, darling?"

"Weren't *you* the one who said the gods were on our side?" Jason asked, smiling.

Lupe shrugged and paused a moment. "Maybe they were."

Jason stretched back and curled his hands behind his head. "Four hundred leagues west of the Pillars of Hercules ... Plato's Atlantis. Do you have any 'feelings' about it?"

"Good ones ... especially if you're there."

Jason Farewey sighed. "When do we leave?"

SENSATIONAL #1 BESTSELLER

THE TALISMAN

STEPHEN KING PETER STRAUB

You are about to take a journey...
a journey into the dark heart of horror...

Stephen King. Peter Straub.
Two of the world's best-selling authors team up
in the ultimate masterpiece of spine-tingling
terror...the most compelling, most talked-about,
most <u>frightening</u> book of the decade...

_____ 08181-8/$4.95   THE TALISMAN

Price may be slightly higher in Canada.
(On Sale Nov. 1985)

Available at your local bookstore or return this form to:

BERKLEY
Book Mailing Service
P.O. Box 690, Rockville Centre, NY 11571

Please send me the titles checked above. I enclose _____. Include 75¢ for postage and handling if one book is ordered; 25¢ per book for two or more not to exceed $1.75. California, Illinois, New York and Tennessee residents please add sales tax.

NAME_____
ADDRESS_____
CITY_____ STATE/ZIP_____
(Allow six weeks for delivery.)   412/B